WOUNDS

OF

TIME

WOUNDS
OF
TIME

STEVIE D. PARKER

atmosphere press

In loving memory
of Christopher

VINCE

I can remember it like it was yesterday: the day before Christmas Eve, 2011. Stock market had just closed, and two of the guys came into my office to grab me.

"Vince, you ready?" Jimmy said.

On that same day every year, a strip club a few blocks away opened early for us brokers. It was our "holiday party." On the drive over, I clearly remember Jimmy asking me, "You going to pretend you like girls today?"

I rolled my eyes. Jimmy was my right-hand guy and my best friend. He was a big guy, 6'5", always well dressed. He liked showing off exactly how much he was worth. His sleeves rolled up just enough to show off the diamonds on his Rolex and carrying a Hermes briefcase that I poked fun at any chance I could. He always insisted on having his driver pick us up, even if we were just going a few blocks. He was extremely good-looking, at least that's what the ladies thought. He never had any problems meeting women, and managed to score at least one number everywhere we went. I never could figure out why he didn't mind paying for the attention of naked girls.

"Hey, if I had his wife at home, I wouldn't be looking at girls either," Tom said.

The guys loved talking about how hot my wife was. Samantha certainly was beautiful: brunette with blonde streaks, green eyes, great body. Always tan, no matter what the season. Cost me a lot of money for her to keep up with her body, between her personal trainer and enhancements. If you compared a picture of her now to when we'd first met, you wouldn't even recognize her. Sure, she was hot—but not the same girl I met twenty years ago. I never quite understood why she felt the need to change so much.

"Hey, I have a sixteen-year-old daughter at home, too—these girls don't look much older than her. Sorry if I'm not creepy enough for you guys," I said. They busted my balls every year, so I was used to it by now. I took off my tie and rolled it up.

"Would you mind putting this in your murse?" I asked, handing the tie to Jimmy.

"What's a murse?" Tom asked, laughing.

Tom wasn't as good-looking or successful as either of us and he was much younger. He idolized Jimmy and me so much, he would have laughed at anything we said.

Jimmy reached out and took the tie from my hand. "Well, Tom, it's a man purse. I think Vince just has briefcase envy." He smiled at me. "Where's your jacket, sweetheart? Would you like me to hold that for you, too?"

"I left it in the office—you get your nails done?" I asked, as I watched him place the tie in his bag. He held his hand up towards the window and examined his shiny nailbeds under the city lights.

"I did, last night. See, that's what I love about you, you notice the small things. On the topic of noticing, the only hard nipples I better 'notice' tonight are the ones on the chick on my lap. So, you'd better at least be wearing an undershirt," Jimmy said.

We kept giving each other shit as we entered the club. The interior was dimly lit, with drums pounding out a slow beat and red lights glimmering off the stage. The guys were already lining up by the stage, jostling each other to get the best view. I headed straight over to the bar to order a drink.

Lou, one of the brokers, rushed over and intercepted me. "No wine at a strip club, Vince." He looked at the bartender and said, "What's your name, honey?"

"Nicole." The bartender batted her eyes and tossed her long wavy blonde hair with pink tips on the ends.

"Nicole, get him a beer—a manly one."

I wanted a scotch, but I accepted the beer that Nicole poured from a tap and handed me.

"Guinness manly enough?" she asked, looking at Lou.

"Personally, I prefer blondes, but you're right. I take Vince here as a stout guy, too," Lou answered.

Nicole grinned before walking to the register to add the drink to his tab.

Lou lifted his glass to cheers me. "You know, up by the stage, they actually take their clothes off," he said, after taking a sip.

I didn't respond, just half-smiled as he walked away. Samantha would be pissed if I came home too hammered. We hosted Christmas Eve at our house every year; I had no room in my schedule for a hangover. I settled on a barstool with my back to the stage. Every once in a while, one of the guys would come over to me, say *Merry Christmas,* and thank me for whatever it was they thought they were thanking me for. They were really just kissing my ass. I was their boss. Actually, I was their boss' boss. If I were anyone else, they wouldn't care enough to wish me much of anything.

Nicole returned from the far end of the bar and paused across from me. "Why are you sitting here all alone?" She leaned over to emphasize her cleavage, as if her shirt wasn't low enough already. She was probably in her thirties, so at least I didn't feel too dirty talking to her.

"Just enjoying my beer at the bar. Why, are you telling me you don't want me near you?"

"I didn't say that, just wondering if you realized I don't take my clothes off?" she said.

I cracked a smile at her joke.

"What does that mean?" I pointed at the Asian lettering inked into her forearm.

"Live for the day."

"Live for the day," I repeated, nodding. "I like that—funny, you don't look Asian at all."

"You gay?" she said.

"No, I'm not gay...I mean, not that I have anything against gay people. But I'm wearing a wedding ring."

She shrugged. "They just legalized gay marriage in New York, so theoretically, you can be married to a man. But, if you're not gay, you should turn around. Not to say that I'm not enjoying your company of course, but the main act is coming out."

I turned my stool around. The opening notes of "Santa Baby" filled the room. A pretty, young Spanish brunette strolled onto the stage from the left. She launched right into her striptease act: shimmying around the stage, grinding against the pole, taking her clothes off. A redhead emerged from the right. Same routine, different side. The two women met at the pole—touching each other, doing the typical stripper thing. The guys up front were eating it up. Dollar bills out, whistling, yelling stuff at the girls. I never understood why these guys got such a kick out of this. Most of them had wives at home. Did they not have sex anymore? I'd never had to pay for a woman to take her clothes off and I certainly wasn't going to start now.

I was about to turn back to the bar when *she* appeared during the third verse, strolling right out to the middle of the stage. The girls to each side started taking the new dancer's clothes off for her. She was the most gorgeous woman I'd ever seen: golden blonde hair, green eyes. And thankfully, not so young that she made me feel like a creep. She had a tattoo of a rose that started on the back of her neck. The thorns wandered down her spine, wrapped around her ribs, traveled down her stomach, and well, I could only imagine where they ended. Her body was a work of art. Extremely fit and defined, with breasts that weren't too small or too big, but perfect. Obviously real. I was instantly mesmerized. Without taking my eyes off of her, I asked Nicole, "Who is that?"

"Bianca. I figured you might like her. Most men do."

An understatement. I couldn't stop looking at her, almost like I was in a trance. Trust me, I tried. I couldn't even finish my drink. I placed the beer on the bar and slowly rose from my stool and walked toward the stage. To this day, I didn't know why, but I started playing with my wedding ring—moving the metal band up and down my finger. Why was I so nervous? No idea. She was a stripper. Her act was what she got paid to do. But I kept fidgeting with my ring, so uncontrollably that the stupid thing flew off.

Damn. I panicked, dropping to my hands and knees and crawling on the floor, frantically searching for my ring. The club was so dark—all of the light was directed at the stage. I turned on my phone's flashlight, but I didn't see so much as a hint of gold anywhere. Samantha was going to flip out if I came home without a ring. I mean, she knew we went to the strip club every year, but she'd wonder why I took it off. She'd be right to wonder. Stupid move, Vince.

I glanced up for a brief moment, and holy shit. There she was—Bianca, on the floor, on her hands and knees crawling toward me. My body stiffened. All of a sudden, her hands were on me. She touched me, urging me to my feet. Directed me into an empty chair. In a daze, I followed her lead and sank into the seat. She was even more stunning up close. On my lap. Dancing for me. So natural, so real. So beautiful, I wondered why she was stripping at all. She could have easily landed a modeling career if she'd wanted one.

While she danced on my lap, the guys cheered her on, whistling and applauding. I almost forgot all about the ring, or the fact that I was even married until out of the blue, she slipped her finger into my mouth. Staring right in my eyes, she seductively slid her finger out, leaving behind a small, hard object with a metallic taste. My wedding ring, in my mouth. She must have seen it fall off, or at the very least, noticed me looking for it. She winked at me and smiled—the most beautiful, most pure smile I'd ever witnessed.

The entire encounter was the sexiest thing I'd ever experienced. I was so turned on that, for the first time in my marriage, I experienced thoughts about being with someone other than my wife. I wanted to take this woman somewhere, anywhere. Just the two of us, alone. I didn't know how or why, but she made me lose control of all of my senses. Like she had some sort of magical power over me. I usually didn't get intimidated by anybody, and yet this girl, who couldn't have been taller than 5'2" in her bare feet, had me shook. I felt like I was in middle school again, crushing hard on a cheerleader. I slid the ring back on my finger and watched as she returned to the stage to finish her act.

BIANCA

When my act was over, I went back to the dressing room, pulled on a t-shirt and a pair of leggings, and got ready to head out. I was happy that I only had the one show. I shuffled through my bag to find the Red Bull that was now warm. I was so tired that I could actually feel the bags under my eyes, as if they weighed a pound each. It was already 6 p.m., and I still had to get home, do my workout, and practice my routine for the 2 p.m. Christmas Eve matinee. My feet were so numb that I could barely even feel them.

There was a knock. I opened the door and there was Frank, the club manager. I was so exhausted that just the sight of his balding head, protruding stomach and nasty expression made me wish he was there to fire me.

"There's a man requesting to talk to you at the bar," he said.

"What does he want?"

"I don't know, must have slipped my mind to take a message. Go find out," he said, his lip curling before he stalked away.

I slid into my jacket, grabbed my things, and walked over to the bar. I spotted him instantly—the poor guy who had been crawling around on the floor, desperately looking for his wedding ring. Wow. Now that I got a better look at him, I could see he was sexy. He wore a light blue button-down shirt that looked great with his dark hair and eyes, and he had a very nicely shaped goatee. Something about him suggested money, but not in an over-the-top, show-off way. He was sporting a really nice Rolex on his wrist and a thin, simple gold chain with a cross around his neck.

I sighed. Sexy or not, I was in no mood to explain to another married broker why I wouldn't give him a private dance. I hurried over to him, impatient to leave as quickly as possible.

"My shift is over, and I don't do personal dances," I snapped.

He seemed a little taken aback with my opening statement. "I'm not here for a dance; I just wanted to say thank you for giving me my ring back."

"You're welcome." I turned to leave.

"Why didn't you keep it?" he asked.

Well, that was just insulting. I'd been warned about broker night—these guys really were something else!

Annoyed, I pivoted to face him again. "Because I'm a stripper, not a thief. Oh wait, of course someone like you would think that if a girl's stripping, she must be so desperately broke that she'd steal." I had to admit, my tone was pretty nasty.

He looked at the ground and made a face like he was embarrassed. Without lifting his head, he shifted his gaze back up to meet mine, like he was thinking of what he could possibly say to redeem himself from that last statement.

"You're right, that was a stupid assumption," he said. "I'm sorry. If I looked like you, I'd probably be prancing around naked all day, too."

I couldn't help but laugh. He was actually quite charming.

"Can I buy you a drink?" he asked.

"No, thank you," I said. "I have a long day tomorrow. I can't drink too much tonight."

"How about food? A meal? Not because I think you can't afford to buy food by any means—just because I'd like to eat something with you. Anything you want... I'm not a picky eater. Please," he said, making a ridiculous pouty face.

Normally I would have turned down an offer like that, but there was something about him that enticed me. His smile, for one thing. He had such a nice, sincere smile. Perfect teeth and a dimple that seemed to appear out of nowhere. Plus, unlike most of the customers at the club, he looked me straight in the eyes when he spoke to me. The truth was, in that moment, I probably would have gone anywhere he wanted.

"I know a place," I said.

As we walked, he told me he wasn't a picky eater, but when I led him over to the little stand, he stared at the gyro cart as if I had just invited him to dumpster-dive. He shook his head and asked, "Seriously. I say anything you want, and you pick street meat??"

I shrugged. "This is some good shit."

"Yeah, sautéed rat—real good shit," he said.

"It's not rat; it's lamb."

He gave me that lifted-brow look. "How many lambs you see frolicking around New York City?"

I ignored him and looked up at the gyro man. He knew me well; I stopped there frequently. "Hey Bruno, two gyros with the works, please."

After Bruno dished them up, I handed one to him. He reluctantly took it, like the platter literally contained a live rat that might jump out and bite him.

"Where are we even going to eat these?" he asked.

"I know a quiet place."

He started following me as I walked toward the club.

"Wait," he said. "Stay here, I'll be right back."

I waited while he ran into the liquor store. A few minutes later, he emerged with a bottle of wine. I led him through the back entrance of the strip club, up the stairs, and to the roof.

"Great view," he said when we reached the top.

It really was, especially at night. New York City all lit up. Beyond our rooftop, the Empire State Building stood majestic, glimmering red and green for Christmas. The lights spread all the way into New Jersey. I think sometimes it was hard for New Yorkers to truly appreciate how beautiful their city was, glowing at night. Even though I visited the roof frequently, I still often felt like a tourist, with the way I was enthralled by the whole scene.

"We're lucky the weather is okay. Remember the blizzard last Christmas Eve?" he asked.

"How could I forget? I was stuck in my house for days. I love this place. I come here to think sometimes," I said.

He pulled out a cheap wine opener that he'd bought in the liquor store and opened the bottle. There was a nook on the roof that we were able to sit on. I was surprised when he sat right down without commenting on the cement being too dirty or cold.

"They didn't have glasses, so I guess we'll have to drink it out of the bottle," he said. "I know you said you didn't want to get drunk, but a little wine won't hurt anyone. Plus, I'm sure you have somewhere to be tonight."

"I don't, actually. I hate Christmas. Also, I hope that bottle wasn't too expensive. I don't know the difference between good wine and bad wine."

He handed me the bottle. "Try it."

I took a swig.

"Wow—that's really good!"

Normally I found red wine to be dry and bitter, but this was very smooth. Not too sweet. Tasted like they'd just blended the fruit together a second ago.

He smiled. "Then I guess you do know the difference. It's my favorite. And by the way, what's wrong with you? Who hates Christmas?"

I avoided his question by asking some of my own. "How old are you?"

"Forty-one. You?" he said.

"Twenty-five." Older, but not too old. "What's your name?"

"Vince."

"Is that short for Vincent?" I asked.

"Yes."

"I like Vincent—does anyone call you Vincent?"

"Not in years. My mother used to but usually only when she was mad, and it was more like, *Vincent Anthony*!"

"Can I call you Vincent?" I asked.

He paused to put his gyro down in his lap. He gazed directly into the eyes. "You can call me whatever you want."

We basically just looked at each other for what seemed like an hour. I barely noticed how much the temperature kept dropping outside. I never once felt like I was sitting there with a stranger. So odd. I knew I would have remembered meeting him, which made me wonder about past lives. I wasn't a spiritual person, but I had no explanation for the attraction and level of comfort I experienced with him.

After a while, he broke the silence, "Does your dad know you strip?"

Well, that was a weird ice breaker. Of all the people to bring up, he chose my dad?

"I'm sure—he's dead, but they say your loved ones watch over you, right? I hope he closes his eyes during some of the shows. Stripping is part-time, anyway. I do it for extra cash and trust me, I make a lot of extra cash. I'm a Broadway dancer. One day, I'm going to be the lead."

"Wow, that's impressive," he said. "And, I'm sorry for your loss."

I shrugged. "It's okay, he died years ago—car accident. He went pretty fast, so no suffering."

"How old were you?" he asked.

"Fifteen," I said.

"I'm very sorry. That must be a rough time for a daughter not to have a dad," he said.

"He wasn't the nicest of guys. Not that I'm saying he deserved his fate, but it was probably better he wasn't around when I was a teenager."

"Did he hit you?" he asked.

"No, not me, but I never gave him a reason to."

Normally I would feel uncomfortable having a conversation about this with someone, but I didn't think there was much he could ask me that I would have felt uneasy answering.

"He hit your mom?" he asked.

I nodded.

He stared at his lap, clearly upset.

"I never understood how a man could hit a woman. Sorry, it just bothers me. Okay, let's not talk about it anymore," he said, and changed the subject.

We spoke about the dream I'd had since I was a little girl, to be a Broadway actress. The gig I currently had was decent, but I wanted to be more than just a backup dancer. He asked a lot about the audition process—what was entailed in dancing and what my workout routine consisted of. He expressed even more surprise that I ate "rat," considering how hard I trained. He seemed genuinely interested in everything I said, which felt good. It was so hard nowadays to have a man hang on your every word. I told him I lived in an apartment a few blocks away. I was proud to say I rented a one-bedroom apartment and not a studio until he told me he lived in the Upper East Side. Then I just felt silly about elaborating on my little one-bedroom.

Vincent told me he grew up in California and moved to New York with his wife when he was in his early twenties, came here to take his Series 7. He had two kids: one boy, nineteen-year-old Nick, and a sixteen-year-old daughter, Casey. He looked way too young to have such old kids. He didn't have any wrinkles, dressed very stylishly, and that smile—so youthful.

I told him I was born in California, too, but when he asked where, I couldn't remember. He found that funny, said California was a big state. I shared that I moved to New York City when I was a little girl to go to performing arts schools. My parents felt the schools here were better for that. I barely remembered anything about the move. My parents were so conservative that they never spoke about, well, anything, really. He was so easy to talk to, that my life story came pouring out. He wasn't arrogant at all, but just the opposite—extremely humble, especially considering how successful he was. We sat on that roof for two hours talking about nothing and everything.

"Do you date a lot?" he asked.

"It's hard for me working two jobs to find time to date. Especially after meeting someone you swipe right on, and then he shows and ends up looking nothing like he did in his picture."

"Swipe right?" he asked, confused.

"It's a dating app. Your kids don't online date?" I asked.

"I hope not! They're both very good-looking, so I can't imagine they'd have to."

I stared at him, a bit offended. "Are you saying I'm not good-looking?"

He hit himself in the head and scrunched up his nose. "Wow, you make me say the stupidest shit," he said, laughing nervously. "No, you're the most beautiful woman I've ever seen. I don't know why I said that."

He started biting the thumbnail on his left hand, while cracking his knuckles with his other thumb on his right.

I smiled and let the comment go.

We continued on with the conversation. When the

bottle was empty, I asked him if I could keep the cork. I told him I collected them.

"Sure," he said, handing the cork to me.

My skin tingled when his hand touched mine. He gazed at me. Intensely, like he wanted to say something more but wasn't sure if he could or should.

"Why do you keep looking at me like that?" I finally asked. It took him a while to answer.

"I really want to kiss you," he said. "Can you kiss on the mouth, or is that against the rules?"

"This isn't *Pretty Woman*, and I'm not a prostitute, dick," I said.

He laughed. "I'm only kidding...about the rules, not about kissing you. I do want to kiss you, badly."

"You want to—but you won't?" Suddenly, I was staring at his lips.

"I mean, I will, if you're giving me permission," he said.

"Man, talk about putting me on the spot!"

He leaned in closer.

"So, is that a yes?" he asked.

I didn't know what to say. This whole asking permission to kiss a girl got kind of awkward at times. His lips were so close to mine, that I could feel his breath on me. I was dying for him to kiss me. I thought that was obvious.

"I guess if you did, I wouldn't be too opposed."

He kissed me right on the lips, holding my face in his hands. Slow, sensual, romantic. Very gentleman-like. His hands were large and manly yet felt so soft on my face, and they didn't try to wander anywhere else.

He was such a good kisser that I could have kissed him

all night. I felt his goatee scrape against my cheek and couldn't help but imagine that scruff on other parts of my body. I could still taste the wine on his tongue. I didn't know what type of cologne he wore, but he smelled amazing. Sexy. Masculine. His whole demeanor intoxicated me.

"I had an awesome time with you tonight," he said, when he finally peeled his lips off mine.

I smiled. "Me too."

I hadn't had that good of a conversation with a man in quite some time. Maybe ever.

He looked at his watch.

"I could stay up here all night with you, but unfortunately, I do have to go. Some people like Christmas, my kids in particular. Luckily since Christmas Eve is tomorrow, it bought me a little extra time. Maybe meeting you tonight was meant to be." He started to walk away but stopped to look at me. "It was really, *really* nice meeting you, Bianca."

"It was nice meeting you too, Vincent."

Butterflies fluttered in my stomach as he walked away. What was wrong with me? I didn't even know this guy!

"My name isn't Bianca..." I blurted out.

He turned and looked at me, confused. "What?"

"I mean it is, now, it's my stage name, I changed it. My real name is Sarah."

I didn't even know why I told him that. No one called me Sarah. My name had legally been Bianca Evans for the past seven years. For the first time, I guess I just felt like someone should know the real me. The me that I was born as.

He started walking back towards me.

"Changed it? Witness protection program? It's okay you can tell me, what did you do?" he playfully asked.

"No, I'm not a trained assassin," I began, laughing. "When I knew it was real, that I was going to be an actress, I changed my name. Bianca is so much sexier than Sarah...don't you think?"

He had such a boyish smile as he glanced down and then back up at me.

"Yes, Bianca is a sexy name, but it was even nicer meeting Sarah," he said.

He moved to walk away again before stopping and turning back, like he'd just had an idea.

"Why don't you meet me here next year, same time?"

"What? That's insane! You won't even remember me in a year," I said.

"Oh, trust me, I will," he said. "Come on, it will give us something to look forward to. I know it will give me something to look forward to, anyway. You can be like my...like my Christmas Fairy."

I stood there, staring at him. I didn't know what to say. It seemed ridiculous to believe that he would still be thinking about me in a year from today. What if I came and he didn't?

"A Christmas Fairy?" I laughed. "Is she related to the Tooth Fairy?"

"Yes! She's her third cousin. Well," he continued, "you can think about it. I'm going to be here on Christmas Eve next year. I hope you are, too. If you are, I'll give you anything you want. Anything—just name it. You have a year to be creative about what you want. I would just really like to see you again."

There was just something about him that was so

inviting and romantic. So sincere. He didn't seem like the type of jerk who was meeting girls on roofs all over New York City. Then again, three hours ago, he'd been crawling around the floor searching for his wedding ring.

"And if you're not here in a year, then you'll have to live with the guilt for the rest of your life of being the only woman ever to stand me up," he said.

That made me laugh. "Okay," I said. "Merry Christmas, Vincent."

"Merry Christmas, Sarah."

It was hard to believe an entire year had passed since that night I met Vincent. I went about my life, working out, practicing every day, and stripping at night to make extra cash. Now here we were, the Friday before Christmas Eve, 2012. I was standing in front of my best friend, Isabel, in the dressing room of the club. Isabel was incredibly sexy. Tall, dark hair, and piercing blue eyes. Curvy in all the right places. The brokers were going to be here soon; they usually arrived shortly after the market closed. I was nervous. I didn't even know why.

"You're seriously going to meet this guy after?" she asked.

I smiled while looking at myself in the mirror.

"Yes, why? You don't think it's romantic?" I asked. "It's like that movie where they meet on the top of the Empire State Building."

I couldn't help it. I was a hopeless romantic.

"I've never seen it, but I'm pretty sure someone gets hit by a car in that movie," she said.

"What? You're lying," I said.

"No, I'm serious. I think that's the whole point of the movie. Someone didn't make it."

Interesting. I had never seen the movie either. Did someone die? Note to self: watch the movie about meeting on the Empire State Building.

The show started. While dancing, I tried to look through the crowd of guys to see if *he* was there. I struggled to get a good look through the red lights shining in my face, feeling self-conscious that by squinting so hard, I was making a weird face. The men all kind of looked the same from where I was standing. Light button-down shirts, dress pants, fancy ties, and wedding rings like some sort of white-collar uniform. By the time the show was over, I still hadn't seen him.

Back in the dressing room, I put on a little red dress I had bought. When Isabel asked if I bought it just for this occasion, I lied and said no. I knew it would have sounded a bit ridiculous to admit that I'd bought a dress to meet some random guy on the roof of a strip club.

"I just thought of something. He said same time, but we went up there at like six and left around eight. What time do you think he meant?" I asked.

Isabel looked at me like she was annoyed by my question. I knew she thought I was crazy for even entertaining this. Vincent had been right, though—his plan did give me something to look forward to. I couldn't help but fantasize about us meeting again from time-to-time throughout the year.

"Go up about ten after six, be fashionably late. If he's not there, check ten minutes after every hour until eight. If he's still not there, well, then I promise I won't say I told you so," she laughed.

She was so different than me that at times, it was hard to believe we were best friends. Not into romance at all.

Hated when guys did sweet things like buy flowers or hold doors.

At ten after six, I slowly made my way up to the roof. I was so nervous. Isabel was probably right, and I was being stupid. Why would this guy be waiting for me after one kiss? Maybe he was drunk when he'd made the plan? He'd been drinking before the wine. On the climb up, I felt like my heart was going to beat right out of my chest.

I opened the door and looked across the rooftop. There he was, standing with his back to me, facing the rest of the city. As I started to approach him, I wondered if he was even as cute as I'd thought, or if I'd just made that up in my head.

He slowly turned, holding a bottle of wine in one hand and two wine glasses in the other.

"I brought glasses this time, thought I'd class it up a bit," he said, with a smile.

I wasn't imagining it at all. He was so good looking that suddenly, I couldn't get the visual of our kiss out of my head.

As I continued walking toward him, he said, "I was starting to think you weren't going to come."

I reached out and took one of the glasses he was holding out.

"I couldn't live with the guilt of being the only woman ever to stand you up. And—I wasn't sure when you said the same time, if you meant six or eight."

"I meant six, but it doesn't matter. You're here now."

We sat on the same nook as a year ago, and he poured two glasses of wine.

"You didn't go to the show?" I asked.

"No, I was more looking forward to seeing you here in

clothes. You look great," he said. "So, there's something that's been driving me crazy all year. I know you're a Broadway dancer, but do you sing? I never got to ask you that last time."

"And that drove you crazy?" I asked.

"Insanely yes. Is that weird?"

"Yeah, kind of. I mean, of course I sing...how could I ever be the lead of a musical if I don't sing?" I asked.

"Go ahead—sing," he dared.

"No way," I said.

"If you make it big, you'll have to sing in front of hundreds of people a night. You can't sing for me?" he asked.

I smiled and drank some more of my wine. "If I remember correctly, you told me you'd give me whatever I wanted if I showed up, not the reverse."

His eyebrows raised. "You're right. I did promise you anything. Did you decide what you wanted?"

I paused for a moment, and he looked extra curious about what I was going to request.

"Yes." I stood and reached down to him. "I want you to dance with me." I was half kidding, guessing he would think my request was corny.

"Dance with you? I'm sure you can get any guy in the world to dance with you. I offered you anything you wanted, and that's the best you came up with?"

"Yes, that's what I want."

"I don't dance," he said abruptly.

"You said *anything*." I was especially determined now for him to grant my request after seeing how opposed he was to it. "I want you to dance with me right here, to my favorite Christmas song before they start talking about banning it for being inappropriate."

I searched my phone and started playing "Baby, It's Cold Outside." The good version with Dean Martin. Vincent laughed, shook his head no, and shooed me away with his hand. I took his hand and pulled him up to his feet. He stood reluctantly, barely moving to the music.

"You going to make me beg?" I asked.

Suddenly he became very serious, staring deep into my eyes. "No, I would never make you beg for anything."

He took our glasses and set them both on the floor. Then, he started dancing. He was very stiff at first.

"Follow my lead."

I moved my face closer into his, trying to assure him. He curled his hand around my waist as I took his other hand and held it in mine. With his fingers lacing between mine, I was reminded of what big, manly hands he had. My other hand rested on the back of his neck, my fingers right under his hair line. He wasn't a bad dancer at all, once he loosened up.

"By the way, how does the girl who hates Christmas have a favorite Christmas song anyway?" he asked.

"Well, it's not really about Christmas. It's about being cold!"

We danced. He even knew the words, half-mouthing, half-singing while twirling me around. The whole thing was pretty amazing, actually. He danced with me, his eyes smiling into mine as he sang the words.

"See, I sing for you. You can't sing for me? Did you think about me at all?" he asked, pulling me in closer to him.

"Maybe a little," I said. "Did you think about me?"

He sighed and looked up at the sky. "A lot more than

I'd like to admit."

The song ended, yet we still stood there holding each other, entranced by what we saw in each other's eyes. Both of his arms now around my waist, and mine across his shoulders. He didn't ask permission this time. He just kissed me.

The kiss started slow and gentle but quickly grew intense, like suddenly we both realized that this moment was all we've been thinking about all year. He backed me straight against the wall, his hands still on my waist, squeezing tighter by the second. My fingers slid through his hair, pulling him close.

He turned me on so much that I ended up making the first move. I needed to know if he was just as turned on as me. I unzipped his jacket and slid my hand down his neck, his chest, between his legs. Oh yeah, he was just as turned on. He moaned a little as I touched him there, and then started kissing my neck while unbuttoning my coat. One of his hands stroked my breasts, then slid around to my back, trailing down my behind, up my thigh, until he was rubbing me between my legs, too. His other hand pressed on my neck, pulling my lips firmly into his. As the minutes progressed, we became more and more passionate. I unzipped his pants and stuck my hand inside, stroking him while he massaged me. Next thing I knew, he'd ripped the crotch of my stockings apart. Right there, right on that roof against that wall, he entered me.

I leaned back against the wall, standing on only one leg. My other one wrapped around his waist as he held me up. I'd never done anything like this in my life, and it was the hottest thing I'd ever experienced. Feeling him thrust inside me, out here in the open, the view of New York City lit up over his shoulder.

He didn't say anything until near the very end, when he slowed down and whispered, "I want to feel you cum on me."

I did, and he followed. He leaned up against the wall and pulled me into him, bringing my head to his chest. He was out of breath and sweating a bit. We stood there for a few minutes, not saying a word.

When he finally caught his breath, he zipped up his pants, walked back over to the nook, and poured us both another glass of wine. I took the glass from him, feeling so embarrassed, I could barely look at him. He patted the spot next to him, so I sat. He put his arm around me as we drank our wine. Then, he leaned forward and kissed me on the forehead. He took a deep breath and looked me deep in the eyes.

"That's going to be hard to get over. This whole year I couldn't stop thinking about that kiss, and now this is going to be running through my mind until next year."

I laughed. "You're already planning on meeting me next year?" I asked.

"Oh yeah, and the year after that." He took my hand and placed it on his lap. "You know, I've never done anything like this. I truly haven't. I've never even cheated on my wife before. There's just something about you that..."

I interrupted. "You don't have to explain anything to me. I'm not judging you."

His expression turned serious. "I know I don't, but I just really want you to know that this was...it was...different. And pretty fucking incredible."

Vincent was right, it was incredible—and so out of

character for me. I sat there staring at him, wondering how or why I was so unbelievably attracted to someone I barely knew. He wasn't even my type, I normally went for blue eyes, not brown. Jocks, not businessmen. Not to mention, he was so much older than me. We sat on the roof, talking for another hour.

"Do you believe everything happens for a reason?" he asked.

I paused for a minute. "Yes, I do."

"The fact that Christmas Eve fell on the weekend these past two years gave us a little more time to spend together. You don't think there's something peculiar about that?" he asked.

It was true. The timing had certainly worked out for us. I smiled but didn't say anything.

Then, like the year before, he had to leave. "Next year? Same time? As in six!"

I sighed. After what had just happened, it was going to be difficult for me to wait an entire year before seeing him again.

"Yes, I will be here at six, but it's going to be pretty hard for you to top this year," I said. He kissed me long and passionately.

"Merry Christmas, Sarah."

About four weeks later. I'd just finished my act at the strip club when Isabel came into the dressing room.

"Bianca, there is an incredibly attractive guy asking for you by name at the bar," she said.

"Another one?" I asked, annoyed. "Did you tell him my act is over?"

"Yes, but he was pretty insistent, said he was a friend of yours."

Baffled, I slowly walked out to get a look from behind the entrance leading into the bar. I stepped back so fast I bumped right into Isabel.

"Oh my God, it's him!"

"Him?" she asked. "As in the guy you were a hoochie for on the roof, HIM?"

I rolled my eyes. "Yes, THAT him—Vincent. Shit, what is he doing here?" I asked her as if she would possibly have an answer.

She started shaking her head. "These married guys are dangerous. Does he have luggage with him? Was he kicked out?"

"Oh God, I hope not!" We both slowly peered our heads out to get a better look.

"I don't see luggage, do you?" I asked.

"No, looks like it might be safe to proceed," she said. "But you do know your roof is covered with snow, right? I wouldn't suggest going up there unless you're planning on making snow angels."

"I look like shit! I need to freshen up my makeup, can you go entertain him?"

"You look exactly how you did the first time he came back," she said.

I released a sigh. I had no time to argue with her. "Please?"

"Okay, go, but hurry. I gotta go back out for the next dance!" she said.

VINCE

"You must be Vincent," the girl who just played gatekeeper said, approaching me.

"Yes, I am. You're the brunette from the Christmas show, right?" I asked.

She tilted her head and rolled her eyes. "Wow, very observant, nothing gets by you, huh? I'm Isabel. Bianca's best friend. She's getting changed. Care for a lap dance?"

I looked at her, almost speechless. "I'm sorry, what?"

She started speaking very slowly. "Would. You. Like. A. Lap. Dance?"

"Um, no thank you. Did she really tell you to come give me a lap dance?" That certainly couldn't have been a good sign. I stared into my glass and moved the ice around.

"Not in those exact words, but she asked me to entertain you, and since I'm a stripper...you got a better idea?"

"How about a drink?"

She sat on the empty bar stool next to me. I glanced at Nicole, who seemed to be very amused by our conversation.

"I'll have another Johnnie Walker Black, and whatever she wants," I said.

"I'll have the Blue," she ordered.

I could feel her looking at me from the side of her eye for a reaction. I didn't say anything. Nicole shifted her gaze to me for approval of the extremely high-priced drink that Isabel had ordered.

"I said whatever she wanted," I reiterated. When the drinks arrived, I lifted my glass to hers. "Nice to meet you, Isabel."

"Same to you," she said as she took a sip. She pulled a face and made a choking sound, as if she'd just tasted gasoline.

"Not typically a scotch drinker?" I asked, laughing.

She tried to give me a dirty look but couldn't help but smile. "Would you like to order another drink? One you're more comfortable with?"

She nodded and ordered a vodka and soda.

When I finished my drink, I pulled her leftover one toward me and took a sip. "You didn't find this to be smooth? I'll have to send a letter of complaint to Mr. Walker."

Isabel turned her seat around so that she faced me. Her expression turned very serious and her voice grew deeper.

"Bianca doesn't have a father, so I'll have to fill in... What are your intentions with my friend?"

I took another sip of my drink and looked over at her, confused. "My intentions?" I slowly repeated.

She started laughing. "Relax, I'm fucking with you. Bianca didn't warn me you had no sense of humor."

"You know, you would love my best friend, Jimmy," I

said.

She leaned closer to me, suddenly intrigued. "Is he as cute as you?"

"I mean, I don't look at guys like that, but from the reaction he gets from the female gender, I'm going to say cuter."

"Is he rich, too?" was her second question.

"He does well for himself," I said.

"Why do you rich guys have a problem using the word 'rich'? Does he also dance on rooftops?"

I chuckled. "I don't know, it never came up. I can find out if you'd like."

"Wait—is he married?" she said.

"Yes." I nodded. "He is married."

"Yeah, thanks anyway, but I don't date married men," she said. "You know *why* I don't date married men?"

I studied her, resting my chin in the palm on my hand, my fingers on my mouth.

"Because we lie?" I asked through my hand, expecting that to be the obvious answer she was looking for.

"No, no. Because you all go home after you're with us and start analyzing your wives and suddenly realize *exactly* what it is they're not doing for you. It's a liability really," she responded.

Luckily, I heard Sarah's voice from behind me, as if she somehow knew I needed saving in that particular moment.

"I'm surprised you're not giving him a lap dance," she said to Isabel.

"I offered, he refused." Isabel stood up, ready to leave.

"Did you really expect her to give me a lap dance?" I asked. Sarah started laughing.

"Oh, FYI—he has zero sense of humor," Isabel informed Sarah as she took her drink, raised it to me as a silent *thank you*, and then walked away.

"Are you stalking me?" she asked as she approached the bar.

I half smiled. How did this girl make me so nervous? What was I even doing there? I had no time in my life for hobbies, let alone a girlfriend. What could I even offer her? My underarms grew wet with sweat.

"Stalking? No, no, not stalking per se, that would be creepy. I mean, I did call the club to see when your act was and I did come here knowing you were getting off at nine, but no, I wouldn't say stalking. Would you? Is that stalking?" I knew I was rambling, but I felt like I was on some sort of emotional roller coaster, between Isabel's interrogation and her stalking question. I had no idea what was a joke and what wasn't, but was extremely relieved when Sarah finally smiled.

"It isn't Christmas Eve yet," she said.

"Yeah, about that...see, I'm not sure if you're aware, but next week is Chinese New Year, which technically makes tomorrow Chinese Christmas and today Chinese Christmas Eve, so I thought that might be relevant information for you to know. I don't discriminate against anyone, especially the Chinese."

She started laughing, watching me with this shy yet captivated smile. She bit her bottom lip. I couldn't figure out if she was being flirtatious, or if she was just as nervous as I was.

"What are you drinking?" she asked.

"Johnnie Walker Black," I said.

She ducked behind the bar and grabbed a bottle. "Tell

Frank I owe him a bottle," she said to Nicole, before glancing at me. "The roof is covered with snow. I live three blocks away, want to come for a drink?"

I nodded. "Yes, I would absolutely love to come for a drink."

We walked over to her apartment. "How do you get off so early?" I asked her once we were at her place.

"I work the first shift on Mondays and Wednesdays because those are my days off from my Broadway job, but I still have to get sufficient sleep for the real show tomorrow. How are you out so late?" she said.

"Every third Wednesday of the month, I play poker with the boys. I figured they wouldn't miss me too much if I didn't show up this one time," I said. I glanced around her apartment, taking everything in. Brought me back to the days I'd first moved to New York and lived in a similar place—except mine wasn't as nice as hers.

Her apartment had that same classic Manhattan feel to it, though. Traditional old radiators, pipes along the walls, cracks in the ceiling and peeling paint. She did a good job of making the best of the space, though. She didn't have a lot of furniture, but the little she did have was nice and in good shape. A fake leather couch faced a TV stand that held a decent sized TV. There were trendy artsy canvass paintings on the walls, along with framed pictures of her and her friends. Bookshelves fit into every corner, each holding a plant. The kitchen counter wrapped around in a U shape, part of the counter space doubling as a bar area for the living room. Three barstools faced the kitchen, and inside was a small table with only two chairs.

"I like your place," I said, sitting down on one of the stools.

She poured a drink and passed it to me, leaning on the counter from the kitchen side. "Yeah, okay," she laughed.

I looked at her, confused. "You think I'm lying?" I asked.

"No, not lying, but being nice. You live in the Upper East Side, and you like my apartment?" she asked disbelievingly.

"Yes, I do," I said. "I didn't always live in the Upper East Side. You should have seen my first apartment when I came to New York. Smaller than this. Wife and two kids in bed with me. Did you find a boyfriend since the last time I saw you?"

"No, I'm still single," she said.

"Got tired of swiping right? You know, if you do it too much, it can cause carpal tunnel, it's a serious health risk." I winked. "It was right and not left, correct?"

"Yes, right—right. I mean correct, right." She gave a nervous laugh.

"I still can't understand how a girl as gorgeous as you is single," I said.

"I guess I have high standards. I have three requirements for a boyfriend. He needs to have his own apartment, his own car, and make at least as much as I do. Not so easy to find nowadays," she said.

"Hey, I have all that!" I smiled and raised my hand.

She giggled. "Yeah, you have more than all that. You have so much baggage you may as well be the claim at the airport".

I started sweating again. "Is it hot in here?"

She straightened from leaning on the counter. "I'm not hot, do you want me to open a window?"

I unbuttoned my collar. "Do you mind if I take my shirt

off?"

She shook her head, no. I felt her watching me as I stood up and took my button-down off and hung it neatly on the kitchen chair. I sat back down on the stool.

"You like Metallica?" she asked, noticing my t-shirt.

"I do," I said. "Do you know who they are?"

"Don't they play that song at Yankees games? What's the name of it?"

"'Enter Sandman,' and yes, they do. You like the Yankees?" I was sort of surprised she'd know anything about baseball. I couldn't think of one woman in my life who showed any interest in a sport, let alone knew the specific details of music played.

"Yeah, why? You didn't take me for a Mets fan, did you?" she replied, acting as if she was insulted.

I laughed. "My company has box seats. If you ever want to go to a game with your friends, I can hook you up with tickets."

"That's cool! I've never even seen the new stadium," she said.

"Wow, seriously? It's gorgeous. Like a museum, really."

She just smiled and bit her bottom lip again. She drove me crazy when she did that.

"Oh, Metallica has that other song too that I like. 'The Day That Never Comes,'" she said.

"That's the newer stuff. I like the older albums. *Kill 'Em All, Ride the Lightning*. When I was in middle school, before you were born, they weren't mainstream. They didn't play their songs on the radio—all underground stuff. Thrash metal was a whole new thing, like nothing anyone had ever done before," I said. I was impressed she knew who they were. Every time she opened her mouth, I liked her even more, as I realized that we actually had similar interests beyond our uncontrollable sexual attraction.

"Aren't they from California too? Did you ever meet them?" she asked.

I chuckled. She really was cute. "You truly have no concept of how big California is, huh?"

"No, I really don't." She laughed and turned red. "I told you I moved here very young. Outside of summers in the Poconos, I never really left New York."

"They're from the San Francisco Bay Area. I'm from Santa Monica. It's about seven hours south of San Francisco," I explained. There was silence for a second, like she didn't know what to say next. "I know I said I'd wait until Christmas Eve, but I couldn't stop thinking about you."

"Well, it's Chinese Christmas Eve, right?"

She walked around the counter and took the glass from my hand, standing between my legs. She placed her other hand on my thigh.

"Do you mind I take a sip?" I took a deep breath and stared into her eyes.

"Nope, not at all. You can take whatever you want." I placed my hand on top of hers. She leaned in closer to me and took a sip of my drink. "So, you like Metallica and the Yankees, what else do you like?"

"I like the smell of scotch on your breath," she told me.

I moved closer. "Do you like the taste of it, too?" I asked.

She kissed me slowly, then licked her lips. "Yes, I definitely like the taste of you." She took my hand and pulled me up from the stool. "Come with me."

I followed her to the bedroom. "I've been dying to taste you," I said, taking off her shirt and leading her to the bed, my tongue in her mouth as she softly sucked on my lower lip. I was unzipping her jeans as she was trying to wrestle my shirt off. I pulled my lips away from hers just long enough to allow her time to lift the t-shirt over my head, and then my lips were on hers again.

"I never got to do that the last time," I said, continuing to take off her pants.

I laid her down on the bed and immediately started pleasuring her with my tongue. She gripped my hair, grabbing it even tighter when I slid my fingers into her. I could have done that to her all night. I didn't think I'd ever been that aroused by a woman before. The more stimulated she got, the more nervous I became that I was going to explode before I had a chance to sink inside. After she orgasmed, I climbed on top of her. She couldn't get my pants off fast enough. I lifted her legs over my shoulders and got even harder when I saw how flexible she was. The faster I went, the harder she told me to go. At one point, I was pumping so hard while gripping the bedpost that I was seriously afraid we were going to collapse her bed.

Lying with her curled against my chest afterward, I looked around her bedroom. It was the smallest room in the house. The bed was only a full but covered nearly the entire wall, only room for one small end table on the side I assumed she slept on. There was a desk with a mirror on it that looked like she did her makeup there, and a dresser. Both pieces of furniture were different shades of brown. Despite the mismatched wood, it didn't look bad. She decorated the room in all earth tones, so the pieces blended nicely, with similar canvas pictures on her walls as in the living room. Everything was very neatly arranged in its own spot, except for a stack of large candles in the corner that seemed completely out of place.

"Planning on a power outage or preparing for a séance?" I asked.

She peeked over my chest to see what I was looking at and then jumped out of bed.

Holding a candle up in her hand, she said, "One of the pharmacies down the block went out of business. These things are normally like ten dollars, but they were on sale for six, and then buy one, get one free..."

She lit the wick and placed the candle on the desk and said with a rebellious tone, "I splurged."

I closed my eyes and inhaled the scent. "Passionfruit?" I guessed.

"Very good!" she answered, crawling back into bed with me.

"Do I get a prize?" I asked. She sat on top of me and leaned into my lips.

"You sure do."

We had sex twice that night. Although the actual act was incredible, I enjoyed just lying with her. Her head on my chest, talking, caressing each other. I ran my fingers through her hair. Our sweat and other bodily fluids mixed together into a somehow hypnotizing scent. I was so comfortable around her, that I felt like I'd known her forever.

She trailed her hand up and down my chest. "I like your body," she said. "Do you work out?"

"Not like you do... I mean, I do pushups and sit ups every morning and run two miles. Nothing too crazy."

"You guys have it so easy to stay in shape." She

laughed. "It's so weird. I feel like I can tell you anything."

"You can," I said. "Not like I can tell anyone anyway." I looked down at her, wanting so badly to tell her exactly what I was thinking, but I stopped myself.

"What?" she asked. "You look like you want to say something."

"I do," I said, looking straight in her eyes, still running my fingers through her hair. "I know I already told you I never cheated before. I've had plenty of opportunities, but I've never even been interested. Not until I saw you that night. I can't explain it, but there's something about you. I can't control myself around you, from the minute I saw you. I'm more attracted to you than I have ever been to any other woman in my life. If I had to build a girl, it would be you."

"You don't think my breasts are too small?" she asked. "You can tell me honestly."

It was hard to believe a girl as beautiful as her would have any insecurities.

"What? No way, not at all. They are perfect. *Everything* about you is perfect. But even more—I barely know you, yet I'm so comfortable around you. Am I making any sense, or you think I'm crazy?"

"No, I don't think you're crazy. I'm been thinking the same thing. I have never done anything like this, like the roof, especially with anyone. There's just something about you that feels—I don't even know the right word."

I just smiled. I understood exactly what she was saying.

Around eleven-thirty, I said I had to leave. I usually got home around midnight on poker night. I didn't want to go. I wanted to lie in bed with her all night. Before I left, she reminded me that she now had a bottle of Johnnie Walker Black in her house should I ever want a drink.

SAMANTHA

Vince was taking longer than usual to get ready for his poker night, and I was getting aggravated. I hosted a dinner party during his poker nights every month. My girlfriends were going to be there soon, and I wanted him to leave already. I walked into the bedroom, where he stood in front of the mirror, buttoning down his shirt. I could smell his cologne from the hallway.

"Did you shower today?" I asked.

"Of course, I showered. Why?" he asked, looking at me through the mirror.

"You smell like you took a bath in a bottle of cologne," I responded. "Are you leaving?"

He rolled his eyes. "Yes, I'm leaving, why you in such a rush for me to go? You got strippers coming or something?"

It actually wasn't a terrible idea. Maybe next dinner party, I *would* hire strippers—that could be entertaining.

"Lisa is coming early to help me set up."

He smirked. "Translation, you and Lisa want to talk shit about all your other friends before they arrive," he said sarcastically.

"Exactly," I said.

"Samantha, look around. This bedroom is literally like six-hundred square feet, why are you breathing down my neck?" he asked.

"It's my intimidation tactic to get you out of here faster. Speaking of, did you happen to notice the changes we made to the room?"

I'd just had the interior designer over. They'd extended the dressing room and changed the floors from carpet to a beautiful marble tile to match the furniture. A white leather loveseat with blue throw pillows that matched the walls was placed under the bay window. He looked around the room like he was just realizing it was different. He walked to the loveseat and threw himself down.

"Your tactic may have worked better yesterday, but having this loveseat now somehow propels me to gaze out the window, perhaps drink a cup of tea?" he said, making a hand gesture as if he were holding a small cup with his pinky pointed up. "I did however notice the twenty-grand taken out of the account, which—by the way—what was the check you wrote for fifty thousand today?"

"Oh, a donation to the animal rescue charity," I said.

He stood up and walked towards me, pointing at the beautiful Maltipoo I was holding. "Fifty thousand on rescue animals, yet I had to spend two grand on Tiny Tim for Christmas?"

He curled up his lip and squinted at the dog.

I pulled the dog close and covered his ears. "Can you stop referring to him as Tiny Tim? He's going to start thinking it's his name!"

"I'm sorry, but I cannot look at a five-pound dog that looks like a hamster, and with a straight face call him Rocky," he replied.

The doorbell rang. Thankfully, Lisa had arrived just in time for me to end the conversation. I practically ran down the stairs to greet her.

Lisa was my best friend. She was a few years older than me. A redhead, who was in extremely good shape and always well dressed. The type of woman who only wore designer clothes paired with five-inch stilettos, no matter what the weather, and who always sparkled from the diamonds visible on every part of her body. Lisa had a very chic and sexy vibe to her and was married to Vince's best friend, Jimmy. She excelled at being rich. Born to rich parents and married to a rich man, it was second nature to her. She was the only one who knew the truth about mine and Vince's past and how we came to be as a couple. Everyone else thought I was older than I was, although I kept both my real and fake age a secret.

Lisa walked in, annoyed.

"Tonight couldn't come fast enough. I needed to get the fuck out of that house with those kids. Heads up, Rachel is down the block, on her way," she said. "Why do we keep inviting that bitch places?"

"How can we get away with not inviting her?" I asked.

"I just find it bizarre that she hits on your husband right in front of you," she said.

I rolled my eyes. "Please, if she thinks he's such a gem, she can have him."

"If she pulls out that sperm donor book, I might slap her," she said.

Rachel, along with the three other women who were coming, were our friends from the country club. She had her own money; she was a successful dentist. Very plain and mousy looking with such frizzy hair that Lisa and I had contemplated taking her to a salon for a treatment. She was eternally single, probably due to the fact she was so irritating to be around. Currently, she was shopping for a sperm donor to impregnate herself and babbled on and on about it all the time, telling us about every donor's bio and asking for input as if her unborn child was a communal vote. Sperm donor shopping was literally the only thing she had going on in her life.

Rachel walked in, holding a platter of cupcakes.

"I brought some cupcakes from that new trendy place down the block," she said.

"Oh, thank you sooo much!"

I took the platter from her and placed it on the counter, both of us knowing full well that not one woman coming over would ever eat a cupcake. Lisa and I shot each other the telepathic *I hate her* looks that we'd gotten so good at communicating. Vince came down, shuffling through the car keys on the wall to pick the vehicle he wanted to drive.

"Hi Vince!" Rachel pushed her chest out and playfully tossed her hair. Lisa and I shared our telepathic look again.

"Hi Rachel," he said, not bothering to glance up.

"I saw the new addition to the family you got Samantha for Christmas. Haven't you ever heard the phrase 'adopt don't shop?'" Rachel asked.

Still not looking directly at her, he said, "If you can pay, why get a stray?" He grabbed his keys and finally glanced up. "Have fun, ladies," he said, and left for poker night.

The other three women arrived shortly after Vince left.

All beautiful women, married to rich men. No one worked, with the exception of Rachel. Their conversations were always about new improvements to their houses, their last gifts from their husbands, and who the best plastic surgeon was for whatever addition or subtraction of our bodies required.

"Ladies, let me share with you the festivities for tonight! First, here's a menu of the entrée, coming directly from the sushi chef in the kitchen," I began, handing out cardboard cards displaying the varieties of fish to choose from.

Rachel interrupted. She always had something to say. "Does he do anything vegetarian?"

Annoyed, I was about to reply with something snippy when Lisa let out a sigh.

"Why don't you ask him for just rice and seaweed?" Lisa asked. "Samantha, please continue."

"Secondly, I've had this very special sake flown in straight from Japan," I said.

The women all moved forward to get a closer look at the bottle.

"Also, I have gifts for all of you," I said, handing out silver and gold gift bags, all nicely decorated with ribbons. Courtesy of Bloomingdales, of course.

The women all started gasping as they opened their bags, each one containing a different colored silk nightgown and an aromatherapy eye mask. I walked over to the attached family room, separated by sliding doors, and opened them. The aroma of lavender and eucalyptus poured out. Inside, there were three massage tables set up, all accompanied by a massage therapist. The room had been temporarily transformed into a spa, dimly lit with candles.

"Oh, Samantha! You outdid yourself this time!" one of the women exclaimed.

I clapped my hands. "I'm so glad you all like it. So, three girls, ninety minutes each, two rounds. You can decide amongst yourselves who wants to be in the first group," I said.

Just then my daughter, Casey, came down the stairs.

"Casey, honey—care to join us?" I asked.

I knew there was no way she would say yes. She thought my friends and I were ridiculous, and tried her hardest not to be home whenever they were over. Casey was beautiful, with blonde hair and Vince's brown eyes. She looked a lot older than sixteen, probably because she was extremely well-developed. I'm not sure where her chest came from, considering I had to pay for mine.

"Oh, no thanks, I'm going out to meet my friends. Have fun, though!" Casey said.

"There's snow outside, aren't you going to wear a jacket?" I asked.

"Mom. I have a turtleneck on. I'm getting right into my friend's car and then in her house, I don't need a jacket," she said.

"There are cupcakes on the counter for you and your brother," I told her. She smiled and walked out without taking one. Lisa let out a chuckle directed at Rachel.

The sake was well worth the money. The rich beverage was chilled to perfection with a crisp apple and grape taste but more importantly, just a few hours later, we all had nice buzzes going. That was when everyone started sharing the first time their significant other told them they loved them. Aside from the fact that Rachel didn't have a story to tell, none were particularly nice enough to even remember.

"Samantha, how did Vince tell you he loved you?" one of the women asked.

I smiled and looked up to the ceiling, as if I were reminiscing about the best day of my life.

"Oh, it was so romantic," I began, playing with my hair. "We were still in California, dating for a while already. He was so handsome that I could barely take my eyes off of him. We'd been shopping all day long on Rodeo Drive. He told me to buy anything I wanted. That night, he had reservations for us at this romantic restaurant on the cliffs of Malibu overlooking the beach. He ordered this fancy bottle of wine, and we gazed at each from across the table. After, he said he wanted to go for a drive. He had this beautiful sports car—a Corvette, I believe. We drove an hour and a half, and he surprised me with a three thousand square foot suite in this hotel in Huntington Beach, directly across the street from the water."

The women were all staring at me in awe, so I continued. "We walked across to the beach later that night, he didn't even care what time it was or if we were trespassing or not. He led me right over to the ocean, just before water could touch our feet. Then, he got down on one knee, and took out this." I held up my five-carat engagement ring. "He told me he was so madly in love with me that he couldn't imagine spending another day without me."

The fairy tale I spun was nothing at all like the real story. The truth was, I'd gotten pregnant at sixteen, back when Vince was still a baseball player. He never spoke about playing baseball to anyone except Jimmy. We got married when my parents kicked me out of the house. He didn't drive a Corvette, he drove a Camaro. It was nice, but not anywhere near the same caliber of car. The engagement ring I was showing off wasn't even the original. We had to pawn the first one to make rent when we were forced to move to New York so that Vince could go for his Series 7. The one I was wearing was the replacement he bought me after his first real bonus.

As far as the first time my husband told me he loved me, it wasn't on the beach. That happened in a hospital two years after we were already married. I wasn't feeling well that night and didn't make it to his game. I was holed up in a hotel room with Nick, who was only fourteen months old at the time. I only left him unattended for five minutes so that I could go to the bathroom, and by the time I came out, he'd gotten into the minibar. Vince had been informed that we were in the hospital during the seventh inning of his game. They gave him a police escort. By the time he arrived, the staff had already pumped Nick's stomach. Vince found me sitting on the floor of the waiting room, sobbing hysterically.

I was only eighteen years old. I had no right being a mother. I hadn't a clue what I was doing. Being a father came so naturally to Vince, and he was so good at it. He wouldn't even change his uniform in the locker room with the other players, instead, rushing straight home to spend time with Nick. In the hospital, he kept trying to calm me down. He assured me that I wasn't a bad mother at all, and that accidents happened, and luckily, Nick was okay. Then he pulled me into his chest and said, "You know what else? You're a great wife too. You cook for me, keep the house clean, come to my games even though it's obvious you hate baseball..."

"Is it really that obvious I hate baseball?" I remembered asking through my tears.

He'd laughed. "Yes, it's extremely obvious. And even though you got stuck with me, you never complain about it. I love you."

I still don't know if he said the words because he meant them, or if he was just trying to calm me down.

A laugh drew me back to reality. I started clearing the sushi plates and bringing them to the kitchen. Lisa followed, helping me with the mess.

"You can write a book on the love story between you and Vince," one of the women commented.

Lisa leaned into me and laughed. "Or you could work on Wall Street," she whispered.

The door opened, and Vince walked back in. The women stared at him with dreamy eyes. He cleared his throat uncomfortably.

"Sorry, didn't realize you were all still here. You look like you just got through watching *The Notebook*." He headed over to the bar to make himself a scotch.

"Samantha was just telling us how you proposed to her," Rachel said.

He smiled at me.

"Oh, that story—oldie but goodie. Thankfully, she said yes!" he said, making his way upstairs. "Don't keep me waiting too long, honey."

Once he disappeared from sight, I looked up at the women and shrugged. "After all this time, we still can't keep our hands off each other!"

SARAH

Vincent's visits became more frequent. He would show up randomly at my apartment. He always texted first, and he always had a reason. "Happy Presidents Day." "Happy St. Patrick's Day." "Happy Easter." "Happy Cinco day Mayo."

This time when I opened the door to my apartment, I held up my cell phone and displayed the text message he'd sent.

"Happy Thursday?" I laughed. "What's so special about Thursdays?"

"Oh, it's my favorite day of the week. Nobody likes Mondays, and Fridays are so overrated. Wednesdays are too in the middle. But Thursday is a pretty perfect day." He walked in and handed me a Nordstrom's bag that was beautifully wrapped with a gold ribbon on top.

"What's this?" I asked.

"Just something I got for you." He smiled. "Open it."

The bag wasn't large but must have weighed five pounds.

"Are we celebrating Thursdays now?" I laughed.

"No, we're celebrating you," he said.

We sat on the couch and I very carefully tried to untie the ribbon without ruining it. He started tapping his fingers on his leg and rocking back and forth.

"Just rip it," he said.

"It's wrapped so nice, I don't want to ruin the bow," I said.

He leaned back and watched me as I continued opening the gift. I reached inside and pulled out a beautiful white candle in a glass bottle with a silver lid. The label said Jo Malone London. I opened the top and sniffed. It smelled like a mixture of fruit and flowers, like fresh apples and roses.

"This smells amazing!" I lit the candle and placed it on the coffee table. "Thank you so much!"

He leaned in closer. "It does smell nice," he said, like this was the first time he'd noticed.

"You didn't smell it when you bought it? What made you pick it out?" I asked.

He stood and walked over to the kitchen chair, took off his suit jacket and his slacks, and neatly placed both items on the kitchen chair so they didn't get wrinkled. There was something about watching him undo his tie that was incredibly sexy.

"If we're being honest, I knew you liked candles, so I just asked the girl in the store to give me the nicest one they had. This was her suggestion," he said, returning to the couch in just boxer briefs and a t-shirt.

"It does smell beautiful," I said.

He leaned in to kiss me. "I'm glad you like it." He pulled his lips back from mine and took my hand in his. "You look really tired."

I let out a deep breath. "I am. I didn't sleep well last night after the club and then went straight to the matinee today after my work out."

"Why don't you quit the strip club already? I'll help you out with money."

"No, I'm not a prostitute. I am not taking money from you," I said.

"Why does everything go back to prostitution? Can't I just help out someone I care about, without it being some sort of quid quo pro situation?"

I just shook my head. I couldn't take money from him. It wouldn't feel right. I had to do this on my own.

"You want me to go so you can get some sleep?" he said.

"No, are you kidding? You're the highlight of my month!"

I led him to the bedroom. As I settled on top of him in the bed and lifted his t-shirt up to expose his bare chest, his phone rang. He apologized and then answered. I must have nodded off on him while he was talking because some time later, I woke up with my face mashed against his chest.

"Oh my God, I'm so sorry! I must have dozed off."

He pushed the hair out of my face. "It's okay, how do you feel?" he asked.

"Like I slept for five hours," I said.

"It was four and a half," he corrected me.

I sprung up and looked at the clock. The time was 9:45 p.m.

"Holy shit! Why didn't you wake me?" I asked.

"You looked so comfortable sleeping on me, I didn't

want to disturb you. You needed sleep." He pulled me back down to his chest.

"How did you get away with not going home?" I asked.

He pinched the bridge of his nose while he looked down at me, as if he were ashamed to be repeating the lie he'd told his wife. "I said I had an impromptu business dinner," he admitted.

"You said that just so I could sleep?" I asked, stunned.

"Yes, is that weird?"

I started kissing him. "No, you're not weird. You're amazing."

Pulling his lips away from mine, he said, "Unfortunately, I do have to go now, though."

He got up from the bed.

"Did you even eat? Do you want something before you go? I can make you a sandwich or something," I offered, following him into the kitchen.

"Oh, no thank you. I'll grab a hot dog on the way."

"I thought you don't eat 'street meat,'" I teased.

He started changing back into his suit.

"Dirty water dogs and street meat are two very different things."

He pulled me close and held me tightly in his arms, like he was never going to see me again. "This is the worst part of seeing you—having to leave you."

I held him by his tie as he leaned in to kiss me. We kissed for a bit and once he left, I couldn't help but look up the candle, wondering what qualified it to be the nicest candle they had. I almost dropped the phone when I saw the price—$495! I immediately blew the flame out. With that price tag, the candle would only be lit on special occasions. Luckily, the description claimed it had two hundred and thirty hours of burn time. So far, I had only used five.

Our affair continued and reached the six-month mark. I couldn't get enough of him, and I think Vincent felt the same. He was always telling me how gorgeous I was, how it was technically my parents' fault for making such a perfect woman. How he couldn't stop thinking about me. When he arrived at my apartment in July for "Happy 4th of July," I pulled open the door. "I couldn't wait to see you!"

He peered behind him, like he was checking to make sure I was referring to him, before turning back to me and holding up a brown paper bag.

"Craving sushi?" He laughed.

He went to the kitchen and began setting the table as I pulled the food out of the bag. By now he was so familiar with my apartment and where everything was, he may as well have lived there.

"I got it!" I blurted. He looked up from the plates, lifting his eyebrows.

"I got the role!" I repeated. "The *lead* role in the new show, *Wounds of Time*!"

He stopped what he was doing and ran over to hug me. He was sincerely happy and proud.

"That's amazing!" he said. "Now what?"

"Well, I'm going to quit the strip club, because now I'll be able to make enough money to focus only on the show."

He blew out a sigh of relief. "That's great! For numerous reasons!"

"I still have off on Mondays and then on Wednesday nights, but I'm required to do the matinee on Wednesday. Every other day, I'll be working. Both shows. My workout routine is going become more intense, so I'm required to do an hour of massage therapy twice a week."

"I can help you with the massage therapy!" he said, rubbing my shoulders before we sat down at the table to eat. "What's the show about?"

"Well," I said, "it's about a woman in a love triangle. She's having an affair and torn between the both of them."

He swallowed his sushi and made a face.

"Most of the show she doesn't know what to do," I continued. "Her husband isn't the same man he once was, and she feels more wanted by the other guy."

He stared at me before bowing his head down a little. Then, he peeked up at me, his mouth slightly open. I knew what he was thinking—basically, I was playing him in the show.

He put his chopsticks down. "How does the story end?"

"Turns out her husband realizes she's having an affair and feels a tremendous amount of guilt. He blames himself. He starts doing all the things he did when he was younger to win her over again." I shrugged. "I guess in the end, the affair essentially makes their marriage stronger."

He jumped up from his chair.

"That's completely unrealistic! He just forgave her after having an affair? No—it's stupid. I need to get with your writers and help them rewrite the ending, what bullshit."

He was quite aggravated, like the entire storyline was a personal jab at him. I hadn't even realized the similarities of the show to us until I said it out loud. His little outburst was honestly adorable.

"How do you propose the story ends?" I asked.

He started pacing the kitchen like he was thinking of

ideas.

"Okay, I got it. She's about to tell the husband she's having an affair, and in love with this other man. But then the husband gets hit by a car and dies, and she doesn't have to tell him, and she and the boyfriend live happily ever after," he said.

I put my hand over my mouth, horrified.

"Vincent! That is a terrible thing to say!"

He looked down, rubbing the back of his neck.

"No, you're right. That's a bad idea... um..." He began pacing again.

"Okay, okay, I got it!" he said, snapping his fingers and pointing up, excited at his new idea. "Turns out, he, the husband is *also* having an affair, and he too met a woman that he is madly in love with. They're afraid to tell each other, but in the end, the husband and the wife are relieved that they both found who they're supposed to be with and part the closest of friends. Like that Billy Joel song where they get married really young, but when they get divorced, they are still friends." He started singing the lyrics.

I cut in and sang the next part.

He turned very animated, singing right to me like he was trying to convey a point.

We both stood there in the kitchen, singing the rest of the song.

By the end, Vincent was getting very silly, waving bye, and playing air guitar. Singing, like he was on an audition to play Mr. Joel himself. By the time we finished, he had his arms around my waist. He suddenly got serious.

"You know this is just one of the many reasons why I love you," he said.

My heart literally skipped a beat. He'd never told me

that he loved me before. I almost didn't know what to say. "Because I know Billy Joel?" I asked.

"Yes! What twenty-seven-year-old knows who Billy Joel is? Let alone the lyrics to 'Brenda and Eddie?'"

I looked directly into his eyes, gazing as hard as I could the way he did to me. "It's called 'Scenes from an Italian Restaurant.'"

He started laughing. "Oh...I'm sorry! Is *that* what it's called? All of a sudden, you're the Billy Joel expert?" he asked

I wrapped my arms around his shoulders and stood on my tippy toes to kiss him. We didn't make it to the bedroom. He took my clothes off right there.

On opening night, Vincent was there, front and center. Luckily, I never looked at the crowd until the end with the bows, or else I'd be super nervous. I was worried that maybe he wouldn't even think I was a good actress. After the show, he met me with a massive bouquet of flowers.

He started showing up so often, the whole staff knew who he was. I wasn't quite sure they knew his title, but they assumed he was my boyfriend. I was okay with that. I mean, in a way, he sort of was my boyfriend. Now that I'd quit the strip club, he came to my apartment every Monday with lunch. We would eat and have sex. He called me often, as any boyfriend would.

A few times a week turned into every day on his way to work. I knew exactly what time he'd be calling, and that was when I took a break from my workout routine and waited for the phone to ring. We'd talk about everything a real couple would discuss: work, friend drama, kids, social lives. The only difference was that he had a wife he went home to, and that wife wasn't me. I knew he was going to be trouble. Especially as the months went on, and I fell for him harder and harder. It was difficult to date other men with a man like Vincent in my life. No one seemed to come close in comparison.

Soon, it was the Monday right before Thanksgiving week. Vincent had asked me what I was doing for Thanksgiving. I'd explained that since my father passed away, my mother and I had a tradition where we would get all dressed up, go to a fancy restaurant for a prix-fixe Thanksgiving meal, and then see a movie. She lived in Brooklyn and hated taking the train so I would meet her there, and we'd always find a new trendy place to eat. Never the same restaurant twice. Brooklyn was very up and coming, so it was easy to keep things interesting.

I immediately regretted asking Vincent what he was doing.

"We have a tradition since the kids were little. We go to the same resort in Aruba every year for the week," he said.

I couldn't help but be envious of his wife. She got to do the real stuff with him. Go out to eat in public, go to the movies, sleep in the same bed as him, go on vacations.

"Is your wife pretty?" I asked.

"Yes, very," he answered honestly.

He spoke about his kids often; he was so proud of them. He spoke about them so much that at times, I felt like I knew them. He never really talked much about his wife, though. Almost like he thought I would be jealous, and he would be right—I was. But I was so into him, my infatuation outweighed my jealousy. I just wanted him in my life no matter what the capacity.

"Why don't you talk about your wife?" I asked, on that

Monday as we were eating lunch.

He glanced up at me—surprised, I guessed, that I would even want to know. "What do you want to know?"

"What does she do for a living?" I asked.

He laughed. "Nothing. Not anymore. When we were younger and trying to make it in New York, she would waitress or bartend—mostly jobs to keep the lights on in the house, at night when I could stay home with the kids. When I started doing so well, she stopped working."

That surprised me. Nowadays, everyone worked, even women. At least every woman I knew did.

"What does she do all day?" I asked curiously.

He looked down and bit his bottom lip, like he was searching for an answer.

"Not sure. I know she belongs to a country club with her best friend and they, I don't know, do whatever women do in a country club." He laughed.

"Do you think she cheats on you too?" I asked.

"Okay, let's stop talking about my wife," he said, lifting his hand to halt the conversation.

"Why? Would you be upset if she cheated on you? I mean, you—"

He interrupted me. "I'd rather not know about it. You're right. If I were to get mad over my wife cheating, it would be a complete double standard. So, if she is, I would rather not know."

I stopped the conversation. If he didn't want to talk about her, I wasn't going to make him.

My mother was impressed with the restaurant I chose for Thanksgiving this year. I'd picked a very high-end Italian place, well decorated with cloth tablecloths, and waiters who sounded like they were really from Italy. My mother was typically very plain and modest. She didn't even dye her hair, kept it gray. She looked a lot older than she was. But she really enjoyed dressing up for our yearly dinner.

During our meal, she couldn't stop talking about the show. She'd watched it twice already—she was so proud of me. She loved bragging to her friends about her daughter, the Broadway actress.

"Are you dating anybody?" she asked.

"No," I lied. The last thing she would want to hear was that I was dating a married man.

"What about that guy from the show? The one who plays your love interest? I've seen the way he looks at you. I think he's smitten," she said.

"Matt? No, Matt's just a really good friend," I answered. I didn't have the heart or the guts to tell her that Matt was gay, that wouldn't go over so well. My mother was so religious and judgmental. When I'd started dating my last boyfriend, she'd bought me a Bible and a crucifix. There wasn't much about my real life that I share. She wouldn't approve of any of it.

SAMANTHA

"Earth to Samantha, you there?"

I looked up from my wine glass. I was having brunch with Lisa at the country club and I must have zoned out. Throughout the years, fitting in became easier, but it was a struggle at first. All these women, sitting there with their designer bags, toy dogs, and diamonds that sparkled so much, you could spot them from tables away. Even the waiters wore tuxedos at noon. Lisa and Jimmy were such a good match; they played the power couple well.

"Yeah, I'm here," I whispered, afraid to let other women hear me. "Can I ask you a personal question? Do you and Jimmy still have sex?"

She looked at me like I had three heads. "Of course. Too much if you ask me—you and Vince don't?"

"No, we do, it's just lately it's different," I said. "Like he's distant, not too into it. Last night it was taking him like an hour, literally an hour, moving me around, changing positions. I finally had to stop him, it was exhausting."

The week before we'd been in Aruba and had only had sex once. Not that we'd ever really had sex every day, but we usually tried to at least a couple of times a month.

"No passion anymore?" she asked.

I took a sip of my wine. "Anymore? I wouldn't have ever called us passionate. He's the only guy I've ever been with. He became my whole family, just us and the kids. Even when we have sex, it's, you know, just sex."

The waiter came over to us with a tray. "Tuna tartare?" he asked.

"Yes please." Lisa accepted a napkin holding the tuna covered cracker.

I shook my head. "No, thank you."

"You must have had passion for him when you were younger, no?" Lisa asked while slowly nibbling on the cracker.

"When I was sixteen? I don't know if I'd call it passion. I was undoubtedly infatuated. So much so that I lied about my age. I never in a million years thought I'd get pregnant. I told him I was nineteen. He was older, a great talker, very charming. Completely different than he is now. Kind of a bad boy. Although I will admit, he's still a good talker." I reminisced, smiling.

"Of course, he is, that's what makes him so successful. It sounds like you were a little bit of a bad girl yourself—lying to a guy about your age to get laid," Lisa said.

"Not really, more like extremely naïve and rebellious. I used to sneak him into my house when my parents weren't home. I would make my little sister be my lookout," I said, laughing. So hard to believe how different we both were now.

"Vince, a bad boy?" Lisa said. "I can't even imagine

that—he couldn't have been *that* bad. I mean, he did the right thing and married you, even after you lied to him."

"Yeah, he did," I said. "I absolutely give him credit for that. He could have gotten into a lot of trouble, considering how young I was and how mad my parents were. The first time they met him was when we told them I was pregnant. Not that they would have liked him any better if I wasn't. We were parents ourselves at such an early age that we never really got to experiment with different things, you know, in bed."

I finished my glass of wine, so Lisa reached into the bucket of ice next to us, poured me another glass, and then topped hers off.

"Jimmy and I like to roleplay," she said, bringing the glass to her lips for a sip.

"Roleplay?"

"Yeah. Like, we'll go into a bar, pretend we don't know each other. He'll pick me up, and then we'll go do it in the car or something," Lisa said.

Now I looked at her like she was the one with three heads. "Like Vince would ever do that in one of his precious cars."

"Look, you guys have been married for twenty years. You need to spice it up a bit. Switch it up, make it exciting. What's he into?" Lisa asked.

"What's he into?" I repeated. "I don't know, normal stuff. I think in his mind, I never grew up, like I'm still sixteen. He still treats me like I'm this fragile being."

"He never mentioned anything that he wanted to do? Or that maybe he did with other girls before you?" she asked.

I paused for a minute and took a deep breath. "When I

found out I was pregnant, I kept trying to call him, but he wasn't picking up. We didn't have texting back then, so I did something really dumb, I showed up at his house."

Lisa leaned in closer, realizing the story was about to get interesting.

"He was there with a girl," I continued. "A woman, I should say, she had to be at least thirty. I was devastated, crying. I felt like such a fool. He awkwardly introduced me to the woman, called her Melissa, who then got pretty upset over his introduction because her name was actually Melanie. He didn't even know her name!" I shook my head. "When she left, he thought I was overreacting, said we'd never had a conversation that we were in a relationship. Melanie was striking. Spanish, huge boobs, really pretty and put together. The complete opposite of me."

"Doesn't sound that different than you," Lisa said.

"Well, then she was. Back then, I was pretty plain. Vince swore he liked me and that sleeping with her didn't mean otherwise. Said she was just easy. A week later, we were engaged. I've asked him about his encounter with her so many times, I might as well have been in the room with them. I wanted every single detail. Evidently, she wanted it rough. Real rough. I asked him if he wanted to do that with me, and he always said no. I think he was traumatized when he found out I was sixteen. He thought I'd be relieved to know that he didn't go down on her, said that was too intimate to him." I shook my head in disgust. "Gotta love men—going down on a girl is intimate, yet sticking your dick in her isn't. To this day, I still can't get her face out of my head."

"So...sounds like some *Fifty Shades of Grey* type shit," Lisa said.

I stared at her, puzzled. "What's *Fifty Shades of Grey*?"

"Are you kidding me?" she asked. "It's like the hottest book of the millennium, everyone is talking about it. Come on. After this, we are going to a bookstore and getting you a copy."

After we finished our meal, we headed right over to Herald Square. I purchased the book that apparently "everyone was talking about." It took me three days to finish the thing. Wow—who knew that so many people were into S&M? Was I that out of the loop?

Next, Lisa brought me to an adult store, and well, I picked up some things there that I would have never imagined myself using.

The following night I decided to surprise Vince. I put on this leather outfit that may as well have been painted on me. With much difficulty, I tied myself to the bed, stuffing this ridiculous thing I'd bought in my mouth. When Vince got home that night, it took him a while to come into the bedroom. I could hear him downstairs, fixing himself a drink, scavenging through the fridge. It was a Friday night, Nick and Casey were away at college. There was no good reason why we couldn't get kinky.

I tried to look as sexy as possible as I heard him walk up the stairs. I sucked in everything that needed to be sucked in, positioned myself in a completely submissive form. He still had the drink in his hand when he opened the door and stood there, staring at me like I was insane. Not a sexy look at all.

When he realized I was tied to the bedposts, he said, "What the fuck is going on in that bed?"

Not exactly the response I was going for.

I tried talking, but turns out, it's hard to speak with a ball gag in your mouth.

Vince approached the bed, drink still in hand, and removed the ball from my mouth.

"What is this?" he asked, turning the object around in his hand, trying to examine it.

"It's a ball gag," I replied.

"And what exactly is a ball gag?" he asked, confused.

I guess I was semi relieved that he didn't know what it was. "It's um...well, it's to muffle my screams when you, you know, get rough or beat me," I said. Wow, that sounded so bad.

He stared at me as if I'd lost my mind. His mouth hung half open, as if he were going to say something, but nothing came out. He downed the rest of his drink, and then looked back at me like he was still trying to figure out what to say.

"Would you rather be the one to get beat?" I asked, hoping he said no.

Now he was thoroughly un-entertained. He shook his head in disgust, and put the ball gag down on the night table. "Why is *anyone* getting beat in this scenario?"

I was mortified. I guess he'd never heard of *Fifty Shades of Grey*, either. I didn't know how to explain. I couldn't exactly admit that Lisa suggested it while I was complaining about our sex life.

"I don't know I just thought maybe it would turn you on," I said.

He untied me from the bed. "Well, it doesn't," he said, and walked over to the dressing room to change his clothes.

He went into the guest room, and I suppose he went to

sleep. I don't exactly remember when he started sleeping in the guest room full time. It had been years now. Vince had never been a good sleeper. He woke up every hour and checked emails regularly throughout the night. He started sleeping in there, so he didn't disturb me during his nightly activities. I never thought anything of it. From everything I'd heard, it was typical for a white-collar businessman to have sleeping issues. He really only came into the bedroom to get dressed or, on occasion, have sex. We never had sex in the guest room, always the master bedroom. If someone was sleeping over and needed the guest room, then and only then would he sleep in the bed with me. During those times, I didn't get much sleep.

The next night, I decided that instead of going full-out freak, maybe I'd just wear a sexy Santa outfit, what with Christmas being so close. Vince was sitting on the couch in the living room, watching TV. I came in with a trench coat and my surprise Santa outfit underneath.

"I have an early Christmas present for you," I said.

He put the remote down, folded his hands together and looked up at me with a grin.

"Oh yeah? What's that?" he asked.

Finally, he seemed interested! He wasn't stupid. He knew I had something sexy on underneath or nothing at all.

I shut the TV off and put the music on. I found the sexiest Christmas song I could find, one that I could strip to. I started dancing around the living room, moving seductively and taking off the trench coat as "Santa Baby" played in the background.

When the music came on, his facial expression changed. He sat up straight and started moving his neck back and forth, biting on his thumb nail. Did he not like this song? For a few moments, he looked like he was still trying to play along. But when I dropped my trench coat and straddled his lap to seduce him, he got this weird look on his face.

"Everything okay?" I asked.

He was quiet for a minute, like he didn't know what to say.

When he did speak, he said, "I have to shit," and then moved me off his lap so that he could rush to the bathroom and lock the door.

I stopped the music and slumped on the couch. I suddenly felt like I was a teenager, getting rejected by the guy I had a crush on. Only difference was I had never been rejected by someone I had a crush on, and also—I didn't exactly have a crush on him. He was my husband. That made his reaction an even bigger burn.

The next day while getting manicures and pedicures with Lisa, I couldn't help but vent. What did I do wrong? What did Vince have against "Santa Baby"? Was I just not attractive anymore?

"Maybe he really did have to shit," Lisa said, trying to justify his actions.

"Are you kidding me?" I asked.

"I mean, you guys have been married so long now—maybe he's just comfortable being that honest with you."

"In the middle of sex?!" I wasn't buying it. Granted, Vince and I didn't have the perfect marriage, but we used to at least have sex. Even if it was just an act to get each other off, we'd been together so long that we could easily arouse each other within minutes. I assumed he cheated, at least once in a while. Why wouldn't he? It wasn't like we were madly in love. At home, though, he always played the game.

The day after that, I was at home watching TV when Vince called me in the afternoon. He never called in the afternoon, so I picked up, concerned. He was yelling so loud that he was hard to understand.

"What? Slow down. I can't understand you—what the fuck are you so mad about?" I asked.

"This is what you and Lisa do all day long? Talk shit about your sex lives?" he yelled.

"What are you talking about?" I asked.

"Answer this, why would Jimmy tell me I should take care of my wife before someone else does? Let me guess, was the ball gag Lisa's suggestion?"

Oh shit. My heart dropped into my stomach. He was furious, to say the least. Wouldn't even let me get a sentence out. "Vince," I began, but he cut me off.

"My job is stressful enough, especially at the end of the year. You think I need this added high school drama? You like the Louboutins on your feet, or your revolving bedroom that's redecorated every month? What the fuck do you think I'm doing all day? *Working*. I know you probably have no concept of what that word means, but that's where your bank account comes from. I can assure you, I have no time for this baby bullshit!" he yelled.

"Can I—" I tried, but he cut me off again.

"Hey, I have an idea. You want to get so kinky? How about we suggest a swap with Lisa and Jimmy, I'm sure they'd be down. Wanna fuck Jimmy? He thinks you're crazy hot, I can arrange it."

Finally, there was a pause. "No Vince, I do not want to sleep with Jimmy," I said in an even tone.

"Aw that's too bad, guess you're still stuck with me!" Then he hung up on me.

He didn't get home that night until after 10 p.m. Vince wasn't a big drinker. Every night like clockwork, he had one glass of scotch and brought it up to his room before bed. I guess the alcohol took the edge off from his day at work. But that night, I smelled the distinct scent on him the second he walked through the door. He must have been drinking for hours. I hated the smell of scotch on him. He walked into the kitchen to pour himself another glass, barely looking at me, not saying anything. I hadn't seen him this quiet in a very long time.

"Can we talk?" I suggested.

He looked up at me. "Oh, you want to talk? You haven't done enough talking already?" He took a sip of his drink. He looked so hurt, like I'd betrayed him, or challenged his manhood. He stared down at the counter, refusing to meet my eyes.

"Vince, I...you're right. I shouldn't have said anything to Lisa. I was just frustrated, so I thought we could try out different things. Spice it up a bit. Trying to make it not so...boring," I said.

He rested his hand over his mouth and looked at me for a minute. "Boring?" He started to approach me.

"Maybe 'boring' isn't the right word," I said, back-peddling. "Routine?"

"Routine?" he repeated, raising his eyes to the ceiling. He grabbed me and turned me over the sink. "You want it rough?"

I clutched the sink as he lifted my nightgown and started having sex with me right there, from behind. Against the sink and hard. *Really* hard. In a way, it was actually pretty sexy. He'd never been that forceful before, with his fingers digging into my hips and pulling me to him.

As I was getting really into it, he reached his hand across the sink and filled his palm with dishwashing liquid. I had no idea what he was planning until suddenly, I got the answer to that question. Using the liquid as a lubricant, he pushed his finger into a hole that nothing ever naturally enters. I didn't know what to do. It all happened so fast. Do I tell him to stop? Let him keep going? I was the one who'd introduced this idea the other night.

Then it happened. His finger disappeared, replaced by him—his penis, in the hole that nothing was ever supposed to enter. It hurt, so bad. All I could think about was Melanie and what they did together. Was he really into this? Had he been lying to me the whole time? I was holding the sink so hard, my knuckles were white. Then, he reached around to my front and shoved two fingers into me there, too. I let him keep going, hoping it wouldn't take him too long to get off.

Luckily, the act must have excited him because he finished pretty quickly. I turned around, pulled my nightgown back down, and looked at him. Speechless.

He zipped up his pants and topped off his drink. "Make sure when you tell Lisa about this tomorrow, you let her know we broke the routine, and I popped in your ass. Are you happy now? Is that what you wanted?" he asked.

I was too embarrassed to reply. He stood there for a few minutes, waiting for an answer. When he realized he wasn't getting one, he shook his head, sighed, and walked upstairs. I stayed in the kitchen, staring at the dishwashing liquid for quite a while, trying to process what had just happened.

After that, we barely spoke until his company Christmas party a few nights later. I guess I was afraid to even bring it up again. I wasn't sure if this type of sex was something that he really liked, and if so, why hadn't he brought it up after all these years? I knew he'd done that with Melanie. I'd even offered in the past, but he'd always said no. Now I wondered: did he do this with other girls?

I walked into the room as he gazed into the mirror, straightening his bowtie, and asked him to zip up my gown.

He zipped me and said, "I don't get my company. We go from one extreme to the next. Either strip joints or black-tie affairs. What about a nice company Christmas dinner? Does no one eat dinner anymore?"

Vince hated this party. First of all, he had to give a speech, and he hated public speaking. More importantly, though, he hated meeting the spouses of the employees. He had a rule not to get to know anyone in the office. Aside from Jimmy, he had no friends at work. He figured if he didn't know them personally, then it would strictly be a business decision and not a personal one when he had to let someone go.

"Do I look okay?" I asked.

He made me do a turnaround. I'd had my hair styled into banana curls and wore a long black gown with diamond-like sequins around the halter top. My stilettos were diamond cut to match the dress, which accented the real diamond Tiffany's necklace and tennis bracelet pair I was wearing.

He smiled as he watched me. "Yeah, you look good.

Really good."

The venue was only a mile away, but Vince made sure he drove his Porsche there. He put on quite the show. He climbed out, opened the door for me, and in we walked, hand-in-hand. He stopped to shake some employees' hands and wish them a Merry Christmas on our way to the executive table, where he was seated right next to the CEO.

"There's the couple of the year!" Phil said, standing up to greet us. "Samantha, how is it possible you look younger and younger every time I see you?"

It had taken me years to get comfortable around Phil. He was very intimidating by nature. In his late thirties, extremely young to be a CEO. Dirty blonde hair and blue eyes, always tan from some excursion that he'd just returned from. He wasn't married and always had a beautiful woman on his arm.

"Thank you," I gushed, kissing him on the cheek.

"I'm a lucky guy," Vince said, extending his hand to Phil.

"In more ways than one," Phil said. "Looks like we're going to end up having a great year. Maybe you can get a nice summer house with that bonus you get."

Vince laughed. "Thank you, but I try to live below my means, never know when my luck is going to run out."

I'd give him that—he didn't live as flashy as he could, considering the number of zeros in his bank account. I was always trying to get him to buy fancier things the way Phil or Jimmy did, but he said he found it unnecessary. Even wearing a nice suit took him quite a while to get used to. If the decision were up to him, he'd be in jogging pants and some sort of band t-shirt every day. He never complained about me spending money though.

Vince was nervous when Phil stood to give the opening speech—squeezing my hand hard, while gulping the drink in his other hand.

"... and without further ado, I'll let the person who handles this more closely come up and speak—my right-hand man, Vince DeLuca," Phil said.

Vince walked up to the microphone. "I'll keep this short and sweet so that you can all go back to eating and drinking. This year was a great year. With three weeks left to go, we're projecting the Nasdaq at a little over a thirty eight percent gain, DOW twenty-six and a half, and S&P up almost twenty-seven percent. Best in a long time. That's the boring stuff. The things that all the hardworking brokers here already know, and your spouses don't care about. I'd really rather take this time to just thank everyone for the hard work they've put in all year long."

He paused to gesture toward me. "Most importantly, though, a special thanks to my beautiful wife, who put up with my 3 a.m. emails and Sunday conference calls. Babe, you're my rock. I love you," he said.

"Merry Christmas, everyone!" he concluded, raising his glass in toast position.

Tom's wife, Christina, leaned over to me. "I am so jealous of your marriage! The two of you are like the real-life Barbie and Ken."

"Thank you. I've been with him since I was sixteen!" I said. In reality, though, sometimes it felt more like I'd been stuck with him since I was sixteen.

I stood as he walked back over to the table and kissed me. Everyone was clapping. He was so good at shooting shit that if he ever decided to quit his job and move to

Hollywood, he would have no problem landing an acting career. He only called me beautiful or said he loved me during his speeches. He was so believable that even I could almost believe him for a second. He sat back down at the table.

"Want to dance?" I asked him.

"No way," he said.

He hated dancing. I would always try to convince him that a slow dance was basically just moving to music, but he never budged.

"Look up Vince, eighty-five percent of the company is on the dance floor," I said.

He looked up at the dance floor. "Yeah, and seventy-five percent of them look like idiots," he replied.

It was a good thing we'd never had a wedding. I didn't know what he would have done when the bride and groom were expected to dance.

The second we got in the car, the show was over. "I wasn't impressed," he said.

"With what?" I asked.

"The steak was too well-done to be called medium rare," he complained.

The truth was that if it wasn't the steak, then something would have been wrong with the pour of his drink or a comment some poor drunk broker said to him. Or the service. There was always something wrong with that event.

VINCE

I laid in bed that night, restless. It was almost 1 a.m., and I couldn't sleep—I couldn't stop thinking about that night in the kitchen with Samantha. What had happened wasn't something that usually turned me on. She'd made me feel so inexperienced that night when I'd walked in and saw that—whatever that ball was in her mouth. Granted, we didn't really talk often, but lately, she seemed to be going out of her way to be extra silent.

The bigger question on my mind, though, was what had gotten into her? She couldn't even stand me, so I doubted she was attracted to me anymore. And then out of the blue, she was talking about us beating each other. Sex outfits? Stripteases? "Santa Baby"? Seriously, of all the songs in the world to pick, she had to pick the one that reminded me of meeting Sarah. The song that she had stripped to that night?

I had full intentions of sleeping with her that night when she came out in that trench coat, but the song just freaked me out. Did she somehow know about Sarah? Was she testing me?

I stood and walked into the master bedroom. Samantha was still up, sitting in bed reading a book. "Hey," I said, entering slowly. She put the book down on her lap and looked up.

"Hey," she responded, taking her reading glasses off and placing them on the night table.

I sat on the edge of the bed. "I'm afraid to ask, but what are you reading?"

"Don't worry—nothing crazy, a murder mystery," she answered.

I took the book out of her lap. "I think you should really stop reading." I laughed. "Also, I think I should probably make Amanda check into my life insurance policy tomorrow."

She smiled and shook her head. "No need to waste your assistant's time with that. Don't worry, Vince. You're still more useful to me alive than dead," she teased.

"Do you want to talk about what happened in the kitchen the other night?" I asked.

Her mouth drooped, and her cheeks turned red. "No, not particularly," she replied. "As a matter of fact, if we never spoke about it again, I would be just fine."

"I just want to explain...." I started, but she cut me off.

"Nothing to explain, I told you to do it rough, and you did."

I looked down. "Did you like it?" I asked, still not looking up.

"I mean maybe the first part, but the second—no, not even a little bit. Did you?" she said.

"I mean, it was okay. I didn't dislike it, but it's not something I would necessarily want or need. You know that already, you've asked me that a million times," I answered honestly. "Look, I just wanted to let you know you looked amazing tonight."

She tilted her head, confused.

"You asked me how you looked before we left, and I said really good," I said. "When I was giving my speech, I saw the way you looked at me when I called you beautiful and realized I don't tell you that enough. So, I just wanted to let you know that you are truly beautiful," I explained, looking directly into her eyes.

I took the reading glasses off the night table and put them back on her. "Actually, I think I kinda like the glasses too."

She slid up on the bed and leaned into me. "How much have you had to drink tonight?" she asked.

"Probably not enough, I can't sleep. I was actually going to go make one now. Do you want one?" I asked.

She said okay, and I went down to grab a bottle of wine. I returned to the room with the wine and two glasses.

"Since when do you drink white wine?" she asked. She knew me too well. I always preferred red. I couldn't even remember the last time I drank white.

"I don't. But it's your favorite, and you hate when I smell like scotch, so I'm am making an exception," I answered, winking at her.

I poured her a glass, and we sat in bed, drinking the wine. I needed something to take the edge off. I knew I needed to sleep with her and was truly afraid I wouldn't be able to.

We sat there, awkwardly drinking the wine together. She seemed just as weirded out by the idea of sleeping with

STEVIE D. PARKER

me as I did with her. "Is there anything different you want to try?" I asked her, afraid of what she was going to reply. After walking into that room with her with that ball gag in her mouth, I could only imagine what else she read.

She took her glasses back off and put them back on the night table. She thought for a minute. "Maybe on the loveseat?" she suggested, leading me there.

I sat down and she sat on top of me, her arms around my shoulders. As we began kissing, I tried so hard to get into it. I removed her nightgown as she moved up and down on me, thinking maybe that would help. It was taking me a while to reach the point of climax, which made me even more nervous—that's what had started this whole mess. So, I picked her up and carried her back over to the bed. I threw her legs over my shoulders, put her back on top of me, turned her over—nothing was working. I could tell she was getting impatient.

Finally, I closed my eyes and pictured Sarah. Pictured being in her apartment, on top of her, inside her. When we were finished, we didn't say much. She rolled over, back to me, and went to sleep. I stayed in bed for a few minutes before returning to the guest room. I experienced more guilt over thinking about Sarah during sex than I even did over actually sleeping with her. Samantha really was beautiful—too beautiful to have a man picturing someone else.

Christmas Eve approached. Sarah found it comical that I still wanted to meet on the roof and have our wine and our dance. Why wouldn't I, though? That was *our* tradition now. Plus, how could she be my "Christmas Fairy" if I didn't see her on Christmas Eve? The kids were going to be home from school on break, so except for our

Monday afternoon rendezvous, the next two weeks were going to be hard for me to get out of the house.

I met her at the club at our usual time. As I walked her to our nook and then opened the bottle of wine, Sarah looked over toward the corner, where we'd done the deed for the first time.

"Imagine someone has us on camera?" she asked.

I handed her the glass. "I'd pay to watch that tape. I bet we'd make great porn stars."

She put our song on, and we danced. I never looked forward to dancing so much in my life, didn't even care how cold it was. When we finished the dance, we sat back down, holding hands and drinking our bottle of wine. I rubbed her hands in mine to keep them warm.

She looked at me, a little dreamy-eyed, and said, "Tell me about your first love."

I chuckled. "That's what you want to know about, my first love?"

"Yes," she said.

"Okay." I launched into storytelling mode "My first love... Well, she was hot. REALLY hot. Gorgeous, in fact. When I would see her no matter what kind of day I was having, she made it better. And when she left, I got this feeling right in the pit of my stomach that I already missed her. My stomach literally hurt."

Sarah smiled at me. She really liked the story. She was very into romantic stuff, which I was okay with. I wasn't typically a romantic guy, but with her, I would be whatever she wanted. I couldn't help but say corny things. That's just what she did to me.

"How old were you?" she asked.

I thought about it for a second. "Forty-one," I replied.

She playfully hit me on the chest, suddenly realizing I was talking about her. "Not me, idiot, your first real love," she said.

"You are my first real love," I insisted.

She gave me a skeptical look. She didn't believe me. "That can't be true. You're married—what about your wife? You don't love her?"

Now that was a harder question to answer. I sat for a second and tried to put my thoughts into words.

"Yes, I love my wife," I said. "But it's different. We didn't fall in love and get married like most couples do. We were young, *really* young, and she got pregnant super-fast, within the first few months. We barely knew each other when we got married. We joke about my 'super sperm' now and how it molded our paths. We love each other, sure, but we kind of grew to."

She didn't seem to like that story as much. "How'd you meet her?" she asked.

"Oh, well, I was a pretty cool twenty-two-year-old, believe it or not. And she had these beautiful green eyes. I was instantly attracted to her".

"Green eyes, huh?" She laughed. "I see you have a type."

"You know what? I never realized it, but you're right. I guess I do," I said, looking into her green eyes. "There's just something about a girl with green eyes. She's Irish like you, too, but most people think she's Spanish. Anyway, I don't tell people about this, but I was a baseball player and one night after winning a game—"

She interrupted me. "A baseball player? Like a real baseball player?"

"If by real, you mean professional, then yes. I played in

California."

Her eyes grew wide and she smiled. Now she was curious. "What position?"

"Catcher," I replied.

"How does a baseball player become a stockbroker?" she asked.

Valid question. "I'm not sure how much you know about baseball, but to be a catcher, you have to have a really strong arm. Be able to throw a ball to second base squatting like this," I said and demonstrated the position for her. "One night in my second season of playing, after going out with the guys, I was driving my car on the freeway, much faster than the speed limit allowed and much drunker than I was supposed to be. Totaled the car. Sucked, nice car too. I broke my right arm in three different spots. Luckily, I didn't kill myself or anyone else. The only thing I killed that night was my baseball career. Even if I'd ever be able to throw that hard again, which was a long shot, the league wasn't having it. They kicked me off. I had some bullshit degree that really served no purpose for anything because I never thought I would have to do anything other than play baseball."

I shrugged and continued. "You know how teachers are with jocks, I passed classes even when I shouldn't have. Now, I had a wife and a toddler son at home and no backup plan. They revoked my license; I couldn't even drive for five years. My uncle was a broker in New York City. He told me he'd be my sponsor, help me get my Series 7. So, we moved. It turns out, I ended up being really good at being a stockbroker."

Sarah looked amazed. "That's an incredible story! Do you miss playing?"

I took a deep breath. "Every day of my life. I played softball for a while when I came to New York, but it's not the same."

"Does your son play?" she asked.

"No," I laughed. "He could care less about sports. Real Brainiac, into science and reading, intellectual stuff. I have no idea where he came from. Both my kids are abnormally smart. I truly have no idea how that happened."

Our bottle of wine was empty, and time was running out. I needed to get home. I hated leaving her. We kissed for a little while, and then she waited with me as I hailed a taxi. As she started walking away, I turned around.

"Hey, Sarah," I called out.

She turned to look at me.

"Just wanted you to know that my stomach is already starting to hurt."

And there it was—the smile I dreamt of seeing every day.

Sarah's birthday was in February. I wanted to take her somewhere special. I suggested a place I knew of in Jersey, so the chances of running into someone I knew were slim. We weren't able to ever go out or do real couple things, so I thought this would be nice. Just so happened, her birthday fell on the third Wednesday of the month, so it was easy to say I was going to play poker. She was real street-smart, living in New York practically her whole life. Wanted to know the exact kind of car I was showing up in beforehand. I could literally see her calling me on her cell phone from my rear-view mirror.

"I'm in the silver Porsche one hundred feet in front of you," I said, laughing. I guessed caution was a good quality.

She came over and slid inside. "Wow... Nice car!" She inspected the interior, checking out the sound system and touching the soft leather seats. "I was always a sucker for a guy with a hot car."

I started pulling out. "And I was always a guy with a hot car, so see we're meant to be together," I replied.

"Where do you park this thing?" she asked.

"I have a four-car garage not far from the house I rent," I replied.

"What other kinds of cars do you have?" she asked, intrigued.

"I have a Cadillac, which is the family SUV, and a classic hot rod that only goes out on occasion, mostly to car shows. Oh, and my wife has a Mercedes that she rarely drives but said she really needed to have," I said, rolling my eyes.

"You must have quite the house," she said.

"Yeah, it's nice."

That was a great night. We went to a nice seafood place in South Jersey. The restaurant had a nautical theme, as if you were sitting on a ship. You could smell the fish broiling the second you walked inside, there was a raw bar and live lobsters in a tank. We had a table by the window overlooking the shore. Sarah loved my black button-down, said I looked good in dark colors that matched my hair. She looked amazing.

That seafood place was the first real public place we had ever gone to together. She was very sophisticated at the fancy restaurant, knowing all the right questions to ask. I ordered the same bottle of wine that we drink on Christmas Eve. I bought her a Louis Vuitton bag. I didn't really know what to get her, but all the other women in my life seemed to like stuff like that, so I figured the purse was a safe bet. It was.

We had a really good conversation that night. Not about the past, not about our current situations, just about regular things any couple would talk about: politics, movies currently playing in the theaters, our week at work. I asked her what she was doing for her birthday, and she was excited to tell me that Isabel was able to get her and her friends into the new trendy Asian fusion restaurant downtown. I knew the place, and she was right; it was hard to get into. The food was great though—I'd been there a couple of times already.

By now, we'd been "dating" for over a year. We were beyond all that first date type banter. When we got up to leave, she tripped, and I caught her fall.

"Remember I saved you! Tipsy or heels?" I asked her, laughing.

"A little of both," she admitted, holding my arm as we went to the car. Right before she got in, she put her arms around my shoulders, and under the moonlight, her eyes seemed even greener.

"I had a really good time with you tonight, thank you for saving me," she said.

As I was driving home on the Garden State Parkway, she started rubbing the inside of my thigh. I looked at her and smiled. "You can't touch me like that, you're going to turn me on," I warned.

"Would that be a bad thing?" she asked.

I didn't think she was serious until suddenly, she was leaning toward me over the armrest and opening my pants. I let her, shocked at what was happening. Then, she started to go down on me as I was driving.

"You're going to make me crash," I said.

She started going faster. Suddenly I was in panic mode. I was trying so hard not to lose control of myself or the car. Finally, my attention went to the rest stop on the side of the road. I pulled over and desperately tried to find a secluded place where I could release myself without worrying about killing both of us. I stopped the car, pulled her head up with my hand, and ordered her to get out of the car.

She didn't have much time to get out before I lifted her onto the hood of my car. She wasn't wearing stockings this time, so I just had to shift her panties over to the side. Holding her legs around my waist, I entered her right there in that deserted lot. I think that memory might have trumped the rooftop one. Penetrating her, on my car, out in the open where anyone could have caught us—that turned me on more than I could have ever imagined.

When we were done, I just stared at her, almost speechless.

"Wow, oysters really are an aphrodisiac, huh?" I remarked. "You drive me fucking crazy."

She kissed me. "Good," she answered.

After that, I never went to another poker night again. Every third Wednesday night became our date night.

SARAH

Vincent was right; the food was incredible. I sat there at my birthday dinner with five of my closet friends. The ambiance was amazing. Asian décor on the walls, all in red and gold, nice Japanese plates with ceramic chopsticks. The wall of the bar changed colors every few minutes and illuminated the bottles of alcohol. The service was on point, too—the second my glass was getting close to empty, a waitress was there asking if I'd like another. The music was more suited to a dance club than a restaurant. The only thing missing that would have made my night truly perfect was him.

When we were done eating, Isabel asked me to go out with her while she smoked a cigarette. "What's wrong with you?" she asked, once we got outside.

"Wrong? Nothing I'm having a great time," I replied.

She looked at me like she didn't buy it. I looked down. "I just wish he could be here," I admitted.

"You know what I love about superheroes?" she asked me, taking a pull of her cigarette.

"The hot guys who play them?" I asked.

"Well yes, obviously, the hot guys are definitely a plus, but even more so- the realness of their situations. Typically, they don't end up with the girl they want to be with. Whether they are protecting their identity, or don't wanna put them in harm's way. Life is like a superhero movie, Bianca. You don't end up with the person you're supposed to be with or want to be with; you end up with the person that makes the most sense. It's a business deal, not a romance novel. It's human nature, it's inevitable. You are always going to want what you can't have."

I looked at her skeptically. "Yeah, the thing about superhero movies is that the men have *superpowers*. I wouldn't put them on the list of top realistic movies."

She laughed. "I mean the 'love story,'" she said, making air quotation marks.

Then she asked, "If you had to wake up in a different time, when would it be?"

I thought about it. "Probably in the past. Maybe the fifties. When there wasn't so much pressure to be a woman, when people didn't expect you to not only be the same but be better than men."

"I think I'd want to wake up in the seventies. Free love, drugs," she said.

"I'm not surprised," I laughed.

As we walked back to the table, the staff was coming out with a cake, singing "Happy Birthday." I figured that was why Isabel had told me to go outside—to give my friends time to secretly tell the waitress to bring it—until I saw the look of confusion on everyone's faces.

"Thank you," I said to the waitress.

"We'll take the check, please," Isabel requested.

"The check has already been taken care of," the waitress informed us. "Happy Birthday."

I looked over at Isabel. She leaned into me. "At least you know even if he's not here, his wallet is," she said, smiling.

It was a really sweet gesture, but I would have preferred him over his wallet any day of the week.

On our fourth monthly Wednesday night out in a row, we were somewhere down the shore of New Jersey at a nice sushi restaurant. A very romantic spot, with candles on each table and relaxing meditation-like music playing softly through the speakers. It was the first time Vincent had ordered me sake, and not only did I like the taste, but boy did it give me a buzz.

He was a real good eater, and liked so many different foods. I was never adventurous when it came to tasting new foods, but he made me try everything. He ordered all these different kinds of sushi rolls: tuna, octopus, eel. By now, he knew exactly what I would like and what I wouldn't. I didn't know if it was the sake, the lighting, or the black shirt he was wearing, but I couldn't stop staring at him. Ever since I'd told him he looked good in black, he'd started wearing a different black shirt every time we went out. He always did sweet things like that. We were really having a good time, enjoying an in-depth conversation when suddenly, he looked behind me, and his face dropped. I couldn't help but turn around to see what he was looking at. A couple was approaching us.

"Vince!" the guy said.

Vincent stood up. "Oh, hey Steve, how's it going? I would never have expected running into you here."

Steve was an older chubby guy with a not-so-attractive

wife. He was balding a bit and seemed quite a bit older than Vincent. I couldn't imagine how they even knew each other.

"My sister has a shore house here. We were spending the day there, and she suggested this place for dinner, claimed the sushi was phenomenal. This is my wife, Jennifer," Steve said, introducing her to Vincent. Then he turned to his wife and said, "This is one of my bosses, Vince."

The woman shook his hand. "I've heard a lot about you!" she said, making Vincent flash a phony smile. I now knew Vincent's real smiles versus his fake ones.

"Eh, only half of it is true," Vincent joked.

There was an awkward silence as the couple stood there looking at me, waiting for him to introduce me. "This is Bianca," he said. "My cousin."

I tried so hard not to show shock on my face when he introduced me as his cousin. The couple very nicely said *hello* and stood next to us, talking for a few more minutes. They ended the conversation with "see you in the office tomorrow."

When they left, Vincent sat back down and started playing with his chopsticks. "Wow, who would have thought I'd run into someone here?" he said, taking another sip of sake.

I didn't say much until we left the restaurant. It was when we were getting into the car that I finally exclaimed, "Your cousin?"

He didn't answer right away. He opened the door for me, and then walked around and got in through his side. Before he started the car, he looked at me and said, "What was I supposed to say? My girlfriend? He knows I'm married, and he knows you're not her."

"Don't you think your wife is going to know that you don't have a cousin named Bianca?" I asked.

"Steve doesn't know her. It won't ever come up," he said.

"Then how would he know I'm not her?" I asked.

"From the pictures in my office," he replied, as if that were an obvious answer.

Until that moment, it had never occurred to me that he had pictures of his wife in his office. I looked down.

"Oh, come on, all husbands have pictures of their wives in their offices. Don't make a big deal about this, please. We were having such a good night; let's not end on a bad note."

He wasn't wrong. I really had no right to be mad. I knew he was married. What else was could he have said? We'd been dating for a year and a half—by that point, I knew the situation I was getting into. We'd never fought before, and I wasn't going to start now. It wasn't fair.

"You're right," I said.

We were silent the entire ride back. It was only 10 p.m. when he dropped me at my house. "Do you want to come in?" I asked, breaking the silence.

He stared straight ahead out the windshield. "Do you want me to come in?" he asked, not turning his head.

I'm pretty sure he thought I was mad. "Yes, I do," I said.

He looked at me, relieved. "Then, yes, I would really like to come in."

Once he was inside, I no longer felt anything but love and attraction for him. The second we started kissing, it was like nothing had happened to potentially ruin the night.

The next weekend was the Tony Awards. I was incredibly tense in my dressing room when Isabel walked in. She was wearing a long black gown with her hair tied up.

"You look great!" I said.

"I feel like a celebrity!. I just need some bling," she answered. "But oh my God, look at you!" She made me stand up and do a turnaround. "Bianca, you look gorgeous! Before we go, I just want you to know that I am so proud of you!"

"I'm so nervous. I feel like I am going to puke," I admitted.

She came over to me and took my hand. "Hey, whatever happens tonight doesn't matter. You are an unbelievable actress and you made it this far! I am so jealous of you. Seriously, no joke—you inspire me."

I looked at her with gratitude. Isabel was never mushy and didn't usually say things like that.

"Hey, if I could sing, I would audition for Broadway too—but I wouldn't want to show you up," she added, laughing. Now this was the Isabel that I knew!

"I'm glad you're here with me," I told her.

"Me too," she responded.

We were seated at our table: Isabel, to one side of me and Matt on the other. We'd been nominated for three awards. Matt was in the Best New Actor in a Musical category; I was nominated for Best New Actress in a Musical category, and the show itself was up for Best New Musical. This was it. This was what I'd worked my entire life for.

I went to shut my phone off as the show was starting,

and there was a text from Vincent: *Wish I could be with you in person, but know that I'm watching and rooting for you. Good luck, beautiful! I love you.*

I smiled and shut my phone off, and the show began. Of the three awards we were nominated for, Best New Actress came up first. My heart was beating so fast, and my hands were sweaty. I'd never been so nervous about anything in my life.

I waited while the actress presenting the award announced the nominees. The second she said, "Bianca Evans, *Wounds of Time,*" Isabel squeezed my hand. Matt looked just as nervous as I felt.

"And the Tony goes to..."

I think the hardest role I ever had to play as an actress was pretending I was genuinely happy for the woman who just beat me out of an award. The award I'd dreamt about since I was a little girl. The award I'd worked so hard for. As she went up to receive her trophy, I smiled and clapped.

I even blew her a kiss when she looked over at me, but I was crushed inside. Matt also lost in the category of Best Actor in a New Musical. When they got up to presenting Best New Musical, Matt and I felt hopeless. I had already wanted to go home forty minutes earlier.

"The next award is for Best New Musical," the gentleman on the stage announced. I almost didn't even understand what he said next until Isabel jumped up in excitement. "*Wounds of Time!*"

Matt and I leapt up and hugged each other. Both of us had tears in our eyes as we, along with the cast, walked up to accept the award. I shook so hard that I could barely walk. Matt held my hand, and the rest of the show was a daze.

When I opened the door for Vincent the next day for lunch, I couldn't even see him over the huge bouquet of flowers he held. He set the flowers down on the coffee table and gave me a big hug and kiss. Then he handed me a Tiffany's box.

"What is this?" I asked.

"Open it," he said.

I slowly opened the box, and inside was a stunning diamond bracelet. I didn't own anything that sparkled that much.

"I'm so proud of you!" he boasted. "Congratulations."

I put the box down next to the flowers. "For what? I lost," I said, disappointed.

He came over to me and pulled me into him. Very sympathetically he said, "You didn't lose, you just didn't win."

I could feel the tears welling up in my eyes. "Is there a difference?" I asked.

He looked straight at me, eye to eye. "Yeah, there's a difference. You were nominated, one of *five*! That puts you in the top five ranking of actresses in New York City. That's amazing! And, you won Best New Musical! Best New Musical!" he repeated. "If it wasn't for you and Matt, that show may not have won. If any other actress was in your role, you don't know what the outcome would have been. The two of you *are* the show. You're twenty-eight years old and the leading actress in a Tony Award-winning show! You should be incredibly proud of that!"

I smiled and hugged him. He always knew the right thing to say. He ended up making me feel a lot better. Not from the Tiffany's box, but from the words that came out of his mouth.

The summer seemed to fly by. Soon it was September, and his birthday was coming up. I wanted to do something special for him, but what did you get someone who had everything? Not like I could even buy him something that he could take home. His birthday fell on a Wednesday, but not the third Wednesday of the month, so he took the day off to spend it with me. He said the only thing he wanted for his birthday was an entire day, together.

So that's what we did. He came early in the morning and we spent the whole day together. Relaxing, watching movies, I ordered a nice lunch for us. I had wanted to make him dinner, but he thought it would be easier to take the day off of work than it would to get out at night. After lunch, I asked him if he wanted his birthday present. He was surprised that I got him something. He was probably thinking the same thing I had—what could I possibly buy him that he could bring home?

"I'll be right back," I said and excused myself into my bedroom. I returned wearing a very skimpy piece of black see-through lingerie with fishnet stockings and garter belts, an outfit I bought especially for the occasion. I finished the look with a pair of heels that I had from my strip club days. On my hip was a silver bow.

"Wow," he said. "Been a while since I've seen you like this." He looked very enthusiastic to "unwrap" his gift.

I stood over him as he sat on the couch. "Take the bow off," I said.

He took the bow off slowly, squinting as he tried to peer through the see-through lingerie. "What is that?"

"Unwrap it," I replied.

He slid the lingerie up and stared in amazement. On my hip, I had a new tattoo: a fairy wearing a Santa hat.

"Since you said I'll always be your Christmas fairy, now you'll always be a part of me."

He just stared silently. "Wow, that is... just *wow*," he said. He pulled me on his lap, let out a little sigh, and said, "Where were you when I was twenty?"

I laughed. "I was four, but let me assure you—I was kind of a big deal on the playground."

"Oh, I'm sure you were," he said.

We had sex right there on the couch. I'd still never told him that I loved him. I did love him, so much, but it was just hard for me to say the words. I'd never said those words to anyone. I always felt like he wondered why I didn't tell him, and wondered if I loved him at all. But at that moment, he knew, just exactly how much I loved him. He was now permanently on my body. I think that night was the happiest I'd ever seen him.

The next day, I grabbed Matt before the show started.

"Hey Matt...," I said, using my most persuasive tone. He knew something was up.

"Hey Bianca..." he mimicked back.

"I need a favor," I said. He looked at me, probably wondering what was going to come out of my mouth next. "Do you have a date to Drew's wedding?"

I hated weddings—especially coworker weddings where I didn't have a date. I'd dragged Isabel to so many different events; it was only a matter of time before rumors started flying that I was gay.

"I'm seeing this guy Dave. Not sure if I'm going to ask him yet. More of a casual sex thing, and I don't want him to get the wrong idea," he answered. "Why, aren't you going with Vincent?"

I couldn't tell Matt that Vincent was married. At least

being gay wouldn't ruin my reputation. Being a mistress to a married man, however, would.

"He has a business trip," I lied.

I hated having to lie to Matt. We'd gotten so close since the show had started, but I had no other choice. I needed a date to the wedding—and that date clearly wasn't going to be Vincent.

SAMANTHA

I'd just finished with my personal trainer and had stopped by the supermarket to grab a few things. I despised running errands after working out. I felt sweaty and gross, so my intention was to get in and out as quickly as possible. All the other women in the supermarket looked like they were getting ready to go out for the night straight after shopping—wheeling their carts with their designer bags and toy dogs in the baskets, wearing high heels.

While I checked the expiration dates on yogurt, I heard a man's voice from behind me.

"Samantha!"

It was Adam, one of Vince's friends from when we first moved to New York. The two of them used to play on a men's softball league together, back when Vince had time to have hobbies. Adam hadn't aged well. He had a big belly and a receding hairline, and it didn't even look like he and Vince could be the same age. He wore dress pants and a button-down shirt, but the buttons were pulling a bit. I was so used to Vince in his expensive suits that I no longer liked the look of men in button-downs without ties.

"You look fantastic!" he said.

I brushed the loose strands of hair out of my face. I was still in yoga pants, a hoodie, and had my hair tied back in a ponytail. I looked far from fantastic.

"Thanks," I said. "I just finished working out. I don't normally look like this." I didn't know why I felt the need to say that, especially since he was complimenting me.

"How are the kids?" he asked.

"They're doing amazing, thanks—both away in college. Nick is studying some sort of computer thing, and Casey is going for a psychology degree," I said. "How have you been?"

"Same shit, different day. Still working at the bank, you know, living the dream." He laughed, implying he was not happy with his job. "Where has Vince been? Too much of a big shot to show up to poker games anymore? Shit, I haven't seen him in months, you need to let him out more. Tell him I miss taking his money."

I never tried so hard to keep a smile on my face. I was in complete shock. Vince hadn't been going to poker games anymore? Then where was he going on those Wednesday nights? I wasn't surprised at the idea that he cheated, but once a month? Was he spending all those nights with the same person? "You know Vince. He gets really consumed in his work."

I promised Adam that I would send my regards, put the yogurt down, and left the store. I didn't know what to do, didn't even know what I was feeling. I headed over to Saks Fifth Avenue and with Vince's credit card, bought myself a lovely pair of Christian Louboutins. Not because

I needed shoes, but because I needed to remind myself of the benefits of my marriage.

I didn't say anything about running into Adam when Vince got home that night. I tried to block the encounter out, but it kept coming into my head. Did Vince have a girlfriend? Casual sex was one thing, but did he have an actual relationship with another woman? I had so many questions that I didn't dare to ask. We had a good life, didn't we? Was he going to try to leave? Was she the one who was into anal? I wasn't even sure I wanted to know the answers, but I couldn't get the questions out of my head. I kept wondering what she looked like.

The next night, I pulled the sexiest dress I could find out of my closet and put it on with my new shoes. I looked in the mirror before leaving. I had to say, I looked pretty good.

I made it to the W around 9 p.m. When I walked in, I spotted a group of good-looking guys at the bar, probably in their late twenties or early thirties. I sat next to them. The one closest to me was exceptionally attractive. He wore black dress pants with a maroon-colored shirt and a nice tie that matched well. His hair was dark, and he had hazel eyes and a very nicely shaped beard.

I kept trying to make eye contact with him, but he was too consumed in his conversation to even realize I was sitting next to him. I began moving my upper body to the beat of the pop music playing—still nothing. Finally, I started the conversation. "What are you drinking? It looks delicious."

He swiveled and smiled, once he realized that a woman was sitting next to him. "A gin martini," he answered.

"I'll have the same thing," I said to the bartender.

The drink was a nice presentation. Big, stuffed blue-cheese olives were skewered across the martini glass on a long toothpick. I took a sip and immediately reared back. It tasted like drinking rubbing alcohol mixed with turpentine, with a hint of olives. The martini was disgusting, but I smiled like the drink was the best thing I'd ever tasted.

"What's your name?" I asked the man.

"Cole," he said.

"Wow, Cole, you have good taste in alcohol," I said.

"And what's your name?" he asked.

"Samantha," I said.

He turned his seat around to face me. "Why are you here all alone?"

"I'm waiting for my friend," I lied. "She's running late."

Cole and I spoke for about an hour. He bragged to me about his job. He was some sort of generic stockbroker—not on Wall Street, but in an office downtown somewhere. He was very proud of his $125 thousand salary like he thought that was a lot of money, so I acted impressed. When he asked me what I did, I told him I was a teacher. It was the first thing that came to mind. I couldn't exactly tell him I was nothing—just a housewife with grown kids and a rich husband. If you could even call me a housewife.

I rubbed my stomach. "I don't think my friend is showing up. I'm starving, do they serve food here?" I asked. He suggested a nice restaurant a few blocks down and asked if I'd like to go. I accepted the invitation, and we left to go eat.

We went to this little tapas place, dimly lit with candles and a rustic theme—very romantic. We shared plates of food and had a few more drinks. He was single, twenty-nine years old, and lived in Brooklyn. He was seven years older than my son. When he wasn't looking down at his cell phone he spoke about online dating, video games, and some new superhero movie that was out. We had nothing in common, but he was cute. He was using a lot of slang I didn't understand, and most of the time I found myself nodding and pretending I knew what he was talking about. I was technically only nine years older than him but felt like there was a much bigger generation gap.

The check came at almost midnight. Cole picked up the bill and read: "$125, so a $25 tip?"

"Sounds about right," I said.

He took out his phone and did some sort of mathematical equation. "Okay, so a hundred and twenty give plus twenty-five is one hundred fifty, divided by two, $75 each."

I looked up, stunned. Was he asking me to pay half the bill?

"If you have Venmo, you can send it that way," he said.

I didn't know what to say. I didn't realize that women picked up their own share on first dates now. I certainly couldn't Venmo him money, where all transactions could be viewed on a public wall for all of your contacts to see.

"I'll have to go to an ATM," I said.

He smiled. "No big deal. I'll wait."

I walked a block down to the closest ATM. I hadn't even prepped my new shoes with sole guards yet for walking on concrete, so they were quite clearly never going to be worn again. Did Casey deal with this sort of thing when she went out with guys? Whatever, I wasn't going to let this ruin my night. I took the money out and returned to the restaurant to pay him.

"What are you doing now?" he asked. "You want to come back to my place?"

I did. I don't know why I did. Maybe I just needed to be with someone other than Vince. Perhaps I'd feel better about what I'd discovered earlier in the supermarket if I slept with someone else, too.

We climbed into an Uber and headed to Brooklyn. He kept trying to kiss me in the Uber, and I laughed, telling him to wait. The Uber driver kept looking at us through the rearview mirror. I started to get worried. I'd never slept with anyone except Vince—were all men the same? Would the same things turn Cole on? He was probably used to sleeping with girls in their twenties—was I even still attractive enough?

The Uber stopped. I was expecting Cole to tell me what half the bill was, but he didn't. I guess now that he knew for sure he was getting laid, he was willing to pay the fare. The block was pretty quiet compared to Manhattan. There was a bodega on the corner, where a group of guys were hanging out and drinking something out of a paper bag. We started walking toward his house, and he put his finger over his mouth and motioned for me to be quiet. He led me through the backyard. Walking on the grass in my heels was a challenge, so I took them off. "Why are we being quiet?" I whispered.

"I don't want to wake my parents up," he said.

I froze right there. "Your *parents*? You live with your parents?"

He seemed annoyed that I was talking after he'd just told me to be quiet.

"No, I don't live with my parents. I have the basement

apartment," he whispered. "They don't come down, but they can hear me coming in if we're too loud. Don't worry, my space is nice, it has windows."

I just stood there. What the hell was I doing? I'd paid half the tapas bill to come all the way out to Brooklyn, to sleep with some kid who still technically lived under his parents' roof?

"You know what, Cole? I should go home. I'm a little older than you," I confessed.

He looked at me as if that was no big shock. "It's okay," he reassured me, "I like cougars."

Cougars?! Now, that was the straw that broke the camel's back. I immediately called an Uber. Cole was annoyed, to say the least. Called me some sort of name that I assumed translated to "tease" and disappeared inside. Fortunately, the Uber came quickly. I was disgusted. How could I ever consider leaving if *this* was what dating had turned into nowadays? The whole experience scared the shit out of me, so much that I didn't care anymore. Vince could do whatever he wanted; I was way too old to start dating again.

When I got home, all the lights were off. Vince must have already been asleep upstairs. I wasn't even sure he realized that I'd been gone. Right next to the door was a vase that we'd bought on a trip to France. I wanted him to see me, I realized. I wanted him to see me walking through that door dressed like I was. Let him wonder where I'd been, the same way I now wondered about where he spent his Wednesday nights.

I took the vase and dropped it on the floor. At the crash, Rocky started going crazy, barking like a lunatic. Within seconds, Vince came running down the stairs, armed with a handgun. It was dark and he couldn't see. I flipped on the lights, and he pointed the gun straight at me. He immediately dropped his stance and looked at me, relieved. "Oh shit, I thought you were someone breaking in—what time is it?"

"2 a.m."

Vince appeared half asleep, like he was still in a daze. He glanced down at the ground and spotted the broken vase on the floor.

"Are you hurt, did you cut yourself?" He barely looked at me, much less seem to notice what I was wearing.

"No, I'm fine," I said quietly, picking Rocky up and petting him. The poor little guy was shaking. I think I'd scared him more than Vince.

He went into the kitchen to get a broom. He returned as I removed my heels and held them in my other hand. He swept up the mess and took it to the kitchen to toss. This time, when he came back, he looked me up and down. Finally, the outfit I was wearing and the time registered.

"Are you drunk? Do you need help getting upstairs?" he asked.

Disappointed at his lack of reaction, I replied, "No, seriously, I'm fine."

"Okay," he said. "I'm going back to sleep—I have to be up early tomorrow. Well, today, I guess." Then, he went back upstairs.

I made my way to the empty master bedroom, my room. I sank onto the bed, replaying the entire night in my head. Vince didn't care where I'd been, or for that matter, who I'd been with. He didn't care that I'd stumbled home at 2 a.m. He must really like this new girl, for him to not even try to sleep with me when I was all dressed up.

He just didn't care anymore.

SARAH

Isabel surprised me at work one night. She hadn't even told me she'd purchased tickets to the show, but when I came out from my dressing room afterward, she was waiting for me.

"You were great!" she said. "Let's go out and celebrate. There's a hot new club in meatpacking. We can probably get there by midnight."

"Oh, I can't," I said. "It's a rough week. I don't have that type of cash flow tonight."

"What's the sense of dating a rich man if you still don't have enough cash to go out on a Saturday night?" she asked. "Don't worry about the money. I have it covered."

"Okay," I agreed. "But I can't drink a lot. I'm not really supposed to be drinking at all."

We went back to my apartment and I searched my closet for something to wear. She wasn't impressed by anything I tried on. Nothing was sexy enough. So, we headed to her apartment, which was only a few blocks away. She had a studio, and her couch turned into a bed.

We stepped over the clothes strewn all over the floor so that she could shuffle through her closet to find something that met her approval. She pulled out a tiny pair of black leather shorts and a sparkly belly shirt. She dug out a pair of stilettos that matched the shirt perfectly.

When we got to the club, there was still a line that wrapped around the corner, despite the late time. It took about twenty minutes before we even saw a sign of a bouncer. We had our arms wrapped around our waists while we rocked back and forth to try to warm up. There was a group of girls in front of us. Not very attractive, but well made up, like they'd paid to have their hair and nails done just to go to the club that night. They were excited in the line, anxious to get in.

"$50," I heard the bouncer say. He looked like a professional fighter.

I looked at Isabel. "Did he just say $50? I'm not paying $50 to get into a club," I said. We stared over at the bouncer in shock. The girls were quite surprised as well and tried to negotiate.

"$50 or go to another club," he repeated.

Disappointed, the girls walked out of the line, leaving Isabel and I to approach the bouncer—even though neither of us had the money to pay the admission fee. The bouncer looked at us up and down, undressing us with his eyes. Then, with a smirk on his face, he announced, "$20."

"You just told those other girls fifty," I said.

He folded his arms across his chest and stared down at me. His biceps looked like they were made of steel. "And now I'm telling you twenty," he said.

I looked at Isabel in disgust. I felt so bad for those other girls who were forced to leave.

"Forget it," she said, and I followed her off the line.

As she raised her arm to hail a cab, the bouncer yelled over at us, "$10."

We looked at each other. Sure, it was messed up, but for $10, we were going to go inside. We made our way through the crowded dance floor to the bar. There were so many people dancing that I quickly went from cold to hot. Isabel ordered us two vodka shots.

"Okay, here's the game plan," she said, holding up her shot. "We're both broke. If anyone offers to buy us drinks, we get shots. We'll get drunk faster that way."

We took the shots and made our way onto the dance floor. The DJ was playing great music, and colored lights blinked throughout. The two of us put on quite the show. The way we were dancing on each other, you'd think we were back on stage at the strip club. Soon we had a crowd surrounding us, watching us dance. Isabel yelled something over the music. I cupped my ear because didn't understand what she was saying. To me, it sounded like she'd said, *Kiss me.*

"I can't hear you," I shouted back.

"Kiss me," she yelled again.

"Kiss you?" I said, still dancing. "Like on the lips?"

She laughed, nodding. "Yes, on the lips—tongue and all! Trust me!"

So, I kissed her, tongue and all. We made out for a few minutes on the dance floor, and the shots came pouring in. I think every man in that club bought us a drink, and even some of the girls. I was so drunk by the time we left, that I could barely walk. The taxi took me home first. As soon as I got inside my house—still on a high from the awesome time at the club—I picked up the phone and dialed Vincent. You'd think by then that someone would have created new technology, just to prevent drunk calls.

Vincent picked up, half asleep. "What's wrong?" he whispered. "Are you okay?"

"Yes, I'm okay," I said. "I'm more than okay, I'm horny, and you need to come here right now."

There was a slight pause.

"Are you drunk?" he asked.

"Yes. Now get over here."

"Sarah, it's 4 a.m. on a Sunday morning," he said. "I can't come there now. You're not even supposed to be drinking, don't you have to work tomorrow?"

My mood drastically changed from happy to mad, almost instantaneously. "Don't lecture me. I don't want to hear that shit. You better come here now."

"Please. I can't argue with you right now, I can't even really be on this phone. Just go to sleep, and I'll call you tomorrow," he said.

Now I was outraged. In that drunk moment, I didn't care that he had a wife, kids, what time it was—I wanted him here, and I wanted him here right then.

"If you don't get here in twenty minutes, never call me again!" I hung up on him.

It took him about fifteen minutes to arrive. "Oh, that's great," he said, as he walked inside. "Your door is wide open, and you're passed out on the floor. Real safe."

I was sitting on the floor of my living room. "I am not passed out, I just can't stand at the moment," I said.

He came right over to me and tried to lift me up. "Sarah, I can't stay here. I need to go. I still have to figure what to say if I get caught walking back into that house at this hour. Let me help you get undressed."

"Yes! Take my clothes off." I lifted my shirt higher than it already was and exposed the underside of my breasts.

He looked down at me. "What the fuck are you wearing? Do you always go out dressed like this?" He didn't sound impressed.

"It was a special occasion," I slurred.

"Really? What was the occasion? National Slut Day?" he asked.

He started bringing me over to the bedroom, while I was stripping off my clothes. "Fuck me," I kept saying. He was getting annoyed and glancing at everything in my room except me.

"I can't. I have to go, please just go to bed," he said.

"If you don't fuck me right now, I will have someone else come and do it!" I said sternly.

He shook his head in disgust. "Fine," he said. And then he walked out.

Suddenly, I started throwing up over the bed, onto the floor. He must have heard the noise, because he returned with the garbage pail from the bathroom to catch the vomit. He held my hair back, directing my head over the pail so as not to make a mess. He picked up my phone and handed it to me. "Unlock your phone," he demanded.

"Why?" I asked, putting my face right up to his. He backed up, nose scrunched.

"You stink like alcohol and vomit—I'm not asking again! Unlock your damn phone," he repeated angrily.

I unlocked my phone, and he found Isabel's number. "You need to come here. I can't stay, and she's really sick," I heard him say.

Isabel showed up five minutes later.

"Hey Vincent!" she exclaimed, walking in as if she still

had the music playing in her head.

Vincent looked her up and down and then hurried out the door without saying another word to either of us.

My head pounded when Isabel woke me up at 11 a.m. the next morning.

"You may want to call out of work," she said, before rolling over on her side of the bed.

I ran to the bathroom and vomited before calling in to say I wouldn't be making it that day.

"Did we have pizza last night?" I asked her.

"Yeah, in the cab, you don't remember? You got sauce all over the seat—the driver was pissed!" she recalled.

The night before was a blur. "Of all the memories to block out, the pizza? Oh my God, Isabel, I called Vincent last night."

"Yeah, I know, why do you think I am here?" she asked.

"I'm such an asshole; he's going to hate me." I was sick to my stomach. Not only from the alcohol and apparent pizza, but also, what I did to Vincent last night. "He's going to hate me!"

"Bianca, Vincent doesn't have a 'Saint' in front of his name. I'm sure he's been drunk before, and I'm sure he's done stupid things, too. I wouldn't worry about it. Oh my God!" she exclaimed, after looking at a text message she had just received.

"What is it?" I asked.

She passed the phone to me. There was a picture of an erect penis. "What is that? I mean, I know *what* it is—*who* is it?"

"Ugh, this guy I'm sort of seeing. What is it with guys and dick pics? I mean, what am I supposed to do with this?

Other than forward it to all my close friends and acquaintances? Has a woman ever in life received a pic like this and said, 'well damn that's a good-looking dick'?" she ranted. "Do you have a picture of Vincent's dick on your phone?"

She already knew the answer. The truth was, I didn't have any pictures of Vincent on my phone, let alone *that* kind. He was way too mature and classy to send something like that.

"Speaking of this guy, I've been meaning to ask you something," she continued. "He wants to have a threesome."

"And you want my blessing?" I asked.

"No, I want you to be the girl, the unicorn."

I could still taste the vomit in my mouth as more was suddenly coming up. "I'm not having a threesome with you, Isabel."

"Why not? We kissed last night—same thing, you'd just have to kiss me somewhere else," she said.

"First of all, even if I said yes—which I am not, by the way—I wouldn't be the one doing the 'kissing.' It's your man, don't you think you should be the one kissing something?"

"You skeeve me?" she asked, sounding insulted.

"No, I don't skeeve you...why would I have to be the one to do it anyway? Why wouldn't you do it? Do you skeeve me?" I threw the question back at her.

"I'm not doing that!" she said. "Where am I going to find a girl who will?"

"I don't know, hire an escort," I suggested.

She sat up on the bed and gritted her teeth. "Look at me. I'm hot! You think I need to pay for pussy?"

"You work in a strip club, so I don't think it will be that hard to find a willing participant. Now excuse me, I'll be right back—I have to vomit again," I said, and then ran back into the bathroom.

"That sounded bad," Isabel said when I returned to the bedroom. She didn't even look up from her phone.

"It tasted even worse. What are you looking at?" I asked.

"I'm on a singles site, looking for a girl," she said very seriously, still not looking up from her phone.

My own phone started ringing. It was Vincent. I walked into the bathroom with the phone, afraid to answer.

"Hi," I finally said, sliding down to the floor to sit against the wall. Just standing made me dizzy.

"Hi... I wanted to make sure you were up for work," Vincent said in a very monotone voice.

"I called out sick," I replied.

"Can you do that?" he asked.

"Yes, they prefer we do that if I were really sick. We have a strict sick policy, and they don't want the entire cast getting sick at once. That's why we have understudies."

"Yeah, that makes sense," he said. "How do you feel?"

I paused for a few moments before responding. "Like a complete asshole—Vincent, I am so sorry—"

He cut me off. "I meant physically," he specified.

"Oh, you know, like my head is in a vise, and I'm throwing up so much that there's nothing left to come up."

"Do you always dress like that when you go out?" he asked.

"No, that was Isabel's outfit. I guess you didn't like it?" I said, half-kidding.

"I'm sorry I called you a slut. I just find it unnecessary for a girl as beautiful as you to have to show off that much of her body."

"Where are you?" I asked, changing the subject.

"Sitting in my car. I brought it to the car wash to have an excuse to call you," he answered. "I didn't sleep after I left your place. It really killed me to leave you there like that. I wanted to stay with you, just to make sure you were okay. Thank God Isabel came. I don't know what I would've done if she didn't."

"I'm so sorry about last night. I know I put you in an awkward position," I said.

"Hey, it's okay. Just get some rest, I will see you tomorrow afternoon for lunch. Eat something greasy," he said.

I went back to the bedroom and collapsed on the bed next to Isabel. She held up a profile picture of a pretty black girl.

"What do you think of her?" she asked.

"Cute," I said, not really looking. "I think I need to go back to sleep."

Vincent never brought up the drunk call. Even though I saw him all the time now, I still looked forward to our Christmas dance every year on that rooftop. He was getting good at our traditional holiday meet-up, too. We had the whole dance routine down.

This year, the weather was abnormally warm for Christmas, in the sixties. When we finished our dance, he asked me, "Does anyone else call you Sarah?"

"Only my mother," I answered. "She refuses to call me Bianca, says it sounds like a stripper name."

"So, I take it she didn't know you stripped?" he asked.

"Oh, hell no, my parents were super religious. I would have been disowned," I said. "And yeah, I stripped, but not really. Like I didn't give lap dances or anything. Just a few shows a night."

"I'm surprised they even hired you, to be honest," he said.

"If it weren't for Isabel, they wouldn't have. But she pushed, and Frank really liked me, so I guess I got lucky."

"I think I'm the one who got lucky," he said. "If you weren't there that night, I never would have met you."

"Eh...you'd be up here with some other chick," I joked.

"I don't think so," he said. "Did I make you at least like Christmas a little more?"

"I don't look at it as Christmas. I look at it as our anniversary," I said.

"I mean, it kind of is." He placed his hand in mine.

"What about your parents?" I asked. "What are they like?"

"Parent," he specified. "I don't have a father."

"He died, too?" I asked.

"No, at least I don't think so. My dad was an executive at a pharmaceutical company, and my mother was a professor at a university. She tried so hard to get pregnant after me, but for whatever reason, she couldn't. Finally, when I was eight, she got pregnant again and was so excited to tell my dad. But I guess he wasn't as excited. He left for work the next day and never came back."

He paused, gazing out into the city, before continuing. "The next week, she wasn't pregnant anymore. I assume she got an abortion but never had the nerve to ask her. My parents quite clearly weren't as religious as yours. My mom never dated again. I think the whole experience made her not trust men, period. But she took really good care of me. She made a good salary. I became the most important thing in her life, and I was okay with that."

"You're a mama's boy?" I asked, surprised.

"Oh, big time! I speak to her once a week, and the first thing she asks is if I ate lunch yet and wants to know what I had." He laughed.

"She must have been devastated when you moved to New York."

"She handled it well. She wasn't too upset. More concerned, I'd say. Not that I wouldn't succeed. I think her biggest fear was me marrying someone I barely knew and then eventually leaving my wife, same way my dad left her."

We stood silent for a few minutes.

"What are you doing for New Year's Eve?" He changed the subject, sipping his wine.

"Matt's having a party. I'm going with Isabel—you?" I asked.

"My best friend, Jimmy, is married to my wife's best friend, Lisa. We go to their house every year. They have two kids, twins—much younger than mine. Hailey and Hayden. They're eleven. I guess they're like my niece and nephew," he said.

"I love the name Hayden," I said.

"I'm not sure he likes it too much, it's different though," he said. "I hope you're going to be looking for an outfit in your closet and not Isabel's for the party," he added.

I playfully slapped him on the chest. "Are you going to bring this up for the rest of my life?" I asked. I knew I deserved it for the way I'd treated him that night.

"No, not the rest of your life, just a large portion of it. I can't help it. I'm jealous—you make me that way."

He put his arm around me and pulled me into him. "Would you rather be with a guy who didn't care so much?" he asked.

"No, I guess not. I just want you," I said.

He kissed me. Afterward, once we finished the bottle of wine, he handed me the cork. The same way he did every year.

"Here's another one for your collection. Happy Anniversary," he said.

VINCE

The day after Christmas, we were sitting at brunch with my mother and the kids at a restaurant in the theater district. The spot was one of my favorite places, and we went there often. Not too fancy, but they did a really good brunch spread with unlimited mimosas and Bloody Mary's. I particularly liked this place because the customers were more New Yorkers than tourists, and everyone knew each other. There was a real old-school neighborhood feel to it: classic jukeboxes at each booth and a newspaper machine outside. My mother especially liked this spot. Even though she was from California, she said she felt like a real New Yorker sitting there.

As a retired college professor, my mother was very well spoken and always dressed like she was going to work. Dress pants with blouses and blazers. I'm not even sure she owned a pair of jeans. She as very attractive for an older woman: dark hair, an olive complexion, curvy. It was a shame that she never dated again after my father left. She would have had no problem getting a man, especially if she cooked for him. No matter how busy her schedule got while I was growing up, she made sure I always ate a home-cooked meal.

Before our brunch, Samantha had informed me that she'd be giving my mother our Christmas gift at the restaurant, and also not to make plans for afterwards. She always took care of all the gifts, so I never thought to question it. As I was drinking my third Bloody Mary, Samantha looked over at me to signal that she was ready. I motioned at Nick and Casey to stop talking while Samantha eagerly produced the gift.

"Mom, we really wanted to get you something special this year—we hope you like it!" Samantha smiled and clasped her hands together. As soon as my mother opened the box and peeked inside, a huge smile spread across her face.

"Thank you so much! I've been dying to see this! When is it, and who's going?" my mom asked.

Samantha clapped her hands. "Me too!" she exclaimed. "Today, at 2 p.m. All of us are going."

I glanced over, puzzled as to where we were going at 2 p.m. Though, I didn't want to ask the question out loud because then my mother would know I hadn't helped pick out her gift.

"Where are we going?" Casey asked.

"The Broadway show, *Wounds of Time*," Samantha blurted.

I almost spit out my drink. My heart dropped and I froze.

"Really? Cool, I heard it's awesome!" Casey said.

Nick didn't seem as excited. Meanwhile, I was still

motionless. In shock, suddenly sick to my stomach.

"Do I have to go?" Nick asked, clearly not wanting any part of this gift.

Samantha and I answered at the same time. As she said yes, I simultaneously said no.

She looked over at me, looking aggravated that I had an opposing answer.

"If he doesn't want to go, he doesn't have to," I said. "As a matter of fact, why don't you make it a girls thing, and Nick and I will do something else."

Samantha shot a look at me that said she wanted to throw her drink straight in my face. "Vince, these tickets were extremely hard to get—you both have to go. Since when do you dislike Broadway so much? You watched the Tony Awards this year!"

"Who's going to feed the dog?" I asked, desperate.

Samantha ran her tongue across her top teeth and leaned over the table toward me. "All of sudden, you're so concerned about Rocky?"

Nick and I both argued profusely. Nick somehow weaseled his way out of going, but she wasn't having it with me. I could feel my underarms dampen with sweat. FUCK. This was so bad.

The theater was only a few blocks down. I kept my head down for the entire short walk over, and while we stood in line. I silently prayed that no one would see me, especially Sarah. It was when we were going through security that one of guards, Joe spotted me. I tried to pretend like I didn't see him, but he hustled right over.

"Vincent, buddy, what's going on? Merry Christmas!" he asked, shaking my hand. Joe was a built guy, in his twenties and had a very thick Brooklyn accent.

"Merry Christmas! And, oh, not much," I said.

"How many you with?" he asked.

I didn't want to answer the question, but Samantha was now staring at us, no doubt wondering how this young random security guard knew me.

"Four," I responded.

"Stay right here. Let me see if I can get you better seats," he said.

"No, no, really—not necessary," I said. He laughed, waving my reply off as he hurried away.

"How does he know you?" my mother asked.

Good question. Think, Vince. How *does* he know me? Um...

"I get tickets for clients all the time." The lie flew right out of my mouth.

"Wow, my dad is a big deal!" Casey said, seemingly impressed.

I didn't make eye contact with any of them. Instead, I stared at the floor, silently praying that there were no better seats. Then Joe came back with an excited expression on his face.

"Follow me," he said.

Reluctantly, I followed him, practically yanking the playbill from usher's hand. He led us down the carpeted ramp and, sure enough, he'd found seats for us right up front. Extremely up front. Like, right-under-the-stage up front.

If this were any other day, I would have been ecstatic. Given the circumstances, I was scared shitless. Sarah couldn't see me. Not there. Not with my wife. The theme song of the show played softly, and the props of first bedroom scene were on the stage. There was still fifteen minutes before the show started, and people stood in the aisles, talking and shifting around to let others reach their seats.

Samantha was seated to the right of me. She squeezed my hand, so excited that my so-called connections had paid off. My cheeks felt numb, and I guessed that my complexion had turned white.

I stood up. "I'm going to go get drinks, who wants one?"

After getting their drink orders, I hurried out and frantically went in search of Joe. I spotted him across the room. I tried to squeeze past the crowd at the bar.

"Joe! Joey, over here, Joe!" I called over to him, waving my hands in the air. He spotted me and came right over.

"Hey man, like your seats?" he asked, with an expression filled with self-approval. I couldn't breathe. I didn't know how I was going to say this to him.

"Joe, listen—I need to tell you something, and it needs to stay between us," I began. "That woman that's with me, the one in the black dress—"

"Yeah, I was going to ask you who that was. She's hot," he said.

"She's, um, well...she's actually my...she's my wife," I said.

Joe's face dropped. "Your *wife*?" He glanced down at my left hand, noticing I was suddenly wearing a wedding ring.

I nodded yes. When he looked at my face, I think he could tell I was in panic mode.

"Damn bro, you a dog," he said. "Does Bianca know you're married?"

This was not a conversation I'd been prepared to have,

not right now.

"Yes, she knows," I said. "I'm not that much of a dog—like a cute little one, maybe a Chihuahua."

Joe stared at me, looking serious all of a sudden, like I'd hit a nerve.

"You know everyone thinks Chihuahuas are so cute, but my sister has one and that little asshole isn't cute. For starters, he humps everything! Also, he's a rowdy little thing! Did you know Chihuahuas are the most vicious breed of dog? Worse than Pit bulls?"

I just stared at him in shock. Here I was having a nervous breakdown, and he was giving me a National Geographic lesson on Chihuahuas.

"Okay, not the best example, but Bianca cannot know I'm here," I said. I think the reality of my situation finally sank in.

"Oh, damn dude, you got bad seats if you don't wanna be seen," he said.

"You think?!" I asked, aggravated.

"You want me to move you?" he offered.

"Well, you can't now—that would be too obvious. I'll figure something out—just please, do not let her know I'm here. *Please*," I reiterated.

Joe nodded, so I thanked him and then turned to head to the bar to get the girls their drinks.

"Hey, Vincent," he said, after I'd only taken a few steps. "In my next life, I want to come back as you, man! You have great taste in women."

He sounded like he admired me as he shook my hand again.

"Gee, thanks," I said, and then left to order the drinks.

I returned with drinks just in time for the show to

start. They were all so excited, especially when they saw that the drinks came in souvenir cups. At exactly 2 p.m. the lights dimmed, and a man's voice came from the loudspeaker.

"Ladies and gentleman, welcome. Please refrain from pictures and live videos. We ask that you take this time to silence your phones. Enjoy the show!"

As if the seats in a Broadway theater weren't tight enough already, being trapped here with my family felt like the walls were closing in on me. Sweat beaded across my forehead while I slouched in my chair, my face buried in my hand. Throughout the show, Samantha kept hitting me to pay attention. She was annoyed, to say the very least. But I remembered Sarah telling me once that she didn't look at the crowd during her performances. Not until the very end, when the cast took their bows. That was my escape plan—when they came back on-stage after the encore, I would excuse myself to go to the bathroom.

Perfect idea! Until the time came. Sarah emerged with Matt as the crowd stood for the standing ovation. I stayed seated.

Samantha grabbed me by the arm and pulled me up. "What is wrong with you today?" she whispered loudly.

"I have to pee," I said, standing up slowly and trying to leave.

"You can wait until they're done clapping," she said.

As she hooked my arm with hers, essentially holding me in place while she reprimanded me, I looked up, and it happened. I made eye contact with Sarah. Her gaze went from me, to Samantha, and then back to me. Her smile faded for a second, but she was a professional. She put that smile right back on and kept waving to the crowd.

I felt her pain, though. I felt her pain run through my heart like a Mack truck. Then, the actors descended, and the girls were finally ready to leave, all of them in really good spirits. They'd loved the show and now wanted to get something else to eat.

"Why don't you go find a restaurant and text me where you are? I'm going to pee and thank them again for the upgrades," I said.

The girls left, and I tried to make my way backstage as fast as I could. Joe led me to Sarah's dressing room. When she opened the door, I saw an expression on her face that I'd never seen before. Anger, mixed with hurt, combined with jealousy—she looked like she was about to cry.

"How could you do this? HOW could you do this, Vincent!?" she demanded, almost in tears.

"I tried not to. It was an accident, I swear! She got the tickets. I didn't know about them! I tried to get out of it but—"

She cut me off. "And your wife? Your wife is gorgeous!"

"I told you she was pretty," I said.

"Pretty? She's stunning, how could you even cheat on her? Yeah, you guys have such a bad marriage...that's why you're out going to shows together," she yelled. She turned her back to me, but I could still see her perfectly through the lit-up vanity mirror on the wall.

"I don't cheat on her. I don't consider you as cheating. It's different. And I never said I had a *bad* marriage—now you're putting words in my mouth." I made eye contact with her through the mirror.

"Do you have any idea how I'm feeling?" she asked, turning back around to face me.

I started to approach her, but she backed up like she didn't want me to come any closer. "Yes, I do. I swear I do, because my biggest fear is running into you out with another man. I assume you date, and whether you do or don't, please don't specify because I can't handle it. If you're dating someone else, then lie to me until absolutely necessary. So yes, to answer your question, I know exactly what you feel, and I am so, so sorry this happened, but I can't talk about this now. They're waiting for me at a restaurant. Can I come by tomorrow before work? 6 a.m.? We'll talk? I'm so sorry, but I really have to go."

"Sure, come at 6 a.m. I'll be there when you're able to fit me into your schedule." She sat down at the mirror and started fixing her eye makeup.

I walked out of that dressing room feeling like the biggest douchebag to ever walk the streets of New York City.

That night, I couldn't sleep at all. To begin with, my mother was in the guest room, so I had to sleep in bed with Samantha. The only time we slept together in the same bed was when we were on vacation, and she hated it. Plus, I couldn't get Sarah's face out of my head. How upset she'd been. I couldn't wait to see her at 6 a.m. the next morning and explain.

Finally, after what seemed like forty-eight hours, morning came. I threw on my clothes and hailed a taxi. It may have even been 5:59 a.m. when I showed up at her apartment.

Sarah opened the door. Her eyes were red and puffy, like she had been crying all night. I felt so bad, my heart actually hurt. I couldn't see her like this, especially knowing that I was the person who caused her pain.

"You look terrible," I said, walking in.

"Thanks, add salt to the wound." There was almost no expression in her voice.

"Look, last night was a complete accident. My wife, she always buys the Christmas gifts, I had no idea she got the tickets. I tried so hard to get out of it, I really did. Then when Joe saw me..."

"Joe saw you?" she said, looking panicked. "He knows? He knows you're married? Great, now he just thinks I'm your side piece. Damn it, Vincent! Joe's got such a big mouth—he's going to tell everyone! They're all going to think I'm a slut. Even worse, this could ruin my career if it gets out!"

Just when I thought she couldn't be any more upset, I managed to get her there.

"He told me he wouldn't say anything. I mean, I don't know him that well, but I believed him. Look, Sarah, I want to clarify some things for you," I said. "I never said I was in a bad marriage. It's not bad. It's just more, well, it's kind of more like a business arrangement. Like I've told you before, my wife got pregnant young, so we didn't really know each other when we got married. We grew to love each other, but not like this. Not like us. Honestly, I didn't even know what real love was until I met you. We don't even sleep in the same room."

She seemed surprised when I said that. "You don't sleep in the same room?" she repeated.

"No—I mean, last night we did because my mother is in from California, but I typically sleep in the guest room."

"Do you still have sex with her?" she asked.

I paused for a second. "Yes. Not a lot, not recently."

I tried to remember. I didn't think we'd had sex since

the Christmas party. Did we? No—not even in Aruba this year. "Now that I think about it, we haven't in months, maybe even a year. And when we do, it's not like it is with us. There's no passion, no lust. It's just sex. With you, it's different. I know that sounds like a bunch of bullshit, but I swear on my kids it's not. I never, ever swear on my kids. We do regular couple things. Go out to eat, have couple friends, regular *public* couple things. At home, we don't really talk. We don't really laugh. We're barely in the same room with each other, especially with the kids away in college. We just....we just live," I said.

"Do you think she knows you cheat on her?" she asked.

I took a deep breath and exhaled. "Knows, suspects, cares? I really don't know," I answered as honestly as I could.

"You don't think she'd care if you cheated on her?" she asked, apparently baffled.

"She's never said it, but as long as her perfect life doesn't change, I'd say no, probably not," I admitted. "I never realized how abnormal that sounds. Not until I just said it out loud. I guess I always thought that was just how marriage was."

She got very quiet, leaning against the kitchen counter. I walked over and wrapped my arms around her waist from behind. "I'll leave. I'll get a divorce. My kids are already in college. There's no reason for us to keep this up."

"No!" she said, turning around to face me. "I will not be a homewrecker. I will not be the cause of your divorce!"

Tears glistened in her eyes again. I could tell she wanted to be with me, but not like this. I pressed my forehead against hers and stared right into her eyes.

"Sarah, I have never in my life felt this way about anybody, not the way I feel with you. I would never do anything intentionally to hurt you. I couldn't sleep at all last night. I just kept wanting to come here and hold you. That was so fucked up, I know it was. I'm not denying it. Let me make it up to you, please."

"Make it up to me?" she asked. "How? By buying me something? Wrong girl—I don't care about your money!"

I backed away from her, frantically scrambling for ideas of how I could make this right. "Let's do something; go away. Can you take a vacation? We can go somewhere close, maybe Puerto Rico. There's a really nice hotel in Old San Juan on the beach. It's not buying you something, it's taking you somewhere. Let's go somewhere where no one knows who we are, and we can do whatever we want, with no limitations."

I could tell she wanted to believe what I was saying. "Please," I said, putting my arms around her waist again. "Go away with me."

"I need to put in notice to take a vacation, at least a couple of weeks. How are you going to get away?" she asked.

"I don't know. I'll say I have a business trip or something, I'll figure it out. We can go Monday through Thursday. Then you only have to take a few shows off. End of January? Weather will be real nice there, much better than here."

She agreed. She even half-smiled.

"Great!" I said. "Let me know the exact dates, and I will make all the arrangements. Wow, I can't wait to be alone with you for four days straight!" Suddenly, I was really excited.

I went out with Jimmy for drinks after work. There was a bar not far from the office that a lot of the brokers went to for happy hour. They knew us well there. Older businessmen sat at the bar with laptops out and talking on cell phones. The younger ones played games that were set up on the tables: checkers, some sort of manual robot-fighting machine. After the bartender handed us our drinks, I pointed at a table off to the side.

"Let's go sit in the corner. I need to talk to you." I hurried to the table to avoid being seen by anyone we knew.

As we sat down, Jimmy said, "Look, if this is about the Justin thing, I'm sorry. I shouldn't have lost my shit with him."

I looked at him, confused. "What are you talking about?" I asked.

"Justin fucked up big time today, so I went off on him, and he reported me to HR. I spent an hour in there justifying myself and apologizing. Is that what this is about?"

"No," I said. "I didn't even know about that, and this isn't about work. I'm not out with you as your boss, I'm out with you as my best friend. On that note, though, I will say—as your boss—you need to calm the fuck down. The workplace isn't what it used to be. You can't yell at people anymore, or you'll get us sued. Have you been going to the harassment classes?"

He put his head down. "Yes, yes. I read the memos, and I know they're mandatory. Okay, I'm sorry. I'll work on the yelling, but honestly though, this whole new generation thinks they can do whatever they want with no repercussions. They don't have business ethics. They want to come to work, do a half-ass job, take five breaks during the day to 'meditate' and get a six-figure salary! They don't want to earn money anymore, they think they are entitled to it."

I didn't answer; Jimmy wasn't entirely wrong. He had a hard job dealing with all the employees daily. I was relieved that they reported into him. He and my assistant were the only direct reports I had, which meant I didn't have to deal with that kind of stuff.

"What did you want to talk about?" he asked.

I took a deep breath. "I need your help, and you cannot under any circumstances tell anyone, especially Lisa," I began. "I'm going on vacation at the end of January. I need you to cover me at work, and if anyone asks—Lisa in particular—I'm on a business trip."

Jimmy looked up from his glass. "Where are you going?" he asked.

"Puerto Rico."

"And with whom are we going to Puerto Rico with?" he slowly asked, realizing it was not my wife.

I downed a gulp of my drink. "Not Samantha," I answered.

"You're going with a girl? Who is she? Is she hot?"

I knew he was going to ask a ton of questions. "Yes, very. You've seen her before, a few years ago. At the Christmas party at the strip club. The blonde in the Christmas show, the one who was dancing on me."

Now he was really impressed. "You're fucking a stripper! Good for you, man! My boy is blossoming!"

He held up his hand to high five me.

"She doesn't do that anymore. She's a Broadway actress."

"Wait," he said, as realization dawned. "That was years ago; how long have you been seeing her for?"

"Well, I hung out with her that same night, but we really didn't start dating until the following year, so two years now," I answered.

"Two years? You've been fucking a girl for two years, and I am just finding out about this now? I tell you about all the girls I sleep with!" He slammed his glass on the table.

"I'm not just fucking her. It's different. Those Monday 'yoga' classes I go to during lunch, I'm really with her."

"This is great!" he said, signaling to the waitress for another round. "You can finally be my wingman when we go out!"

"No, I am not going to be your wingman. I am not going to cheat on her," I said.

Now he got serious. "Cheat on her? Let me get this straight: you will cheat on Samantha, but not on this girl?"

I took another sip of my drink. "Jimmy, I'm in love with her." I was afraid to look up at him.

He sat there, stunned. "In love with her? Are you insane? I feel like I'm talking to a chick. Only you would fuck a stripper then fall in love with her—do you even have a dick? You have a wife. What are you going to do? Leave Samantha?"

I looked down again and he winced.

"Vince, you *cannot* leave Samantha. She'll take you for everything, especially over infidelity. Nothing is worse than a woman scorned. You love this girl enough to lose everything? To be broke?" he asked, now getting very serious. "How old is this girl? Is she in love with you too?"

I knew he'd have something to say about that. "Yeah, I

think she is. She hasn't said it, but I'm pretty sure she loves me back. She's twenty-eight."

"Twenty-eight? Vince, let me tell you a story about these young girls. They're fucking nuts. I fucked this girl a few months ago, the one from the Hamptons," he began.

"The hot tub girl?" I asked.

"Yes, exactly, her. Young, real young—twenty-three. She got obsessed with me after only one night. She made a fake social media page with my information. A fake profile, Vince! Who does that? I don't even know how she got my picture. She found Lisa on there, told her. Put some crazy shit on this page."

I was in shock. I had never heard anything like that. "A fake profile? I like how you tell me the details of the act but not the drama that happens after. What did Lisa say?"

The waitress came over with fresh drinks.

"Thanks honey," he said, smiling at her, and then went right back to his stern tone. "She was pissed! Not so much that I slept with the girl, but now it was blasted all over the Internet. She just wanted the page down. Made me swear not to tell you. She was too embarrassed for Samantha to find out. We went to the cops. Do you know what it is? Freedom of fucking speech! They couldn't do anything. What would you have done?"

I picked up the new glass and took a rather large gulp. "I have no idea. I can't even comprehend that. Maybe send a cease and desist?"

He looked at me like that was the stupidest thing I could have said. "A cease and desist?" he repeated.

"Yeah, okay, maybe it's freedom of speech, but there's also slander, defamation of character—"

He cut me off. "Vince she was twenty-three years old,

what the fuck was I going to sue her for?"

"I don't know, what did she do for a living?" I asked.

He took another sip of his drink and gave me a sarcastic smile. "I don't know, it didn't occur to me to ask for her resume as she was sucking my dick."

"So, what did you do?" I asked.

"I paid her."

"You gave her money?"

"Yes, Lisa just wanted it to go away. I had no choice. Twenty-five thousand dollars. Most expensive blowjob I ever got," he said, shaking his head in disgust. "I'm just telling you to be careful. These young girls are truly crazy."

"She's not like that. She would never do that," I argued.

He shook his head again and put his hand up to motion me to stop talking. Then he laughed. "Leave it to you, can't even cheat right, falls in love with the girl. She must be one good lay if she has you so pussy whipped. What am I going to do with you, Vince? I'm not telling you to stop seeing her, but be smart about it, please," he said firmly.

Jimmy's story shook me. It was a scary story. Crazy, in fact. But Sarah would never do that to me. She did love me, I was sure of it—and, even if she didn't, she was too mature for that.

SARAH

"How do you think he's going to get away with coming home with a suntan?" I asked Isabel as we were eating Chinese food at my place that night.

She stopped pushing around her fried rice with her fork and looked up at me. "Bianca, I think it's time we had a serious talk about Vincent. I understand your attraction to him, I really do. He's rich, charming, sexy, and judging by the way you glow after he leaves here, I'm guessing a hell of a fuck. Any woman would be attracted to that. But, he's MARRIED—to someone else. You saw her this weekend and you said it yourself, she's gorgeous. He ain't leaving her."

"He said he would if I wanted him to, but I didn't want him to—"

She threw her hand up in the air and interrupted me. "I'm sure he did say that and would have said anything he needed to at that point after what happened, but saying he's leaving his wife and actually leaving his wife are two very different things."

"You're just anti-love," I argued.

"No, Bianca, I am not anti-love. I'm a realist. Men in that caliber never leave their wives. You ever hear the expression, 'It's cheaper to keep her?' And women who are married to men in that caliber don't give a fuck what they do. As long as they stay flossed, they know it comes along with the territory. These men have licenses to cheat." She stood up and walked over to the counter and made us another drink.

"So, what exactly are you saying? I shouldn't go to Puerto Rico with him?"

She turned her head to face me and rolled her eyes. "What, are you stupid? Of course, you should go to Puerto Rico with him. I'm just saying you have to slow down a little with the feelings—date other men. Don't put all your eggs in one basket, especially in an unavailable basket. His son is closer to your age. Do you know what he looks like? Maybe you can get with him. Then Vincent will be your father-in-law and you can fuck him on all the holidays. Why stop at just Christmas Eve?"

"That's disgusting," I said, shaking my head. I sipped my drink.

"Look, that guy, Chris I'm seeing has this friend, Brendon. The guy is like obsessed with you. Keeps asking about my blonde friend in my profile pic with me. Up my ass about it, really. Go out with him—we can go on a double date so it's not awkward. You can still see Vincent on Mondays and give yourself some options. Next month you're going to be in the last year of your twenties. Don't waste your entire life on a man who is essentially going to break your heart. Plus, it will be fun to date best friends."

She had a point. It would be nice to be able to go out

with someone in public without driving to Jersey, especially on a double date.

"Fine," I agreed. "One date but no promises."

Vincent had a car pick me up that morning to take me to the airport. He was already at the gate waiting.

I walked over to where he paced in front of the gate, holding a garment bag in his hand.

"That's all you brought? What's in there?" I asked.

"Just a few suits," he replied.

"Suits? Little overdressed for Puerto Rico, no?" I asked, surprised.

"Well, I couldn't exactly pack summer clothes—I'll buy some when we get there," he answered.

"Where does she think you're going?" I asked.

"I have a huge client in Miami, just in case the sunblock fails me," he answered.

That solved the mystery of how he was going to explain a suntan. He glanced around.

"Are you afraid to be seen with me?" I asked.

"No," he said. "I'm afraid to look like I'm in love with you. A lot of people fly out of Newark. It may be weird to be gawking at my cousin."

I pointed at the screen that said Puerto Rico, 7:15 a.m. On time.

"May also be weird to be going to Puerto Rico with your cousin," I said.

He laughed. "You're right. We'll just say you're my daughter. She has blonde hair too. You can pass."

"Ew, that's gross that you think I look like your daughter?" I asked.

"No, you don't look like her, she just happens to have blonde hair, too. So, if you were turned around and someone saw me with a little blonde girl, they might assume it's my daughter—you know what? Now you're grossing me out, forget I said it."

"Your hair is so dark—how did your daughter end up with blonde hair?" I asked, as the flight attendants started boarding the plane.

"My wife is naturally blonde; she dyes it...you know what, before we board, I would like to institute a rule. Effective immediately! Once we get on that plane, and I successfully make sure no one knows me, there's no talk of wives, kids, work, friends—just us. This whole trip is just us, like no one else exists. Deal?"

I smiled at him. He couldn't have said anything more perfectly. "Yes, deal," I said.

He had got us first-class tickets. I'd never flown in first-class before—I couldn't even remember the last time I was on a plane. Once we found our seats, the flight attendant came over to us. "Mr. DeLuca, care for a beverage before takeoff?"

"Yes, I'll have a Bloody Mary, please. Sarah?"

My eyes went wide in disbelief. "It's seven a.m., isn't it a little early to start drinking?"

He leaned over to me. "Baby, we're on vacation. There is no such thing as early or late for the next four days."

He looked up at the flight attendant. "Two, please."

After we'd reached a safe flying altitude, Vincent got up to go to the bathroom. He started heading to the back of the plane when the flight attendant stopped him.

"Sir, you can use the first-class bathroom in the front."

"I know, I prefer using the one in the back, if you don't mind," he responded.

I knew exactly what he was doing. He was scouring the

plane to make sure he didn't know anyone.

When he returned to his seat, he seemed relieved and took my hand in his. "I can't wait to be alone with you. I'm going to tell you now though—I'm a real bad sleeper, I get up a lot at night. So, I apologize in advance if I keep waking you," he warned.

The lobby of the hotel was tremendous: crystal chandeliers hanging from the ceilings, beautiful marble floors. The concierge offered us both a glass of champagne and apologized that the room wasn't ready yet.

Vincent was very cool about it. "We'll leave our bags with the bellhop and go hit the beach. Do you want champagne before we go?" he asked me.

"Are you having some?" I asked.

"Nah, not the best thing to mix after Bloody Mary's," he said.

I turned down the offer as well and then went to open my suitcase to dig for my bathing suit.

Vincent stopped me. "Don't worry about it. I have to go shopping anyway. I'll get you a bathing suit. Come on, let's not waste any time."

We were staying at an extremely fancy hotel, so needless to say, there were some very high-end stores. He told me to get whatever I wanted and then headed over to the men's section. I had a bikini in my hand when this beautiful dress caught my eye. The fabric was the prettiest shade of coral I'd ever seen. I leaned in to get a closer look. Holy shit! The price tag said eight hundred dollars! I immediately started backing away, as if I might be charged for touching it, when I heard Vincent.

"Can she try that on?" he said.

I whirled around and saw that he was right behind me.

"Oh no," I said. "It's okay. I don't want that dress."

"You don't want to try it on? It's a really nice dress. I bet you'd look great it in." His dimple appeared.

I flashed the worker an embarrassed smile before peeking up at Vincent. "It's way too expensive," I whispered. "Plus, I would have nowhere even to wear a dress like that. Seriously I don't want it."

He looked at me with a stern expression. "Okay, rule number two on this trip—we don't look at price tags. You see something you like, you get it. I don't even want you to look at how much anything costs, is that understood?"

I didn't know what to say. Meanwhile, the worker sized me up.

"You look like a size four or six. I'll bring you both, and we'll see which one fits better," she said.

Vincent was shuffling through a rack when I came out wearing the dress. He stopped immediately and stared in awe.

"Wow!" he said. "Looks like we have to find a really nice restaurant tomorrow night to give you a reason to wear that dress."

I cannot even put into words what an amazing day it was. We relaxed on the beach until lunchtime, and then ate at an outdoor restaurant overlooking the ocean. Afterward, we walked around and checked out the sights, and he even coaxed me into trying parasailing. Later, we watched the sun dip into the ocean as he stood behind me, arms wrapped around me, kissing the back of my neck. The water was so blue, but now also reflected the red and purple rays from the sky. If I could freeze that one moment in time for eternity, I would. As promised, we spoke of nothing but us. For that short period of time, I was truly convinced we were a real couple.

"Want to go up to the room and get ready for dinner?" he asked, once the sky had darkened.

I wanted to anything he wanted to do. "Yes," I said.

As he opened the door to our room, I stood frozen. The room—no, the suite was bigger than my entire apartment. It was so classy, with a balcony that overlooked the beach. There was a full refrigerator stocked with full sizes of everything: water, wine, beer. There was a living room, an office space, and a huge bathroom, which by itself may literally have been the size of my apartment. Inside the bathroom was a hot tub, a bathtub, a shower, and *two* toilets.

I looked at the toilets, confused.

"That's called a bidet," he said.

"What's a bidet?" I asked.

He started laughing. "It's what rich people use to wash their private parts," he explained.

"Really? Do you use that?" I asked.

He was shaking his head, still laughing. "No, but I know what it is. I'm half-kidding. It's a French thing." He obviously thought my question was very funny.

"What would you like to eat for dinner tonight?" he asked.

I draped my arms around his shoulders and started kissing his neck. "Oh, I have a few ideas," I said, as I ran my hands down his chest. He groaned as I pulled his shirt off.

"Ah, room service, yeah, I thought so too," he said.

We didn't make it out of the bathroom—we had sex right on the sink.

I woke up the next morning with our bodies

intertwined: his arm over my waist, his leg around my thighs. I didn't understand why he'd said he was a bad sleeper. He was a perfect sleeper. Didn't snore, didn't drool, barely moved. The other perfect thing about him, I realized right then...his hair. How did a forty-five-year-old man have such perfect hair? Thick, full, not one gray. I was going to be twenty-nine next month and yet I was already dying grays—did he dye his hair? I started obsessively running my fingers through the dark strands, searching for some sort of indication as to why his hair was so perfect. I tried not to wake him, but his eyes slowly fluttered open until he was gazing at me.

"I'm sorry, did I wake you?" I asked.

He pulled me close and smiled. "You know," he said. "You are the last face I see at night before I close my eyes to go to sleep, and the first face I see in the morning when I wake up. It is so nice to have you here in person, waking up to your real face and not the image of it."

I practically melted in his arms. "How do you have such perfect hair?"

He touched his head, feeling his hair. "I'm sure it's not perfect right now."

"No, really. I inspected it while you were sleeping. Not one sign of a gray, how is that possible?"

He chuckled. "You like gray hair?" he asked.

"Salt and pepper's nice," I said.

"Okay, we'll go to a salon today, and I'll throw some gray in my hair for you," he said, still smiling.

"You would dye your hair gray for me?"

He got really serious. "I would dye my hair blue for you."

I didn't say anything, so he continued. "You're like a

drug, you know that? I haven't slept through the night in years, maybe decades. You're like a natural mood stabilizer."

I laughed. He shook his head. "You don't get it, do you?"

"Get what?" I asked.

He paused for a second, almost as if he wasn't sure whether he should say whatever he was thinking. Then he plunged ahead. "I'm not kidding. When I'm having a bad day, in a funk, or just not in the best of moods, you know what I do? I listen to the soundtrack of *Wounds of Time*. I listen to you sing and immediately, I'm in a good mood. I know every word to every song in your show."

I stared at him. "Vincent, you have to stop saying things like this to me," I said, shifting my eyes off of his.

"Why? I thought we could tell each other anything," he said.

I inhaled deeply. "You are going to make me fall so madly in love with you."

He pulled me in closer. "You're not already?" he asked.

I felt my face turn red.

"Are you blushing?" he asked, surprised.

My gaze locked with his. "No, no, I'm not blushing—am I?"

He started laughing.

"Yeah, you're blushing." He moved in even closer, his mouth so close to mine that I could feel his breath against my lips when he repeated the question, "You're not already?"

What was wrong with me? Why couldn't I say the words? "You know how I feel about you."

"Say it," he said.

"Why do I have to say it?" I asked.

"Because I want to hear it. I *need* to hear it." His lips were so close, I could taste them.

"I love you," I finally said.

He immediately started kissing me and without taking his lips off me, muttered, "Say it again."

"I love you." It came out so much easier the second time.

He stopped kissing me and stared. "I would tell you I love you, but it's not enough. You can't even begin to understand how I feel about you. You consume my entire brain. You're all I think about: all day, all night, every day, every night. I'm possessed by you, if that's possible. You are somehow IN me."

It was the most beautiful thing I'd ever heard anyone say, especially to me.

"Have you slept with a lot of women?" I asked.

He rolled over on his back and gazed up at the ceiling, resting his hand on his forehead. "Well, that's a bizarre question to ask after I profess my love to you."

While still lying on his back, he turned his head to the side to look at me.

"I'm serious," I said.

"Not as many as you probably think. I don't know. I can probably count on one hand, maybe a little more."

"Do you think it's just the sex? Maybe that's why you're so into me, because we have such good sex?" I asked.

His expression suggested that my comment was the stupidest thing he'd ever heard.

"No, it's not about the sex. Yes, we do have incredible sex, but even if we never had sex again, I'd still feel the same way," he said.

"Yeah, okay!" I said sarcastically.

"Oh, you don't believe me? Okay, I'll prove it. No sex anymore. Sex ban, starting now," he said.

"No!" I shrieked.

"What? I'm proving a point that it's not about sex. How am I going to prove that if we still have sex?" he asked.

"You can't do that," I said, running my hands down his bare chest. "I have needs too!"

He rolled over on top of me.

"Oh, you have needs?" he asked playfully now, kissing my neck, up to my ear. Then he whispered, "Tell me what you need."

I slid his hand down my body until it reached between my legs. "For starters, I need your fingers here."

He started rubbing me, moving his lips from my neck, down my chest, over my breasts.

"Tell me what else you need."

I dictated his every move, until we both orgasmed.

After breakfast, we laid on the beach for a while when I noticed him staring off at the ocean. Boats, jet skis, people parasailing.

He shot me a sideways glance and said, "Let's go jet skiing."

I looked at him, unmotivated. *How did a man his age have so much energy?* I wondered to myself. "No way, I don't know how," I said.

"You don't need to know how—I'll drive the jet ski, you just hold on to me."

"Nope, not happening. I've been in a car with you. I know how fast you drive, definitely not. I'm afraid of deep water," I explained.

He looked at me in disbelief. "You hate Christmas, and you're afraid of water? What were you raised by? Gremlins? Don't make me beg," he pleaded. "We'll do whatever you want afterward."

He was very convincing. An hour later, I gripped his waist for dear life as he sped across the ocean on this jet ski, driving like a lunatic. He stopped midway through the ride and hopped off. Standing in waist-deep water, he said, "Jump off."

"I can't." The thought of jumping off this jet ski and landing in the water terrified me.

He laughed, obviously finding this all very amusing. "I'll catch you," he said. "I am literally in three feet of water."

After about ten minutes of him trying to persuade me to get off that thing, I finally give in, and he caught me, just like he said he would.

Standing in his wet arms, he gazed at me and said, "I told you I'd catch you. I will never let anything happen to you."

We stayed in the water until he decided he wanted a drink, and then we rode back. After having a cocktail, we made our way back to our room to get changed for dinner. I emerged from the bathroom wearing the new coral dress.

"Wow." He stopped buttoning down his shirt and stared at me. "You look amazing, like that dress was literally made for your body!" He started tucking his shirt into his pants.

"No, leave it out," I said.

"Leave it out?" he repeated.

"Yes, we're going to dinner, not a business meeting. It looks better out." I could tell he was hesitant, but he kept it out.

He picked a very nice restaurant on the water where I wouldn't be overdressed in my new, extremely expensive dress. They served authentic Puerto Rican food, with Spanish guitars playing softly in the background. I had no idea what they were singing, but the music made me want to dance. I bopped my body to the rhythm while we waited to be seated, pointing out all the men who were wearing their shirts out. I could tell seeing them made Vincent feel better about his own appearance, which made me happy. He looked so handsome; I didn't want him to be uncomfortable.

The hostess approached us. "Mr. and Mrs. DeLuca, your table is ready."

I couldn't help but laugh.

"What are you laughing at?" he asked.

"She thought I was your wife," I said, still laughing.

"Don't laugh. You're going to be one day, so get used to it now," he said as we took our seats.

"You really think we're going to get married?" I asked.

"Yes, I am going to be buried next to you." He said this so seriously, that I almost believed him.

"What is that? It smells amazing!"

I peered over at the table next to us while Vincent tried to be more subtle.

"Looks like grilled octopus, you want to try it?" he asked.

I shook my head no.

"You'll like it trust me, it's very tender and juicy." He went ahead and ordered some as a tourist-hunting photographer came over to us to snap our picture.

When the octopus arrived, I had to admit that he was right. It was delicious; all marinated in a spicy sauce with chopped tomatoes and onions mixed in. I was amazed at how good he was at predicting what I would and wouldn't like.

"Why do you love me?" I asked him.

He took a deep breath, like that was a hard question to answer. "It's kind of hard to pinpoint one specific thing. I guess your willingness to try anything. Food, jet skiing—no matter how afraid you are of something, after enough convincing, you finally try it. The same way I am going to eventually convince you to marry me," he said, smiling. "What about me? What do you love about me?" he asked.

I thought for a second, and then I looked at him and said, "The way you look at me. Are you always going to look at me like that?"

Before he could answer, the photographer came over and showed us the picture, which had turned out great. She asked him if he wanted to buy it and he shook his head.

"No, thank you," he said.

I pretended to study my plate of food, but he noticed my expression. "It's a really nice picture, but I can't do anything with it. Do you want it?" he asked.

In that second, reality sank in: we weren't really a couple. Once we flew home, we'd be going right back to the same situation as before. He'd go home to his wife, and I would be going on a third date with Brendon to appease Isabel. I felt so stupid.

"No, I don't want it," I said.

We finished dinner, and he suggested going to a tiki

bar that wasn't too far away. He claimed that we had been in Puerto Rico for two whole days already without having a real homemade piña colada.

When we walked out, hand-in-hand, I said, "You know what? Let me just go pee real fast before we go to the other place."

He said okay and waited outside the restaurant. I hurried back inside, desperately searching for the photographer. I found her at another tourist's table and waited patiently for her to finish. The young couple seemed very excited about their picture. As she turned to leave, I rushed over, telling her that I'd like to purchase my photo, after all. I slipped the picture into my pocketbook without even looking at it again and then went back outside to meet Vincent. I wasn't sure why I bought the picture. It wasn't like I could hang it anywhere, either. Those past two days had been so amazing, though—I think I needed something to remind me of them when I was an old lady.

We barely made it back in the room when he started pulling the spaghetti straps down my shoulders.

"This dress is the best thing I've ever bought," he said. He grabbed the neckline and yanked it down, exposing my breasts. He kissed them and pushed me back toward the bed, while his hands stroked up my thighs. Then, he flipped me over onto my stomach and held me down on the bed. From behind me, he lifted my dress and slid my panties off. With my dress bunched around my waist and my shoes on, he had me right there.

Luckily, he was careful not to ruin the dress. I was hoping I would be able to wear it again one day.

VINCE

When I woke up the next morning, Sarah wasn't in bed. I got up, still half asleep, to see where she'd gone. It was only 5 a.m. so what could she possibly be doing? When I reached the archway of the living room, I saw her. There she was, on her back, legs stretched over her shoulders in an extremely flexible position. Leave it to a Broadway actress to bring exercise clothes on vacation. I observed her in an upside-down position for a little while, before she spotted with me and realized I was watching her.

"Why are you staring at me like a creep?" she asked, not breaking her stance.

I walked into the room. "I think the term 'gazing adoringly' is a better fit, but hey if you think it's creepy..." I shrugged. "Wanna go for a run?"

She sat up and laughed. "You think you can keep up with me in a run?"

"Are you kidding me? I run every morning and was a baseball player, remember? Of course, I can keep up with you," I said confidently.

Now she looked at me like it was a challenge. "Sure, Mr. Baseball player, let's go for a run."

The cargo shorts I was wearing were definitely not suitable for sprinting, and running on sand was not as easy as running on concrete. Not to say I'd have been able to keep up any better if we were, in fact, on concrete, or if I were wearing the proper attire. As I worked my hardest to stay close, huffing and puffing the entire way, she turned around to face me, running backward. Taunting me.

"There are two types of girls in the world," she said. "The kind that lets their man win out of pure respect for his pride, and the ones who watch them lose and laugh. I'm the second girl."

"Oh yeah?" I tried to squeeze the words out between my gasps for air. "Well, there are two types of men in the world. The ones who are proud of their women for being able to accomplish such a feat and the ones who..."

I grabbed her and pulled her towards me. She tripped from being stopped so abruptly. I caught her midair and picked her up and, with her legs around my waist, started carrying her toward the water.

She playfully yelled, "No!" as she realized what I was about to do.

"...and the men who just won't let them win," I said, as I submerged her in the water. I carried her all the way in until the water reached waist deep. The sun hadn't come up yet and the water was freezing. I could see the hairs on her arms bristling from goosebumps. Her nipples were hard. With my arms around her waist, I pulled her into me and said, "Try running wet."

"Oh my God, we're soaked!" she exclaimed. She put her arms around me, shivering.

"Do we need to go shopping again?" I asked, laughing. We stared at each other, and I said, "Let's not go home. Let's stay here forever. We can get a house, open a tiki bar. Bartend at night and make love all day."

She stared into my eyes lovingly and said, "I wish."

"Would you leave everything for me?" I asked.

Without hesitation, she sighed. "Yes."

I couldn't control what came out of my mouth next. "Then why won't you let me leave everything for you?"

She pushed away from me and began walking towards the sand. She stripped off her soaked sneakers and socks and rolled her pants up. "You said we wouldn't talk about this Vincent—it was your rule. Before even getting on the plane."

I started doing the same, taking off my wet socks and shoes.

"I'm not talking about them. I am talking about us: you and me. Our future," I argued.

She stood there trying to look away from me, wrapping her arms around her waist. "Then what exactly are you talking about when you say *everything*? I already told you I would not be the cause of your divorce."

"You're not the cause of my divorce," I said. "The cause of my divorce will be that we aren't in love. That we don't really have a marriage."

She kept shaking her head. The more I spoke, the more upset she was getting.

"Okay, I'm sorry," I said. I lifted my hand in the air in swear position. "I promise I will never bring it up again. Not until you do. But know this, the second you tell me to pull the trigger, I will."

She nodded in agreement and unfolded her arms. She

glanced down at her soaked clothes. "Let's go take showers," she suggested.

"Showers sounds like a complete waste of water. We should take a shower, one, together," I proposed.

That was a shower to remember.

Afterward, as I stood in the mirror shaping my now three-day-old facial hair, she walked up behind me. "You should keep the sides on around your goatee," she said.

Puzzled, I looked at her and handed her the razor.

"What do you mean? Show me," I said.

She hesitantly took the razor. "You trust me with a blade to your face?" she asked.

"I trust you with anything," I replied.

She sat on the sink with my body now nestled between her legs. I held on to her thighs as she shaved me. She kept the sides along my face the same length as the goatee. Said it was more modern.

I felt weird, when she made comments like that. Like I was so old in comparison—and yet she made me feel so young.

The next day after lunch, we returned to the room to get ready for our next adventure. She came out of the bathroom, wearing only my t-shirt. That shirt had never looked so good. I heard my phone go off, so I looked down, and there was a text from Jimmy.

Call me.

I inhaled an exasperated breath. "I'm really sorry, but I have to call the office real quick. Shit, I can't even take a few days off."

I went into the living room. She sat on the couch and watched me talk on the phone. Jimmy was speaking a mile a minute, telling me about a tip he'd had just received and whether or not we should buy. The call went on longer than I would have liked. I had to go into detail over who needed to be called, what needed to be said, and how much they should buy. Jimmy put me on speakerphone, so that the brokers in his office could listen to my instructions. Sarah stared the whole time, looking impressed. She always told me that I was so smart. She loved hearing me talking about work. I argued that I wasn't that smart, I just knew money.

As I talked to the guys, carefully detailing every step that each of them needed to take, she crawled over to me and unzipped my shorts. I waved my hand, trying to shoo her away. I couldn't be distracted. She apparently found that funny. She kept going, started going down on me while I tried my hardest to concentrate on what I was saying. I couldn't let her bring me to the point of climax. I couldn't get off while on a conference call with my staff.

Her mouth turned me on so much, though. I had to tell my staff, "Hold on one second," and put the phone on mute. I pulled her mouth off of me.

"Are you nuts? Give me a few minutes, let me finish this call," I said, laughing and frustrated, at the same time.

She pouted her lips. "You're no fun." She walked over to the desk and sat on top, watching me and waiting for me to finish the call.

When the call was over, I looked at her with my shorts still hanging open. "I'm going to kill you." I stalked over to the desk where she'd arranged her body into an extremely seductive pose.

"What am I going to do with you?" I asked, knowing full well I was about to ravish her.

"I don't know, what *are* you going to do with me?" she

asked daringly, biting that bottom lip. She must have known that was my weakness.

"Do you masturbate?" she asked, out of the blue.

I stopped. "Why would you ask that question?"

"You're just so sexual and ready to go at any time, I was curious if you masturbated," she said.

"Obviously I masturbate. I'm a man," I answered.

She looked at me, surprised by my answer. "What does being a man have to do with masturbating? Women masturbate too."

I looked at her. I had never thought of women masturbating. I'd always assumed it was a guy thing. Suddenly, all I could envision was her touching herself.

"They do?"

"Of course they do." She laughed.

I closed the distance between us. "I'd like to watch that."

She pulled the t-shirt of mine she was wearing over her head and threw it at me. Now, she sat on the desk, only wearing a bra and panties. "Here's your shirt back...come here."

I stood right between her legs as she kissed me—slow. Sensual. She slipped her pointer finger into my mouth, moistening it. Then, I backed up and watched as she very slowly ran her hand down her body, trailing down her neck, between her breasts, down past her belly button. She shifted her panties over and started caressing herself. Just when I believed I couldn't get any more turned on, I began throbbing—so hard, I felt like I could orgasm without even being touched.

"Do you think about me when you do that?" I asked.

"Yes."

I watched for a few minutes, mesmerized.

"Explain to me what you think about," I said, as I dropped to my knees and let my mouth join her private party. She went into explicit detail of what she pictured me doing to her when I wasn't there.

Those four days were incredible. I don't think there was a square inch of that suite where we didn't have sex. She was right—the sex was amazing, best I ever had. But it was so much more than that. I was so in love with this girl. Obsessed. There wasn't one thing in the world she could ask me to do that I would say no to. I'd never felt that way about anybody.

Friday afternoon back in my office, I was staring at my computer screen. Looking at numbers, but only seeing Puerto Rico. Sand, water, Sarah, piña coladas, and coral dresses. I was in a complete trance when there was a knock on the door.

"Come in," I said, snapping myself out of my fantasy.

Jimmy walked in and shut the door. "Vince, we have a problem."

I stood up, rested my hands on my desk, and sighed. I ranted, "Jimmy, one day someone is going to knock on that door, and when I say come in, they are going to have something positive to say. It's going to be 'Hey Vince, something incredible just happened,' or 'Hey Vince, look what I did,' or even 'Hey Vince, how was your weekend'? It's not always going to be 'Vince, we have a problem.' Why does everyone feel the need to come here with their problems? Do I look like the fucking therapist around here?"

Jimmy stood there with his mouth hanging open. "You're right, I'm so sorry—that was completely insensitive of me. How was Puerto Rico?"

"Amazing, wish I was still there," I said.

"Oh good, that's so reassuring—I'm really glad you had a good time," he said, sarcastically, while putting his hand over his chest. "Now that we've covered that, can we get back to business? To answer your question, no, you don't look like a therapist, but you do look like the boss, and we have a fucking problem. It's Benny. He needs to be fired."

I dropped my head into my hands and groaned. "How bad are his numbers?"

"Bad—very bad. To say extremely bad would be a gross understatement. Not only is he not covering his own salary, but his last mistake cost the firm $40 million. We have brokers down there busting their asses to make up for his mistakes."

He had a point. Benny had been a problem for a while now; it was only a matter of time before we needed to get rid of him. Any other problem I'd been mentally prepared for, with the exception of the termination of an employee. Why today? Why on my day back? Why me?

"Can't human resources do it?" I asked. Of all the stressful things someone in my position ever had to do, firing employees was by far the worst. You never knew how long it was going to take, or how they were going to react. You had to choose your words carefully, with a witness in the room to avoid any type of misinterpretation. I'd watched grown men cry and plead, swearing that they'd improve.

"Vince, the guy worked here for over twenty years. Don't you think he at least deserves the courtesy of you telling him?" he asked.

And just like that, the sand blew away. The water,

drained. No more piña coladas and no more coral dresses. I was back in real life, getting ready to go ruin someone else's.

A few months passed, and then it was June 19th. I remember the exact date because it was Casey's twentieth birthday. We had a tradition every year. We would go to the same Italian restaurant and then I would buy her whatever she wanted for her birthday. Everything was low key, not too fancy. The restaurant was like a glamourized pizzeria with a counter up front for takeout. The dining room in the back was tiny, but Casey loved their eggplant rollatini and especially liked that the owner always knew it was her birthday when she walked in. What she didn't know was that every year, I called ahead to remind him.

"Still seeing that guy, what was his name? Ethan?" I asked her as we were eating.

"No, I broke up with him." She stared down at her pasta.

"What happened? Do I need to kick his ass?" I asked, half-serious.

"No, you don't need to kick his ass." She laughed. "I'll be fine. He cheated on me. I guess he didn't like me as much as I thought he did."

I sat there, silent for a minute. I didn't even know what to say to that, considering I was cheating myself.

"Most guys are just assholes," I began. "Doesn't mean it had anything to do with you at all. You're so young, and you have so much to offer. Any guy would be lucky to have you. You're going to find the right guy one day, who appreciates you, and you shouldn't expect anything less. You're too beautiful and too smart to settle for just anyone. You did the right thing by breaking up with him—you're too good for that."

She looked at me and smiled. "You're my dad. You have to say that kind of stuff."

"Yeah, I am your dad, but that doesn't mean what I'm saying isn't true. I'm also a man, and trust me, we can be assholes."

"You are far from an asshole!" she argued.

I wondered how her thoughts on me would change if she knew my situation.

"Now, did you decide what you wanted for your birthday? Go ahead, hit me with it," I asked, changing the subject.

My daughter was good at picking expensive gifts. Gucci bags, Tiffany jewelry. Who could forget the BMV convertible on her eighteenth birthday that I paid the monthly storage rent for while she was away at school? So, judging by her previous taste in gifts, I was shocked when she told me she wanted a tattoo. In a weird way, I was flattered that she wanted me to go with her to get it. Most twenty-year-olds nowadays already have tattoos that they kept hidden from their parents.

I asked her what she design wanted to get and where she was going to put it. She pulled out a picture on her phone of a dainty little daisy and said she wanted a small one, on her wrist.

I glanced at the picture. "You know, I've been thinking of getting one too."

"Really?" she said, surprised. "What do you want to get?"

"I haven't put much thought into it," I lied. "Something around my bicep. Barbed wire, maybe?"

"No—way too nineties." She shook her head, shooting

me down.

"How about thorns?" I asked, as if I'd just come up with the idea.

"Like rose thorns?" she asked.

"Yeah, no roses, just thorns." I pictured my arm wrapped around Sarah and how my thorns would match the thorns that wrapped around her ribs.

"I like it," she said. "Can we go tonight?" She was excited. Really excited.

"You don't think I'm too old to get a tattoo?" I asked.

"Too old?" she laughed. "You're the youngest dad I know. All my friends talk about how hot you are."

"Really?" I laughed. "That's kind of gross, but I guess a compliment in a twisted way."

"You think it's gross for you? Imagine how I feel when they say stuff like that!" she said.

I made her a deal that I would get her the daisy tattoo, but she couldn't get it on her wrist. She had to get it somewhere less visible, since she had no idea what her career was going to be yet. She settled for her hip, and so we went to get tattoos.

The tattoo parlor wasn't what I'd imagined it would look like. I expected some kind of dirty, underground space, but this place wasn't like that at all. The interior was brightly lit, with clean white tile floors and pictures of designs decorated the walls. Nineties alternative music played in the background. Mixed in with the designs were framed photos of famous people; old Hollywood icons, all tattooed up. I thought I'd be the oldest guy there, but I wasn't by far. An artist worked on an entire sleeve on a man who looked so old, he could have been my father. As Casey flipped through the stencils on the wall, I watched the artist work.

"First tattoo?" he asked, when he realized I was looking.

"Yes," I laughed. "How can you tell?"

He smiled. "I'm warning you now; they get addicting," he advised.

I watched Casey while she got hers. They sat her on a chair, behind a mobile curtain. Then they went through a whole tutorial, showing her the package before opening it, proving the needle was brand new. They explained in detail about how we could tell they were using fresh ink.

Casey took the whole process like such a champ. It made me wonder if this really was her first tattoo. I didn't like how the artist had positioned her, or the way her shorts were pulled down so low, and I started second-guessing my decision of making her put it somewhere so hidden. Once hers was finished, Casey stayed next to me the whole time while the artist worked on mine. After the initial shock of the needle, my arm turned numb pretty quick. It felt more like scraping than anything else. I could see why tattoos could get so addicting.

When we got back to the house, Casey couldn't wait to tell Samantha. "Mom! Dad and I got tattoos!"

Mom was *not* happy.

"Dad and you did what?" Samantha exclaimed. She stood in the kitchen, glaring at me like she wanted to stab me right there, dead on the floor.

As if realizing what was now about to happen between Samantha and me, Casey kissed me on the cheek, thanked me again, and escaped upstairs to her room.

Samantha looked at me, outraged. "What the fuck is wrong with you?" she yelled. "How could you let her get a tattoo?"

"Sam, she's twenty years old. She's an adult. She doesn't need either of our permission to get a tattoo, so be happy she asked me to go or it would have been on her wrist." My voice rose to her level.

"And you? What did you get?" she asked, looking me up and down as if she had some sort of x-ray vision and was examining my body.

I lifted the sleeve of my polo shirt and peeled aside the bandage, not realizing how gross everything would look. Covered in blood and excess ink, it probably wasn't the best presentation.

Her face dropped. "Are you losing your mind?" she demanded. "Are you having a mid-life crisis? Who the fuck gets tattooed at forty-five years old?"

"Oh yeah, I'm having the mid-life crisis—because a tattoo is really so much different than the silicone in your tits!" I yelled. "Actually, it is different, because this didn't cost me ten grand. Twice!"

Oh, she was so mad! She got right up in my face and sneered. "You fucking disgust me. Get out of my face."

"Fine," I said. I quickly made my way upstairs. I went into the room and threw on a pair of joggers and a t-shirt. I grabbed a baseball hat, threw it on my head, and then went back down to tell her I was going for a jog. That was when I smelled something horrible—a very pungent, minty aroma. Almost astringent. I couldn't figure out what the terrible smell was.

"I'm going for a run, what the fuck is that smell?" I asked, walking into a cloud of smoke in the kitchen.

"Sage," she responded. "There's something really negative in this kitchen because every time we're here together, I can't stand you more and more. So, I'm cleansing the area."

I looked at her like she was insane. "Yes, that's exactly what it is—kitchen demons!" I said sarcastically.

"Get the fuck out of my sight," she said.

I slammed the door behind me.

I ran about five blocks before I stopped and picked up my phone. I couldn't wait to show Sarah my tattoo. She answered, sounding surprised that I was calling her so late on a Saturday night.

"Hey baby, what are you doing?" I asked.

She told me she was at a lounge in the village that was kind of lame, but it was Isabel's birthday. I asked if I could meet her there, if she could come out for a few minutes. She said okay, so I took a taxi over. I called her when I was on the corner outside, since I was nowhere near to being dressed appropriately to walk into a bar.

Sarah walked out, and her gaze traveled up and down my body. "*Damn*, you look sexy!" she said.

I was taken back. No one had ever told me that I looked sexy in joggers. "You like the bum look?" I asked.

"You don't look like a bum. You look hot. The joggers, the white t-shirt, hat—very New York," she said.

"I want to show you something," I lifted my sleeve.

Her jaw dropped, and then her mouth widened into a huge smile. "Are those thorns? Is that real? You got a tattoo?"

"Yes, it's real. And yes, those are thorns, I got it to match yours. Do you like it?" I asked.

She threw her arms around me and kissed me. "I love it! You look *so* hot!"

"You know, it's amazing what you find attractive about

me. The smell of scotch on my breath, joggers, tattoos—just the complete opposite of what I hear at home," I said.

"I'm guessing the tattoo didn't go over too well?"

"No, not at all. She's currently performing an exorcism in the kitchen," I said.

"An exorcism?" Sarah said.

"Yeah, sage-ing out the spirits in the kitchen that make us fight when we're in it." I laughed, shaking my head. "We have crystals all over the house. Magical crystals, all holding different superpowers."

She laughed too. "Do you happen to have a crystal on you that will allow us to transport to my apartment miraculously? I can give you a hands-on demonstration of just how turned on you make me," she said enticingly.

I wrapped my arms around her again. "I wish, but I don't have that type of time."

As we stood there talking, I noticed a guy come out of the bar and stare over at us from down the block. "Do you know that guy?" I asked.

She turned around to look. "I'll be right in!" she yelled over to him. We watched him walk back inside.

"There's a bunch of people in there. It's Isabel's birthday," she explained.

"It's okay. I just really wanted to show you, and I couldn't wait until Monday. I have to go back—maybe the demons are all gone by now. I'll see you on Monday."

She turned my baseball cap backward on my head and gave me a long, hard kiss. I hailed a cab. "Tell Isabel I said happy birthday."

SARAH

Once Vincent left, I went back into the bar and headed over to our table with a stupid grin on my face.

"Who was that?" Brendon asked.

"My uncle," I said, winking at Isabel. "Who, by the way, wanted me to tell you happy birthday."

She smiled back at me, realizing what had just happened. "Well, you make sure you tell Uncle Vincent I said thank you."

"He was looking at you a little inappropriately to be your uncle, no?" Brendon said.

I didn't answer him. The truth was, I would have left them all right then if Vincent had been able to go back to my apartment. Like he'd asked me in Puerto Rico—that night, I would have walked away from everything.

The next day, I was in my dressing room when there was a knock on the door. Matt walked in before I could even respond. "I didn't say come in yet," I said.

He rolled his eyes. "Girl, there is nothing you have that I'm interested in," he said, laughing. "I need a favor."

I knew this day would come—payback for the time I'd asked him to be my wedding date.

"What's up?" I asked, throwing on my robe.

"So that guy Dave, the casual sex one? He wants to go out for dinner. Like on a date. I'm afraid he's going to try to get serious, can you and Vincent come?"

I didn't know what to say. I knew I would have to pick a Wednesday night, because that was when Vincent and I were together.

"Let me check his schedule and get back to you," I said. "But it shouldn't be a problem."

We went out and did our performance. I kept worrying about how I needed to convince Vincent to go on the date when he returned the next day for lunch. By this time, I was living a double life, too. I had my career life, where everyone in the show knew Vincent as my boyfriend, and my personal life, where Isabel and I were dating friends. I didn't mix either of the lives, though it was hard. Brendon was a nice guy, made a good living, and was very good-looking. He was tall and built, with dark hair and light eyes. In many ways, he was the complete opposite of Vincent: immature and extremely short-tempered. He spent most of his time playing video games and enjoyed things like comic book conventions. He and his friend Chris would even dress up for the conventions, which was something that didn't interest Isabel or me.

"How exactly are you going to get them to agree to leave Manhattan?" Vincent asked, when I brought up the subject at my apartment the next day.

"We're the lead actors in the hottest, Tony Award-winning show in New York right now. I'll tell him I'd rather not be seen. You're not the only big deal in New

York City anymore. Maybe we can go to Brooklyn," I suggested.

"Brooklyn is very up and coming, there are a lot of brokers that live there," he said.

"We don't have to go downtown. We can go to Bay Ridge, there are a lot of nice restaurants there, too," I said.

"Bay Ridge like *Saturday Night Fever*?" he asked.

"Is that the one with dancers?" I replied.

He shot me a condescending look. "You don't know what *Saturday Night Fever* is?" he asked.

"I know what it is, I've just never seen it," I admitted.

He shook his head, disbelievingly. I think the generation gap got to him sometimes.

"Well, do you know what *Dirty Dancing* is?" I threw back at him, expecting his answer to be no.

"I have a twenty-year-old daughter; of course, I know what *Dirty Dancing* is. I've seen it about five times more than I would have liked to. And NO, before you get any crazy ideas, I am NOT learning that dance routine with you, no matter what holiday it is!" he said.

"Not even on a Thursday?" I asked, pouting.

"No, not even on a Thursday," he said.

"So..." I continued. "You know, you can't say anything about being married or having kids, none of it. I trust Matt, but I don't even want to go there,"

"I assumed as much, I'll think of something," he said.

Plans were made for the third Wednesday of the month. Vincent picked me up in this huge black truck.

"This is the family SUV?" I asked, jumping in.

"Yes, why?" he asked.

"I wouldn't call it an SUV."

"What would you call it?"

I peered over my shoulder, into the back that seemed never to end. "A bus?" I laughed.

"Speaking of," he began, "I hope they have valet; it's a bitch to park this thing."

We drove over to pick up Matt and Dave. The second they climbed in, Matt exclaimed, "Oh shit, Vincent, you're driving! I legit thought you sent a limo service when I saw this thing outside."

Vincent laughed. "Yeah, I get that a lot," he said.

We ended up at a trendy hookah lounge for dinner that Dave had picked out. The smell of different flavors of smoke mixed with thick curry spice lingered in the air, and big hookahs sat on every table.

"I have an announcement to make," I said, as we sat down.

All three men looked up at me, looking curious as to what I was going to say.

"If you're going to suggest the coconut flavored shisha, I was thinking the same!" Dave said, holding up the tobacco menu.

"I'm not smoking that thing!" I exclaimed.

"Nor am I, we're both singers, remember?" Matt added, pointing at me.

"I'll do it with you," Vincent told Dave.

I looked at Vincent a little surprised that he was going to smoke it, but at the same time, somehow turned on by it.

"You don't have to inhale it—you kind of just move the smoke around your mouth to taste the flavor. Like a cigar," Dave explained.

"Really?" Matt asked, looking directly at Vincent for verification.

"Well, you're not supposed to," Vincent said. "I personally find it hard not to inhale because I used to smoke cigarettes, so I find myself inhaling, even on cigars sometimes."

"You used to smoke?" I turned to him and asked, surprised that I was learning anything new about him at this point in our relationship.

"Yeah, for like ten years," he answered.

Suddenly I felt a little prudish, saying I wouldn't smoke. "I'll try it," I said.

Vincent shook his head. "No, don't. Would it make you feel better if I don't smoke?"

"No, you can. I don't care," I said.

"Anyway, what was that announcement?" Matt asked me, trying to intervene into our awkward banter.

"Oh, what I wanted to say is that Vincent is going to learn the finale in *Dirty Dancing* to dance with me!"

Vincent looked up from the hookah menu.

"Oh, hell no," Matt said dramatically. "Vincent, you're a nice guy and all, but she's *my* work wife, so if anyone is going to be having the time of their life with her, it going to be me."

I giggled; I just knew Matt would be annoyed by that.

"And by the way, I don't need to *learn* the routine, just throwing that out there," Matt continued, moving his fingers in air quotations around "learn."

Vincent gave an exaggerated sigh. "Damn, I was *so* looking forward to that lift scene."

"Do you guys ever do that? Like, learn different dance numbers from movies, just messing around?" Dave asked.

"We haven't but not going to lie, I am kind of inclined to now," Matt answered.

We were having a really good time. I couldn't help but watch Vincent as he smoked the hookah. His bicep hardened, and a hint of his new ink peeked out of his shirt. He had this vein in his forearm that bulged every time he held the pipe to his mouth. I was never attracted to smokers before, but for some reason, watching him blow that smoke out of his mouth was unbelievably sexy.

Dave was doing a lot of the talking. I think Matt was right when he said that Dave was really into him; I could tell he wanted more than just casual sex. Matt quickly changed the subject anytime a topic got too serious.

"Okay, Vincent, what's your story?" Matt asked.

Vincent looked up from his plate. "What do you mean 'my story?'" he asked.

"How old are you?" Matt said.

"Forty-five," Vincent answered.

"Forty-five, balling, hot," Matt continued.

"Aw, you think I'm hot?" Vincent said.

"Oh stop, you know you're sexy as fuck, so why are you single? What's your deal? What's *wrong* with you?" Matt said.

Vincent put his fork down while I watched, waiting for his answer. This was the big moment—what was he going to say?

"Well," he began. "I dated a girl for a really long time. Seven years. I was so in love with her. We were engaged, practically married. We had an apartment in the village, and I was best friends with her brother. Really nice girl, extremely smart and very pretty. She was a nurse. We were already up to planning the wedding, and then I came home early one day, and well..."

He paused, like he was suddenly getting sad.

"She was in bed with another man. In OUR bed with another man. Needless to say, we broke up. I was devastated. Not only did I lose the love of my life, but I also lost my best friend, because her brother never spoke to me again. I can only imagine the story she must have told him. Now, I'd just turned thirty-five and after that, I was kind of turned off to women in general. I became a bit of a playboy, thinking I could never trust another woman again."

Vincent turned to look at me and took my hand in his. "And then I met Bianca, and well, she made me forget any other woman even existed except for her."

I sat there in shock. I couldn't believe the amount of bullshit that had just spewed from his mouth so naturally. The guys were really impressed by the story.

"So, you think this is it? You think the two of you are going to get married?" Matt asked.

Vincent shook his head. "What's wrong with you? You don't ask a man a question like that in front of his girl. What if I wanted to propose tonight? You would have ruined the surprise!"

"Oh, he's a keeper!" Dave said to me, smiling. I smiled back.

"He sure is," I answered.

On the way home, Matt and Dave did most of the talking in the backseat, and I stayed quiet most of the ride. We dropped them off and then headed to my place. Vincent pulled over in front of my apartment. "I think that went well, you?" he said, sounding proud.

I shot him a dirty look.

"Are you mad at me?" he asked, surprised.

"You're such a liar!" I exclaimed.

"You told me to lie!" he said

"Yeah, but I didn't know you'd be so good at it!"

He started shaking his head. "I'm confused—you wanted me to lie, but you're mad I did it too well? Would you be happier if I'd been less convincing?" He seemed defensive.

"If you can lie that easily about something so stupid, how do I know you aren't lying to me when you say half the shit you say to me?" I asked.

"Sarah, I'm a stockbroker. We are basically salespeople. You're an actress, is it that much different? Are you looking for a reason to fight? You asked me to lie, and I did, this was your idea. Sorry if I'm so good at words!" His face turned red.

"I guess not. Stockbroker, actress, same thing, right?" I asked sarcastically, only half kissing him goodnight.

When I got inside, I couldn't help but wonder: if Vincent was that good at lying, what could he have been lying to me about this whole time? So, I did a google search on him, determined to find something he'd lied to me about. It was amazing, what you can find out about somebody by Googling them. I found his address, his phone number, his income, how much his house was worth, his family members. That led me to his daughter's social media pages. Wow, she was gorgeous—no wonder he was so proud of her. She had some family pictures on her page, but mostly photos of her and her friends dressed in skimpy outfits at college parties.

His son was quite the looker as well. He was the spitting image of Vincent, only clean shaven with green eyes. Same hair, same dimple when he smiled. Then, I found the articles from 1993. Headlines like "Falling Star,"

"California's Biggest Error of the Season," and "The Catcher in the DUI."

I read every one of them. The articles said such horrible things about him, tore him apart. Really awful things. I felt so bad. I didn't find what I was looking for, but the mean things they wrote about him in the articles upset me. The reporters wrote how he was going to amount to nothing, and called him a waste of talent. A quotation from the judge who'd stated that he'd spared Vincent jail time for his children's sake—one of those kids being his wife. The articles made me think a lot about myself. What if, God forbid, I got hurt? What would I do if I couldn't dance anymore? I had no backup plan in life. I laid in bed restless that night, feeling really depressed.

When Vincent met me for lunch on Monday, he proceeded with caution into my kitchen. I guess he was worried that I was still mad at him.

"I brought your favorite," he said, and pulled two gyros with the works out of a sack. I smiled, as he took his suit jacket off and put it on the chair.

"You hate gyros," I said.

"Yeah, but I love you, and sometimes we have to do what we don't want to do to make the people we love happy," he said, as he started rifling through the utensil drawer for forks. "Are you still mad at me?"

"No, but I have to be honest, I stalked you," I admitted.

"You stalked me?" he said, now turning his body completely around to face me.

"Well, I Google stalked you," I specified.

"You Google stalked me? Does that mean you're too lazy to show up at my house or job like an authentic, old-school stalker?" He laughed and shut the drawer, leaning back against the counter with forks in hand. "What did Google tell you about me?"

"Too much," I said. "I can't believe all this stuff is just out there on the Internet. I got your home phone number, your address, your salary information, how much your house is worth, even pictures of it, which by the way, looks sick."

"All stuff I could have told you—you didn't have to waste your time researching me."

"I saw your daughter's profile page, she's gorgeous. I see why she's your favorite," I said.

"Thank you, but she isn't my favorite. I don't have a favorite child." He sat down at the table across from me.

"Oh, come on, yes you do! You glow when you talk about her," I said.

"She's not my favorite. I can't explain it. You wouldn't understand. As a father, your bond with your daughter, with your little girl, it's just so different than with your son," he tried to explain.

"Did you want a girl?" I asked, surprised.

"No, not when she first got pregnant, I wanted a boy. But by the time the second one came along, I was happy she was a girl," he responded.

"I also found the articles about your baseball incident," I said sympathetically.

"Again, I told you about that, too." He stood up and walked into the living room—like he didn't want to revisit that time. He started undoing his tie.

"I know, but you didn't tell me what brutal things they said about you," I said.

He rolled up his tie and placed it on the coffee table before picking up the candle. Then, he turned the candle around and around, looking at it instead of me.

"Sarah, I did a terrible thing. I was drinking and driving. I'm fortunate that all I had was a revoked license, unemployment, and some bad press. That judge could have thrown me in jail if he'd wanted to. Or worse, I could have killed somebody," he said.

"I just find it so amazing and admirable that you survived all that. You moved forward. Became successful enough to buy a $20 million townhouse in the Upper East Side."

He set the candle back down and smiled. "Thank you, but I bought that house ten years ago for a little over eight million, Google didn't tell you that part? It turned out to be a really good investment." He laughed. "Come here."

When I got close enough, he pulled me to him, holding me tight. He looked me straight in the eyes. "Sarah look, I guess you're right. There is no difference between being a good liar and just being a liar. I lie at work, I lie to my wife, I lied to Matt, but I have never, ever lied to you. You are the one person in this world that I can say whatever I want to. You don't judge me. You don't overreact. Well except for Wednesday night—I think that was a bit of an overreaction. But justified, I get it. I have zero reason to lie to you. It's part of why I love you so much. I can just be myself around you," he explained.

"I know, I'm really sorry," I said, putting my arms around his shoulders. Staring back into his eyes, I told him, "I just love you so much, I know you're going to hurt me one of these days."

He brought his face closer to mine, until we were eye-to-eye. "I will never, ever hurt you—I promise you that. Now come on, your sautéed rat is getting cold. Eat it while you can still convince yourself it's lamb," he said, pulling me back into the kitchen.

He barely touched his gyro, but as I devoured mine, he took off his button down. He lifted his t-shirt sleeve to show me his fresh tattoo.

"Is this normal?" he asked, touching the peeling skin. "It's been weeks already."

"Have you been lubricating it?" I asked.

"I put the A&D ointment on it for the first few days," he answered.

I went to the bedroom and returned with a bottle of hand lotion. I started rubbing the lotion into his tattoo, explaining that he needed to keep lubricating it every day.

He kissed my hand as I was rubbing the lotion into his bicep and pulled me down onto his lap. "If this is how I get you to rub me down with lotion, I'm going to start getting tattoos everywhere," he joked.

"You know Isabel says you got this for her birthday." I laughed.

"Crazy, her and Casey have the same birthday, no wonder why I like her so much," he said. "So, speaking of birthdays....in three weeks, it's my wife's fortieth."

"Are you throwing her a party?" I asked, trying not to sound too jealous.

"No." He smiled. "How can I throw her a fortieth party when she's been thirty-three for the past seven years? Before long, you're going to be older than her. But she is going away with her best friend to celebrate. She'll be gone for a week. I have a get out of jail free card, can you take that weekend off so we can do something? Maybe go to Atlantic City? Do you gamble?"

"No, I don't gamble, but I'll go. I'll have to call out sick though. I don't get any more vacation days, so I won't get paid for it," I answered.

"Okay, let's do it. I'll make up the money you lose on those days," he offered.

"You don't have to give me the money, I have a little bit saved for a rainy day."

"How much do you have saved?" he asked.

I jumped off his lap and moved over to my chair, pushing the gyro meat around the container with my fork. Although I was impressed by my rainy-day fund, he certainly wouldn't be.

"$2,500," I reluctantly answered.

"You know, if you have $2,500 saved, you should throw that into a good mutual fund. I can help you with that. You can earn a pretty substantial rate of return," he suggested.

I laughed at him. "You're such a stockbroker, I wouldn't even know how to manage that, plus what if I lose it all? It took me a year to save it," I said.

"A mutual fund is safer than stocks, and you won't have to manage it. They do that for you."

"So, Atlantic City, huh?" I said, changing the subject. When he spoke about the stock market, I felt so stupid around him.

"Yeah, Atlantic City. I'll book a room. We'll have fun, and better yet, I can wake up with you again," he said, leaning his elbows on the table and smiling at me.

When that Friday came, Vincent left work early and we drove down to Atlantic City. There was a lot of Jersey Shore traffic that night. A typical two-and-a-half hour drive took almost four hours. Starving, the first thing we did once we arrived was go eat. We went to a nice steakhouse in the casino. All you could hear was the sound of the slot machines, even inside the restaurant.

"Do you gamble a lot?" I asked him as we sat down to eat.

"Not too often, but when I do, I get pretty into it," he admitted. "You ever have an oyster shooter?"

"No, what is that?" I asked.

"It's a shot, like a Bloody Mary, only there's an oyster at the bottom. Really good—we'll take a dozen," he said to the waiter.

Those shooters were delicious, and high in alcohol content. I was already feeling the alcohol by the time we left the restaurant. When we entered the casino, Vincent headed right over to the craps table. I hugged myself.

"It's so cold in here!"

"That's a strategy, intentionally done to keep gamblers awake. All casinos are cold. Do you want to go to the gift shop? I'll get you a sweatshirt."

"No, thanks, I'll be fine," I said.

He pointed at the slot machines. "Look at the set up...see how it's like a maze? Also done purposely to keep gamblers from leaving."

Vincent played for a while, doing really well, I think. All I knew was that he had a lot of chips on the table; he must have had forty thousand dollars out. He played for an hour or so, and then he decided he wanted to play blackjack. When he cashed out, he handed me a thousand-dollar chip.

"I told you, I don't want you to give me money," I said, trying to hand the chip back.

"I'm not giving you money—you earned it. That is craps etiquette; if someone is with you giving you luck, you tip them. Ask anyone, it's true," he said. He took the chip from me and tucked it into my back pocket. "Remember to cash that out before we leave."

I wasn't allowed to sit next to him as he played blackjack, but I was able to stand nearby. After he played for a bit, a security guard came over to me and asked me for ID.

Once the guard left, Vincent smiled, leaned over, and said, "That shows I'm doing well; they're trying to throw me off by ID'ing you."

I watched him in amazement. I'd never been out with a real gambler before. I couldn't even comprehend what it was like, to gamble that type of money. I started fidgeting in my heels—my feet were now hurting from standing so long.

"Come on, let's go get a drink at the bar," he said, noticing I wasn't comfortable. We made our way over to the bar.

"I'm going to go to the bathroom," I said.

On my way back to the bar, a guy who looked a little older than me asked if he could buy me drink. Vincent glanced over with him and said, "She's with me." Very matter of fact.

"Oh, I'm sorry man, I thought you were her father," the man replied mockingly. Vincent's jaw clenched. "Oh, you thought I was her father? Nah, she just likes men, not boys." There was an arrogant tone in his voice.

"Just curious, how much Viagra does it take to keep up with someone so young?" the guy asked, obviously trying to pick a fight.

Vincent turned his whole seat around, like he was accepting the challenge the guy had just conveyed. I put my hand on his leg and looked him in the eyes. "Stop, don't let this prick bother you," I said, squeezing his thigh.

"Must be nice to be rich, there's always a gold digger around that you can score." The guy sneered and further egged him on.

Now I was just as angry as Vincent. I turned to the guy and said, "Oh, he's not rich, he just has a huge dick."

Then, I turned back to Vincent. "Come on; let's go."

I took him by the hand, and we made our way to elevators. By the time we got back to the room, it was 2 a.m., and Vincent's eyes kept closing. He laid down on the bed, fully clothed, and pulled me down with him. He wrapped himself around me. "I want to do so many things to you right now, but I'm so tired it will have to wait until morning. I thought it was because I had a long week, but now I know it must be because of my geriatric age," he said. He was still bothered by the father comment.

"Oh stop, that guy was a jealous asshole. You are so much better looking than him, did you see all the girls checking you out at the bar?" I asked. I wasn't kidding either. There were about five different women I caught checking him out.

He laughed. "You're the only woman I care about checking me out," he replied, and then kissed me. "Look, I'm sorry I got so nasty with him. I'm usually not like that; I'm really not. I know you must deal with this a lot when I'm not here—and I'm not here more than I am here. It's very frustrating, makes me think I did something wrong in a past life, and you're my punishment."

"You look at me as a punishment?" I asked, not sure how to take that comment.

"Why'd you come so late? Or so early? Why now of all

times? It's like you're being dangled in front of me. This girl that I love so much, that I want to be with so badly, all the time. But, sorry, no, Vincent you can't. It's like, look but don't touch. I promised myself years ago that I would never be broke again, and I worked so hard to get to where I am—only to realize it's not where I want to be. My kids have good lives. My wife has a good life. I would give up everything I own to live in a cardboard box, though, if you were sleeping next to me."

I pulled him to me, pressing his face against my chest while my lips touched his forehead. I ran my fingers through his hair and lightly stroked his head. I'd never thought of things that way, but what he said made sense. Why had the universe taken so long to bring us into each other's lives? Why bring us together at all?

The next morning, we didn't even speak. As promised, he made up for the lack of sex the night before. We were all over each other, the second we opened our eyes. Afterward, we went downstairs to order breakfast. As we were eating, I heard someone yell, "Bianca!"

We both looked up.

"Brett?" I jumped up to hug him. "How are you?"

"Doing well, thanks. This is my wife, Vanessa." He introduced me to the very pretty girl he was with.

I shook her hand. "Hi, Vanessa, nice to meet you. This is Vincent," I said, as he stood up to shake Brett's hand.

"I saw you landed a leading role on Broadway!" Brett said excitedly. "Good for you! You deserve it, you worked so hard."

"Yes, I did, thank you. Have you seen the show?" I asked.

"No, not yet, but we want to," Brett answered. "You

still have the same number? Maybe the four of us can go have dinner tonight and catch up if you're still here."

I told him I did have the same number, and he said he would text me later. They politely said their goodbyes to Vincent, and then we sat back down.

"He looks like he could be a football player." Vincent said.

"Actually, he was in high school, he's a cop now," I replied.

"Oh, so you went to high school with him?" he asked, taking a sip of his coffee.

"No, believe it or not, my performing arts school didn't have a football team." I laughed. "He's my ex-boyfriend."

Vincent put the coffee cup down and studied the plate in front of him. "How long did you date him for?" he asked.

"Three years," I replied.

"So, your ex-boyfriend was not only extremely good-looking, but was also a football player and owns a pair of handcuffs?" he asked.

I smiled and shook my head. Vincent was always so confident. I'd never seen him so insecure over another man before. It was reassuring to know that I wasn't the only jealous one. I didn't bother to answer his question. I didn't think he really expected me to, considering that the answers were obvious.

"Does it bother you that I'm so much older than you?" he asked.

"No, not at all. Does it bother you that I'm so much younger than you?" I asked, realizing he was still probably upset over the father insult from the night before.

"No," he said. "I mean, not that you're younger. But I wish I was younger, too." There was a bit of silence. "We are definitely not going out with them later."

"Why, are you really *that* jealous to go out with Brett and his wife?" I asked.

"No, I just don't need to stare across a dinner table at a guy who knows what you taste like. Would you want to go out with my ex-girlfriend and her new husband?" he asked.

I realized there was nothing I could say at that point to change his mind, but I joked anyway. "Depends...is she in a nursing home?"

He laughed and shook his head, and the conversation ended. We would not be having dinner that night with Brett and his wife.

I watched him gamble some more, and later, we had a very nice dinner. Vincent made sure we didn't get back to the room so late so that he'd be too tired to perform. We got on the road to Manhattan early Sunday morning, to avoid the summer traffic.

"How did you end up doing last night?" I asked.

Watching him gamble was exciting but confusing at the same time. I couldn't ever tell if he was up or down.

"Not good," he replied. "I'm better at poker, but I didn't want to go into a room and leave you alone."

"How much did you lose?" I asked.

"A little over twenty," he replied.

"Thousand?" I asked, shocked. He nodded, and my heart sank. I couldn't even imagine what it would be like to lose that type of money. "Are you upset?" I asked, as he pulled up in front of my place. He looked over at me and smiled.

"No. Trust me, I can lose a lot more in the stock market at any given time. I had a really good time with you this weekend," he said. "Worth every penny."

It had been a really nice weekend. The very best part was being able to go to sleep and wake up beside him.

"The weekend isn't over yet, and it's still early. Do you want to come in?" I asked.

"Let me go find a spot," he said. "Be back in a few."

SAMANTHA

"Did you know a midlife crisis is a real thing?" I asked Lisa, as we sat at the country club after getting massages.

"Still not over the tattoo?" she asked.

Months had passed since Vince had come home with that stupid ink on his bicep. I shook my head. "No, it's not about the tattoo, it's not even about him. It's about me."

Lisa put down her champagne glass, signaling that she was listening.

"If I tell you something, you can't tell anyone. We both know what happened the last time you opened your mouth to Jimmy," I warned.

She rolled her eyes. "Oh, please, that was the hottest thing I ever heard. You should be thanking me," she said.

"What? You like anal sex?"

"Oh yeah," she said. "A lot of women do, believe it or not. I love being dominated by Jimmy. He's so big. I feel tiny when he's throwing me around. The rougher he gets, the better," she said, lifting her robe to show me a bruise, like the mark was some sort of trophy. "I'm not going to lie," she continued, "I think about that kitchen scene sometimes when Jimmy and me are in bed."

"You think about Vince and me while you're having sex?" I asked, appalled.

"Stop acting so surprised. You're a hot couple. I'm sure a lot of people think about you and Vince in bed."

I shook my head. "Changing the subject...I went on a date with a guy," I admitted.

Lisa looked up from her phone. "What? When?" she asked.

"Last year. If you can even call it a date, since I paid half the bill. There's something about it though that I can't get out of my head. He asked me what I did for a living, and I said I was a teacher. I mean, Lisa, I'm nothing. I'm going to be forty in a few days. I'm just a mom and arm candy to a successful man. Is that what I'm going to be remembered as? I have nothing that defines me as a person. I was thinking of maybe going back to school," I said.

Lisa looked at me like I was insane. "School? To do what?" she asked.

"I don't know—something. I'm just so bored, especially with the kids being out of the house. What am I supposed to do? Fire the cleaning girl and clean the house?"

Lisa gasped at something on her phone, interrupting me. "Oh my God! I'm monitoring Hayden's social media accounts. There's a girl in his class that, for whatever reason, is being bullied by, well, almost everyone. Not Hayden, not yet. That's why I keep looking. Listen to this, written on a public wall: 'I'm going to shove my cock into your mouth until you choke on it, you slut bitch.'"

Her mouth twisted. "These kids are twelve! I don't

know if I feel worse for the poor girl or this douchebag's mother, who can't even yell at this kid without ACS knocking at her door. Be happy your kids are grown, Sam. This is the bullshit I deal with all day long. We pay almost fifty thousand dollars a year to have these kids in private schools, and this still happens! Kids are truly brutal nowadays. Anyway, I'm sorry, continue," she said, shaking her head in disgust.

"I just don't know what to do with myself. I'm not getting any younger. Remember when we were in our twenties, and if we were late for our periods, we were calculating when the last time we had sex was to make sure we weren't pregnant? Now when I'm late for my period, I'm afraid it's menopause. I actually get excited to get my period now, like whew, it's not time yet," I ranted. "I'm bored, Lisa and I miss California. At least in California, you can go to a beach or something. The winters here are miserable."

"So why don't you move somewhere warmer? You guys looked in Florida before. You think Vince will move? Not like he can't retire now," she said.

"No way. Vince is way too New York. He's become such a city guy. He didn't want to move to Florida, even back then. We only looked because he was nervous he was going to lose his job with the crash. That was him in panic mode. He always has a backup plan. We were fortunate to recover from the hit, and now that the economy is doing so much better, no way he'd move," I said.

"You know what you need?" she said. "A boy toy. Nice blue-collar guy. Someone who works with their hands. Mechanic or firefighter. They are so much better in bed. They don't have the things running through their heads these guys do. Not thinking about meetings, or PowerPoints, or stock performances, just focusing on what's under them- or over them!"

"Why do you cheat on Jimmy if you have such good sex with him?" I asked.

She thought about it for a second. "I don't know; maybe it's the thrill."

"Maybe you're right. I was so nervous with that guy from Brooklyn—I should have just slept with the Uber driver!" I joked.

"Hey, if you're so bored, I can give you Hailey's page to monitor. Trust me; it's a full-time job, watching their socials media accounts."

"Thanks, but I'll pass. That sounds stressful," I said.

"Come on, let's get dressed. We'll go get lunch and cocktails and then do some shopping. I'm sure you'll feel a lot better about yourself with a new Chanel bag," she said.

I laughed. "Okay," I agreed. "I am always down for retail therapy."

"We'll be on a beach in Ibiza in two days to celebrate the seventh anniversary of your thirty-third birthday. We're going to have a great time!" she reassured me.

The flight to Ibiza was so long that, as a birthday gift, Vince had chartered a private jet for us. I gripped the railing tightly as we walked up the ramp to board.

"Haven't mastered these steps in heels yet?" Lisa teased.

As we took our seats and prepared for takeoff, the flight attendant appeared.

"Welcome and Happy Birthday Mrs. DeLuca," she said. "For lunch, we'll be serving a branzino, lightly marinated in olive oil with a side of fresh vegetables. For snacks, we have fresh caviar, along with a variety of cheeses with crackers and fresh fruit. On board we have Grey Goose or Belvedere vodka, Patron Tequila, Sapphire Gin and Bacardi One-fifty-one. We also have plenty of mixers, should you want a mixed drink. There are three bottles of champagne chilling, let me know if you'd like me to open a bottle."

As we listened to her spiel, we fastened our seat belts.

"We're taking off shortly and request that your chairs be in the upright position. Once we've reached a safe flying altitude, anything goes. Please let me know if you need anything." The flight attendant handed us both a pair of cashmere socks. We took our heels off and slipped them on.

It took about twenty minutes before the flight attendant informed us that we'd reached a cruising altitude. At that point, we unbuckled our seatbelts and moved to the couch.

"I got you a present," Lisa said. She dug into her pocketbook and extracted a cigarette box. She snapped the box open, pulling out a very nicely rolled joint.

"Is that pot?" I asked.

She started laughing. "Sure is—I made Jimmy get it for us!"

"Good thing we didn't have to go through security, or we'd be spending my birthday in jail."

I laughed and watched as Lisa lit the joint, took a pull, and passed it to me. I hadn't smoked in years, and I started choking on my first pull.

"You okay?" she asked.

"Yeah," I said, trying to catch my breath, half-laughing and half-choking.

"Okay, we need a story," she said.

"What kind of story?" I asked.

"Once we get to that hotel, we are thirty-three years old, single, and well, we need careers. What are we?" she asked.

I thought about it. "Um....what are we? Maybe sales reps?" I suggested.

"No, too boring," she said.

She passed the joint back to me. I took a hit and didn't choke this time.

"Public relations?" I asked. "Party planners—we're party planners! We do weddings, bar mitzvahs, private parties..."

"Yes! I love it!" she said. "We're party planners! My name is Marie," she said.

I started giggling, already incredibly high. "Okay, okay, and I'm Alyssa!"

We devised our plan for about an hour before we both passed out, high as kites.

The flight attendant woke us as we were reaching our initial descent. When we landed, there was a limo waiting for us on the runway. Marie and Alyssa showed at the hotel just in time for lunch.

"I cannot believe I smoked pot!" I said, as we sat down to eat.

"I don't know what you're talking about. You didn't smoke pot, Alyssa did!" she said, turning her head to gaze at the water. "Look at that beach—so different than New York. I hope you brought a sexy bathing suit...we're getting wild this week!"

After lunch, we changed into our bathing suits and spent the rest of the afternoon on the beach, drinking rum runners and pretending we were in our early thirties. There were a lot of American guys there. A lot of nice-looking American guys. All much friendlier than that jerk Cole had been. We were getting approached a lot. It had been a long time since I'd gotten that much attention. One pair of guys invited us to a club that night, and we accepted. We showed up at the club around 10 p.m., Ibiza time, and stayed until they closed. I hadn't partied like that in years. Taking shots, dancing with each other until we were slick with sweat. The next morning, we woke up and headed back to the beach.

"That guy was really into you last night," Lisa said. "Maybe you should lose the ring, it's hard to say you're single with that rock on your finger."

I looked down at my finger. Maybe I should take my ring off. Not that I thought a man would care that I was married, but the size of the diamond could be intimidating. I was pretty sure Jimmy and Lisa had an open marriage, but she'd never admitted as much to me. Vince had always been convinced that they were swingers. Either way, I didn't think either of them cared what the other one did, as long as they came home to each other.

"I'll put it in the safe when we get back to the room," I said.

"Good." Lisa sighed. "Look at all these young guys. So many to choose from."

I laughed. "You know we're cougars," I said.

She gave me a dirty look. "Bite your tongue, bitch! We are not!" she exclaimed.

"Yes, we are, I looked it up. Thirty-five and older!" I answered.

"See, we're thirty-three, so not yet," she said, and then

laughed.

That night, we attended a "singles party" hosted by the hotel. So many men approached me that I had wondered why I hadn't taken off my ring sooner. Lisa immediately hit it off with one of the guys, so I made my way over to the bar to get myself a drink.

"I'll have a rum runner," I said.

"And you can put that on my bill," a man's voice from behind me said.

I turned around. Standing there was a very attractive guy: mid-thirties, blonde hair, blue eyes, insanely built body, and tattoos covering his entire arm. Basically, the complete opposite of Vince.

"I'm John," he said.

"Alyssa," I replied. "Thank you for the drink."

"You owe me a dance now," he said, placing his hand on my waist.

A man hadn't asked me to dance since, well, maybe never. Vince didn't dance, and I never made it to my prom, so there was really nowhere that I ever could have danced. I had such a good time that night, dancing with him. The man was so energetic, full of life. He truly enjoyed dancing with me, even if he wasn't that good of a dancer. When Lisa said she was leaving with the guy she'd met, I told her that I'd meet her back at the room. I stayed him for the rest of the party, and not once did he ask me to split the bill!

John did, however, ask me if I wanted to go back to his room after, and I accepted the invitation. We were barely inside when he started kissing me and unzipping my dress. Once the dress fell to the floor, he looked me up and down and said, "Damn, you're hot!"

He started kissing me everywhere, removing my bra and panties and unzipping his pants. He guided me to my knees and then took out a Magnum condom. He handed the condom to me and told me to put it on him. Vince wasn't small by any means, but this guy was twice his size. I was embarrassed, but had no clue how to put a condom on a man. John ended up retrieving the condom and rolling it on himself, before sitting down on the couch and placing me on top of him, so that I was facing backward.

He yanked my hair and guided me up and down on him, all while talking extremely dirty. He kept saying things like, "You like that, you little slut?" It was so different than any sex I had ever experienced with Vince but, at the same time, a complete turn on. As John got rougher, his enormous size hurt a little more. The more he watched me squirm, the more aroused he seemed to get. I silently hoped that he wouldn't be crazy enough to try to slip into any other body part. Luckily for me, he didn't.

It lasted about twenty minutes before we both orgasmed.

"You're so fucking hot," he said, when it was over. He asked if I wanted to have lunch together the next day, so we exchanged phone numbers before I made my way back to our hotel. When I got there, Lisa stood on our balcony, holding a bottle of wine.

"Well, you're home late," she said. "Have fun?"

I went inside to grab a glass from the room and then joined her on the balcony. I poured myself a glass of wine. Staring over the railing, I was watching the waves hit the sand, reflecting the moon off the water.

"Holy shit! You got laid!" she said, after studying the smile on my face.

"I sure did, and it was fabulous! He was so into me, so different than anything I've ever experienced! We're having lunch tomorrow!" I said, clapping my hands in excitement.

She gave me a skeptical look. "I'm really happy you had a good time, but don't get yourself too worked up. You're not having lunch with him tomorrow," she said.

I turned around, changing my view from the beach to the lounge chair where she sat.

"Sam, we're in Ibiza," she said. "We went to a singles party where people go to hook up. He's not calling you, no matter how much fun he had. It's called a one-night stand."

I sank onto the other lounge chair, and gazed into my wine.

"Tomorrow, we'll meet new guys. Plus, even if he does call, you don't bring sand to the beach," she explained.

Lisa was right. John didn't call the next day, but by then, I didn't even care. We had a routine now. We went to the beach during the day, and a party at night. I was having a fantastic time. I felt so young and attractive, in a way that I hadn't felt in years. On our last night in Ibiza, we were at a club when another good-looking man approached us and asked if he could buy us drinks.

He introduced himself. "I'm Mike."

"I'm Alyssa, and this is Marie," I said.

"Where are you ladies from?" he asked.

"New York," I replied, "You?"

"I'm from the States too! Austin, Texas," he said. "You were in the red bikini on the beach near the water, right? I've been watching you for three days." He smiled.

We were hanging out with Mike for a while when

another man stole Lisa's attention away from us. Soon, Mike had me taking shots with him. We were flirting heavily. He was a little older than me; very in shape and with the prettiest colored blue eyes I'd ever seen, but there was no way I was going to sleep with him. After my night with John, I was happy enough to go back to real life. I'd gotten what I'd needed to out of my system and felt good, even though John hadn't called. I was honest with Mike and told him I was married. Turned out, he was as well, and his wife was there with him, in the room with his kids. As we danced, he kept grabbing me and pulling me into him, trying to kiss me.

"Stop, I'm married," I kept saying, playfully pushing him away.

"So am I!" he kept insisting.

"You just like the chase. It's not going to happen." I looked around for Lisa but couldn't find her through the crowd of dancing people. I finally excused myself to go to the bathroom. Once in the bathroom, I realized I was drunk, *really* drunk. I splashed water on my face and attempted to sober myself up. I called Lisa twice, with no answer.

Finally, I texted her:
Where are you? I'm in the bathroom.

I refreshed my makeup and tried to look as sober as possible as I opened the door to walk out. Mike stood waiting, right outside the bathroom. Before I knew what was happening, he pushed me inside and shut the door and started kissing me. I instantly froze, like I couldn't move. I felt like I was in one of those dreams where you're trying to run, but you're legs just won't budge.

"Mike, stop," I pleaded. "I'm married. I can't do this."

He lifted my dress and tugged the straps down over my shoulders. "I don't see him here—damn, you are gorgeous!" he kept saying.

Then, he pinned me to the sink. He opened his pants and tried to force himself inside of me. I didn't know what to do. He was too big to push off, too overpowering. I started to cry. I didn't know if it was the tears streaming down my face or if there was an angel sitting on my shoulder, but he suddenly lost his erection. He held me captive with one hand and stroked himself with the other, trying to get erect again. Suddenly, there was a knock on the door. He jumped back and zipped his pants up.

I ran to the door half-naked and threw it open. Lisa was there.

"What the fuck is going on in here? I got your text," she said holding up her phone, her eyes narrowed on Mike.

"Nothing," I said, wiping my eyes. I fixed my dress and said, "Let's go."

I was so drunk that I passed out almost as soon as we got back to the room. When we woke up the next morning, I was unbelievably hungover. Still stumbling, I threw things into my suitcase, not even sure what I was packing. I didn't even care; I just wanted to go home. I was very silent.

Lisa finally said something when we were back on the jet, to break the silence.

"Samantha, I know what you're thinking," she said. "But I am telling you, this is not your fault."

I looked up at her disbelievingly. "How could it not be my fault? I was flirting with him," I replied.

"I don't give a fuck if you were giving him a lap dance. You said no, over and over. You told him you're married.

The second you said no, it should have been no. Samantha, he said he was watching you! For three days! That's so scary. We were so drunk that we didn't even realize what that really meant. This guy didn't show up accidentally, he was following you. We need to do *something*!"

I couldn't get it out of my head. I felt guiltier about him than I even did about John.

"What if I didn't start crying?" I asked. "What if he didn't lose his hard-on, what if you didn't come in when you did? What if I'd been raped? What would we have done?"

"Samantha, this is you and me. If he raped you, we would have killed him," she said. She poured champagne and orange juice into a glass and handed it to me.

"You do realize that is exactly how *Thelma and Louise* started, right?" I asked.

"We should report him," she said.

"Report him? How? We don't even know his last name, and he technically didn't rape me," I reasoned. I took a sip of the drink and immediately put it down. "I can't drink this. It's going to make me vomit."

"I'm sure they have security footage," she said.

"Security footage? Are you nuts? You want Jimmy and Vince to see how we acted out in a club? Vince cannot find out about this. He would not be cool with any of it. Both of us, all over guys—not to mention that we both cheated! No way. We have daughters! Do we want Casey or Hailey to think it's okay to act like this?" I asked.

"Would you rather the reverse? That they think it's okay for a man not to take no for an answer, even if they were acting like that?" she argued.

"Let's just be thankful you came in when you did, and

nothing happened. This could have been a lot worse. No one can know about this Lisa—promise, no one. This goes to the grave with us!"

We made a pact right there. No one would ever know what happened in the bathroom that night in Ibiza. I reclined my seat into bed position.

"My entire body hurts, I'm too old for this shit," I complained.

Lisa followed my lead, putting her seat into bed position before looking over at me.

"You know what else?" I asked. "I'm over being thirty-three. I think I'm ready to be forty."

Just like that, I left my thirties in Ibiza.

SARAH

My mother was super excited to meet Brendon for Thanksgiving. Me, not so much. She hadn't met a guy that I'd dated since Brett, and by the time she'd grown to accept *him*, we'd already broken up. I had no idea how she was going to react to Brendon. I didn't even notice what he was wearing until we got out of the car and he took the ticket from the valet guy. He had a new car, but it wasn't flashy, or even noticeable.

"You're wearing sneakers?" I asked, surprised.

He lifted up his pant leg to give me a better view of them. "Yeah—they were like three-hundred dollars, why? What's wrong with them?"

"We're going to a nice restaurant; you really think sneakers are appropriate?" I asked.

"A nice restaurant in *Brooklyn*, sneakers are fine," he argued. "I wore a button-down. I don't think it's a problem."

As we walked into the restaurant, I couldn't help but feel embarrassed. Everyone was dressed up: men in sports coats, women in dresses, even children in cute little suits. No one was wearing sneakers. Even the maître de who escorted us to our table looked like he'd just shined his shoes. The tables were filled with plates of steaks and seafood towers. There were beautiful chandeliers hanging from the ceiling. Brendon's shoes were completely out of place. My mother had already been seated, and was also all dressed up. She didn't have many fancy clothes but the few she had, she enjoyed wearing to events like this. Today she wore a very nice purple dress with matching shoes, I could tell that she'd put time into her outfit. She was even wearing the pearls my father had given her as their wedding gift; the ones she only wore on special occasions. She stood up as soon as she saw us.

"Brendon!" she exclaimed. Her tone grew less excited when she spotted his sneakers. "It's so nice to meet you finally...I've heard so much about you."

"It's nice to meet you too, Mrs. Evans," he said, and kissed her on the cheek.

As we sat down, she looked at me and said, "My name isn't Mrs. Evans. It's Mrs. O'Malley—Sarah, didn't tell you that?"

Brendon glanced sideways at me, taken aback. "Who is Sarah?" he asked.

There was an awkward silence, so I motioned to the waitress to order drinks. After only a few minutes, we were already on strike two.

"Sarah?" my mother said, raising her eyebrows at me and waiting for a response.

I looked at Brendon, who also stared at me, equally confused. I placed my elbow on the table and rested my face in my palm.

"I'm Sarah," I said. "I mean, I was, when I was born. I legally changed my name when I turned eighteen. No one calls me Sarah."

"I do," my mother said. "I'm the one who gave birth to you, don't you think I should have had the right in naming you? And take your elbows off the table."

I dropped my arm to my lap and looked down at the table, secretly wondering if I could crawl under it. Brendon took my hand. He could tell I was getting upset.

"Sarah is a beautiful name," he said to my mother. "Maybe if we have a daughter, we can name her that."

When the waitress approached with drinks on her tray, I practically jumped out of my chair to grab mine. I took an enormous slug. Did he just say *our daughter*? I was now literally feeling under the table with my foot, measuring if there was enough room for me to fit. I wasn't sure if Brendon was trying to appease my mother, or if he seriously thought we were going to have kids together. I'd always wanted children. But in the past few years, that dream had been retired to the back of my head— considering I was in love with someone who already had his own kids, and they were both grown. Would Vincent even want to go through all of that again?

My mother smiled cynically.

"I have a daughter, and she was named Sarah," she said, shifting her gaze from me to him. "But a granddaughter would be just as nice. Are you Catholic?"

"Yes, ma'am," he answered. "I'm Irish, too, went to Catholic school as a kid and all." He instantly redeemed himself with that statement.

I couldn't help but wonder what the conversation would have been like if Vincent were with me instead of

Brendon. Even if he were single and didn't have kids already, my mother would hate that he was so much older. She would hate that he was Italian, too, but she would like that he called me Sarah. She would also like that he'd have enough class to wear real shoes and not sneakers.

During the meal, Brendon and my mother spoke a lot about his parents, his upbringing, my father. By the end of dinner, she was impressed by him. She told me how handsome he was, and how he made a nice catch. That Irish Catholic comment really saved him. I couldn't help but wish I was as impressed by Brendon as she was. He dropped her off after dinner, and we headed back to his place. Once we were in the car alone, he started yelling at me almost immediately.

"Really? When were you planning on telling me that your name wasn't really Bianca? Or were you never going to tell me that? You know what a dick I felt like?"

"Brendon, relax, no one calls me Sarah but her. It's not that big of a deal," I insisted.

"Not that big of a deal?" he continued, raising his voice even louder. "We've been dating for almost a year! I don't know your real name, you won't let me come see your show—is there anything else you're not telling me?!"

He was getting angrier by the minute. The madder he got, the faster his foot pressed the gas pedal.

"I explained to you already—I get nervous when people I know are in the crowd. And the name thing is ridiculous, okay? She named me Sarah, but my name is Bianca now. You're being outrageous, just calm the fuck down!" I said, getting just as loud as him.

"Don't tell me to calm down!" he yelled, and punched the radio. He winced afterward and shook his hand. I took pleasure in the fact that he'd hurt himself.

"Maybe I should just go home," I said. "Why don't you drop me off?"

"Oh, now you want to go home? Because you're a liar?!" he screamed.

"Can you pay attention to the fucking road before you get us both killed? I'm not a liar. I didn't tell you one thing, that doesn't make me a liar."

He pulled up in front of his house.

"I told you to take me home," I said.

He stared at me before opening his door and climbing out. After slamming the door, he said, "If you want to go home so bad, you can walk, *Bianca*."

"Fine." I started walking up the street. I was already to the corner, lifting my hand to hail a cab when I heard him yell.

"Wait!" He ran over to me while the taxi pulled up. "I'm sorry, just come in," he said. His whole tone changed dramatically.

"I just really want to go home." Tears welled in my eyes, and he put his arms around my waist.

"You getting in?" the taxi driver asked impatiently.

Brendon waived his hand to motion him to leave.

"I'm sorry," Brendon said again, once the taxi pulled away. "I'm just so in love with you. You make me crazy. I don't understand why you didn't tell me what your real name was. Just come inside, please."

I wiped the tears off my face. At that moment, I couldn't help but think about how Vincent was currently in Aruba with his wife, doing God knew what. So, I followed Brendon inside his house, where he made us drinks. I stood in the studio room, staring at the mess before me. His place was a real dump. Not only messy, but dirty, too. Dishes all over the coffee table and end tables, clothes all over the floor. He didn't even have a couch, just a twin-size bed that doubled as one. There were holes in the walls, mostly due to him getting mad over some sort of video game drama. I was always afraid to put down the expensive pocketbook that I'd gotten for my birthday. I rarely brought him to my place, mostly because I liked when my sheets smelled like Vincent's cologne. Plus, I didn't feel right bringing him there.

Brendon handed me the drink. Before I could even lift the glass to my mouth, he came over to me and started kissing me. It was so hard to get into kissing him. All I could think about was Vincent. How he would never yell at me like that, and how every time we were together, I couldn't take my hands off of him. Brendon was okay in bed, but there was no passion, no lust—sex with him made me think of how Vincent had described sex with his wife. Brendon was also very rough, which made me wonder about Vincent. Was he rough with his wife? Did he talk dirty? Did she do things with him that I wouldn't do?

Suddenly, I couldn't get the visual of Vincent on top of his wife out of my head. I knew I had no right to be jealous—he was technically her man, not mine—but I was. Insanely jealous. The vision of them having sex haunted me all night.

The next day, I climbed up to the rooftop of the club and sat in the nook. I texted Isabel to meet me there.

"You're not going to jump, are you?" she asked once she arrived, approaching me slowly.

I shook my head. "No—it just feels like forever since I've been up here to think. I used to love coming up here."

"Well, who told you to make it your personal sex roof?" she asked, pointing at the wall where we first had sex. "What's wrong?"

"Brendon told me he loved me last night." I gazed over the rooftop at the view of New York City. The buildings looked so different in the day versus the night. Sure, they were tall, but without the billboard lights illuminating them, there was nothing really special to them at all. The structures just looked like ordinary skyscrapers.

"I'm confused, is that a bad thing? I mean, he's everything you wanted: great on paper, has his own apartment, his own car, makes good money. He's really cute too, so what's the problem?"

I stared up at her without saying a word.

"Is this about Vincent?" she asked, throwing her hands up and rolling her eyes.

"He's just so different," I said.

"Yeah, most men are going to be. It's not a fair comparison. Vincent is older, grew up in a different time. You want to get married, right? Have kids? Vincent ain't the guy you're going to do that with. What are you going to do—have a kid who has a dad every Monday for two hours? I mean, even if he did leave his wife, he's so much older than you! You want a guy that old to be the father of your kids?" she asked.

"Brendon is just so...so, ugh, I don't even know the right word. I like him, I really do, it's just he flips out all the time, over stupid shit. The other day, he almost beat the shit out of someone for checking me out," I said.

"Didn't Vincent almost get into a fight with someone over wanting to buy you a drink in Atlantic City?" she pointed out.

"Yes, but that guy was a prick and started it. And I was able to calm him down. Immediately. Brendon doesn't calm the fuck down. I'm afraid I'm going to get a call one day that he's in jail."

"Look, you may never be as attracted to another man as you are to Vincent. The two of you have some crazy chemistry, I'll admit that. You were attracted to him since the second you saw him but, you have no idea how Vincent would be if he were your man, because you're not with him all the time. You think you'd still be as attracted to him if you woke up next to him every day?" she asked.

I shifted my attention back to the plain skyscrapers. Was Vincent just being illuminated in my head, same as New York City at night? No, he wasn't. He couldn't be.

"Yes," I said. "I would be. I get more attracted to him every time I see him. It's crazy, really—you'd think by now that would have slowed down. I think about him while Brendon and I are having sex. Is that normal?"

"Yes, it is. A lot of people fantasize about other people in bed. That's normal. I do it all the time," she said, trying to cheer me up.

I started pacing the roof, raking my hand through my hair. "I just don't know how much longer I can do this. I don't understand how so many people can live double lives this easily. Brendon keeps wanting to come to my show. Isabel, he can't come to that show, everyone knows Vincent as my boyfriend. How do people do this?" I cried.

She wrapped her arm around me. "Relax, everything will work out the way it's supposed to. Let's just pray that Vincent and Brendon don't show up at your apartment at the same time. My bet is on Vincent, though—I think he'd kick Brendon's ass." She laughed. "Come on. I'll make you feel better."

She picked up her phone and put on the song, "Baby, It's Cold Outside." She started singing the words and pulling me toward her to dance. I laughed and pushed her back.

"Would you rather me be the man?" She started singing the guy's part instead. Then, she grabbed my hand and twirled me around. I had to admit: in that moment, dancing with her up there like an idiot did make me feel a lot better.

When I got home that night though, my mind spun with everything that was happening to me. My entire life, all I'd wanted to do was be an actress. So much so, that my ambition was the reason Brett had broken up with me. He'd claimed I was too focused on my career and had no time for love. I figured I'd never be able to love someone else, and then Vincent came along and changed my entire way of thinking. I kept remembering Puerto Rico. How he'd asked if I'd leave everything for him, and how tempted I was. I hated his wife, and yet felt bad for her at the same time. I didn't even know this woman, whose life I could potentially ruin.

SAMANTHA

I was unenthused, to say the least, about Aruba this year. "Dreading" was a better word. I didn't want to pack, didn't want to get on that plane, didn't want to share a room or bed with Vince. I didn't want to smile and pretend to the staff who knew us so well that I was into any of this. The resort we stayed at was a gorgeous, beachfront paradise and, now that the kids were older, they didn't even hang out with us except during dinners. We were forced to entertain ourselves together—something that should have been fun but had turned into a huge chore. Vince and I had nothing in common anymore.

At least when the kids were young, we could take them to do activities. Now we barely spoke, and we didn't have sex. We didn't even share the same interests. I would lay on the beach for hours, reading a book while he stared off at the water sports that I refused to try, like jet skiing or parasailing. He did convince the kids to go zip lining with him on our first day there, which left me some time to shop by myself.

The next day, I grabbed Casey to go shopping and get some lunch. We found this nice little restaurant on the beach outside the resort. I was feeling nostalgic, watching the children playing in the sand and building little castles. I missed our kids being that young—back when they still needed us and wanted to do things with me. While we ate, I observed the young couples kissing and holding hands. I couldn't take my eyes off of this one couple in particular. They frolicked in the water with their arms around each other, gazing at each other like they were madly in love. Vince and I had never had that, I realized. I couldn't even fathom what it felt like, to be that into someone.

Searching for a distraction, I asked Casey if she was seeing anyone. She didn't answer, but by the way she smiled, I could tell that she liked somebody.

"I want to tell you something," I said, and she looked up at me. "If you're ever out with friends, or a guy, no matter what you're doing, even if you're being inappropriate—if you tell a guy no, it's no. I don't want you ever to feel like you have to do something you are not comfortable doing, no matter what you've already done with him."

Casey stared at me like she had no idea what to say. "I'm not *comfortable* having this conversation with you, can we stop now? We're on vacation!"

I shook my head. "Casey, I know this may be difficult to talk about, but you need to know—"

She cut me off. "What is going on with the two of you?" she asked. "Did something happen with you and Dad that you guys aren't telling me?"

I gaped at her. "What do you mean?"

"Dad just had the same conversation with me when I

was home for the summer. Date rape, drugs, harassment—
what exactly do you guys think I do in college?" she asked.

I was impressed that Vince had bothered to have the
same conversation with her. I knew for whatever reason,
our daughter was more comfortable talking to him, so I let
it go.

By the third day at the resort, I felt like it was the third
week. I suggested that next year, we should try to convince
Lisa and Jimmy to travel with us, and Vince agreed. Of
course, first he made some stupid comment about Jimmy
"at least being fun."

"What did you guys do last night?" Vince asked the
kids that night at dinner. They looked at each other and
smiled.

"What's the joke?" I asked.

"Nick left me hanging to go get laid," Casey said. Vince
and I looked at each other and then at Nick.

"You got laid?" Vince asked, putting his steak knife
down and leaning over the table towards him. "What did
she look like?"

It got to the point that whenever this man opened his
mouth, I truly envisioned myself killing him. Nick started
to go into detail about the girl when I interrupted.

"We're your PARENTS. We don't need to hear about
your sex life. You shouldn't even be having sex," I said. All
three of them shut up. Vince started laughing to himself.

"What exactly is so funny?" I asked him.

"He shouldn't be having sex?" he repeated, picking his
knife back up and going right back to his food. "When you
were twenty-three, they were both already born."

Silence. Tension. Casey tried to lighten the mood.
"How about we take a family Thanksgiving shot?" she

suggested. I looked at her, appalled.

"You're not even twenty-one yet, maybe in a few months."

Vince rolled his eyes and lifted his hand in the air to summon the waitress.

"Shots! Please," he ordered. "ASAP." He looked over at the kids and said, "What kind of shots are we taking?"

They both answered simultaneously. "Green tea shots!"

"Green tea shots," he repeated to the waitress. "Four of them."

After three "family Thanksgiving green tea shots," the kids departed to do their own thing, leaving me at the table with Vince. I was really buzzed. I held the shot glass up and turned it in a slow circle. "What do you suppose is in a green tea shot, anyway?"

"Let's find out," Vince said. He picked up his phone and Googled it. "Hmmm, well, apparently it's peach schnapps, sour mix...oh, and Jameson," he said, letting out a laugh. "That explains why you can suddenly stand being at a table with me."

I wanted to argue with him, but I couldn't. I was just drunk enough to be around him. I lifted my hand in the air and called for the waitress.

"Can we have two more shots, please?"

Vince smiled. "Now you're getting fun!"

When the round arrived, I held up my glass towards his. "To Jameson," I toasted.

He clinked his glass on mine. "Yes, to Jameson!" he repeated.

We had two more shots there, and then he suggested we go to another bar. We left, making our way to a much livelier scene.

"Is it me, or are crowds getting younger and younger?" I asked, pushing our way through the mob of people, toward the bar.

"No, we're getting older and older. You shouldn't mix too much, I don't want you to get sick. You want Jameson? I'm going to get mine neat, no need for the other shit."

"Sure," I agreed.

We'd been drinking there for about an hour when a band started playing in the back. Vince took my hand to lead me through the crowd to get a closer look. Suddenly a man—or boy, really, since he couldn't have been too much older than Nick—groped my ass as I was passing him.

I dropped Vince's hand, whirled to him and said, "What the fuck?" He was drunk, sloppy drunk. Came right up to me and put his arms around my waist, slurring about how hot I was. He was practically drooling on me.

When Vince realized what was happening, he hurried over and pulled him off.

"Hey, that's my wife, asshole, get back in your lane," he warned.

"Or what?" the guy asked, taunting him. "If that's your wife, you shouldn't let her walk around looking like a hoe."

All of a sudden, Vince shoved him and then punched him in the face. The guy hit him back, and a fistfight broke out. He had got one good shot on Vince, but I really thought Vince was going to kill him. I tried to pull him off the guy, but he was drunk and yelling at me to stop holding him back. Security came and broke it up. They grabbed Vince by the shirt and told us we'd better leave before they called the cops.

We exited to the beach, where I watched him growing angrier by the minute as he paced back and forth on the sand. I hadn't seen him this infuriated in years. The worst thing that guy could have done was call me a hoe. It was like a trigger point for Vince; some sort of longstanding guilt for taking my virginity, like he was somehow responsible for stealing my innocence. The only other time I ever saw him get physical with someone was the night we told my parents I was pregnant. My father called me a slut and hit me so hard that I fell to the floor. In that second Vince lost his shit and punched my dad in the face. Until then, he'd had no idea that my father was abusive. When we made it back to his apartment that night, he made me so many promises. He promised I would never have to see my dad again; he would never let another man hurt me. He would never walk out or abandon his child, like both our fathers' had done to us. From then on, it would be him and me against everyone else.

Now on the beach, Vince was still pacing and cracking his knuckles, ready to go back for round two. I tried to calm him down, but nothing was working.

"This fucking guy!" he kept repeating, over and over.

Suddenly, I started laughing. Cracking up uncontrollably.

He shot me the dirtiest look.

"What the fuck is so funny?" he asked, his pacing coming to an abrupt halt. "You okay with the fact he called you a hoe? You don't find that to be disrespectful? Come on. He deserved to get punched in the face!"

"Vince, we just got kicked out of a club. Kicked out of a club! When was the last time we got kicked out of a club?"

215

He paused and looked up to the sky like he was trying to remember. I guess he realized how ridiculous that sounded because he too started laughing.

"If I had to guess I'd say twenty-four, twenty-five years," he answered.

"What would you have done if you got arrested in a different country?" I asked.

"What, they don't have bail here?" he replied, still laughing. "You know, I used to be pretty badass."

"Oh, I know," I said, "A real rebel."

"I was!" he insisted.

"I know, I remember. I'm agreeing with you. You. Were. A. Rebel," I said slowly, smiling at him. I could picture him in his twenties in that baseball uniform, coming home all dirty and sweaty after a game. He would sneak me into clubs, let me drive his car, taught me how to drive a stick and how to shift gears. He would spontaneously race other sports cars on the street and afterward, we'd have sex in the back seat of that Camaro. He would smoke in places where he wasn't allowed, and didn't have a care in the world about rules.

As he stood there smiling, the thoughts of his glory days running through his head; I realized suddenly he had this dimple when he smiled. That, somewhere along the way, I'd stopped noticing. I wasn't sure if it was the alcohol, the fight, or seeing how single men acted now after Ibiza, but for the first time in years, I was extremely attracted to him. I leaned into him, stood on my tippy toes, and kissed him.

He was taken back at first, but kissed me back. "What was that for?" he asked, as I pulled my lips off of him.

"Do I need a reason to kiss my husband?" I asked.

He ran his fingers through his hair and stared down at the sand. Then, looking back at me, he answered. "No, I guess you don't."

I kissed him again, this time slower and more sensual. We stayed there kissing for a while, with his arms wrapped gently around my waist and me using the back of his neck to pull him closer. I reached over as we were walking back to the room and took his hand in mine.

"I'm going to take a shower," I said, as we went inside.

He lounged on the bed, reading emails on his phone. "Okay," he said, now very distracted in his work.

When I got out of the shower, he had dozed off. I sat on the bed, took the phone off his chest, and nudged him slightly.

"Vince, wake up," I said.

He opened his eyes. "What's wrong?"

"Nothing." Then, I slid my robe off and, in my bra and panties, climbed on top of him. Rubbing myself up against him, I started kissing him again. His hands held my hips, and he guided me back and forth on him. He was visibly aroused. He lifted me off, rolled me onto my back, and removed my panties. His fingers plunged inside me while his tongue stroked its way from my neck, down my chest, down my stomach, and in between my legs. He wasn't especially passionate, but he was skilled. If there was one thing he excelled at, it was getting me off with his tongue, and he knew exactly how I liked it—with his right hand holding my breast.

As I pushed his head against me, he squeezed my breast a little harder. It had been so long since I'd had a man do that. I was so turned on; I couldn't control myself. Before long, he'd brought me to orgasm. Then, he climbed on top of me and thrust inside. I felt every thrust like I'd never felt one before. Everything about this was so different than what had happened with John. Vince was the perfect size for me; he knew exactly what to do to turn me on. It was so comfortable, so familiar. So much better than some stranger I barely knew.

I was really getting into it when suddenly he was about to orgasm. He yanked away and, well, made a mess all over me and himself.

"Shit." He jumped up to get a towel from the bathroom, and then rushed over to clean the mess off of both of us.

We stayed in bed, staring at the ceiling while my mind whirled. Almost twenty-four years of marriage and never, not once, had he pulled out. I was in complete shock.

Finally, he broke the silence. "Was that weird?" he asked.

"Um, yeah, a little," I replied. "Something new you learned? If you pulled out twenty-four years ago, we wouldn't even be here now."

Another awkward silence followed.

"I mean, you're forty, I'm forty-six... you don't want to get pregnant again, do you?" he asked, turning his head to look at me.

I glanced at him and realized at that point; it didn't matter what I wanted. I wasn't even thinking about stuff like that, but he was, and he was making sure he didn't tie himself to me or us for any longer than he had to. My excitement turned into fear. If he was thinking along those lines, that meant he was thinking of leaving me. I'd never even imagined a life without him. We'd grown up together. I truly believed death was going to do us part, not another woman.

I didn't answer him. Suddenly, all I could picture was him and his girlfriend. Was he "intimate" with her? I had accepted years ago the fact that he might cheat, but until now, I'd never really pictured it. The thought of his tongue on someone else made me feel disgusted that I'd even kissed him. I rolled over and went to sleep without saying another word.

A few days after we returned home, I was walking through the living room to get a glass of water from the kitchen when the picture hanging on the wall caught my eye. I stopped and went over to look. There was me and Vince smiling, ten years ago, back when we thought everything was okay. We were young and didn't know any better—had no idea that everything was not okay. Everything was never okay. This wasn't what a marriage was supposed to be. We'd been so caught up in fighting the world together that we never stopped to fall in love. We were cheated out of romance. We went straight from kids to adults, without experiencing everything we should have or could have.

I changed my mind and opened a bottle of wine instead. I poured a glass and sipped, still staring at that picture. Then, my engagement ring grabbed my attention. I stared at the huge diamond on my finger and suddenly felt tears trickle down my face. I didn't even know why I was crying. It wasn't like I was *unhappy*; I just wasn't necessarily happy, either. What should I do? I couldn't be single again, not in this new world. I wouldn't be able to online date, and I didn't think I would ever be able to walk into a club again. I felt like I was losing my mind.

VINCE

Three weeks had passed since we returned home from Aruba. By the way I was running that night, you'd think I was being chased down the streets of New York City. I ran so hard, and so fast, I could barely breathe. I felt like I was having a breakdown. I stopped on the pier and looked up at the sky. Now I really couldn't breathe. I really thought I was having a heart attack.

I'd avoided seeing Sarah for three weeks. I missed her so much—I needed to see her. While showering that next morning after sleeping with Samantha, it had hit me. An enormous amount of guilt. I felt dirty, like I'd cheated on her. This wasn't normal; this was bad. I felt like I was cheating on my girlfriend with my wife. I had to do something. I couldn't keep denying Samantha sex, but also, I couldn't feel like this whenever I slept with her. Samantha and I hadn't really spoken since we'd come home. She barely even looked at me. That whole pulling out thing had really gotten to her. Meanwhile, I was afraid to look Sarah in the face.

I held my chest and stared up at the moon, like I expected it to give me some sort of cosmic answer. I started frantically shuffling through my playlist, searching for that song. The song she sang in the show right when her character was breaking up with her lover. Such a great song, about everyone wanting what they couldn't have. Was that it? Did I want her so badly because I couldn't have her? I listened to her words, her voice. Singing to me. Right then, I knew what I needed to do. I needed to leave her. I needed to end my marriage.

I picked Sarah up at 5:30 p.m. Wednesday night. I couldn't wait to see her; it felt like an eternity since the last time. When she got in the car, she wasn't her usual bubbly self. She seemed kind of sad. I kissed her and started driving.

"You okay?" I asked.

"Yeah, where are we going?"

"Steak house, it's really nice. They make great seafood too. They have that octopus you like," I replied.

"Was it hard to get into?" she asked.

"No, not too hard."

"Are you able to cancel the reservation?"

I twisted to look at her. "You don't want to go?" The guy behind me started honking at me to go. The light had turned green. I pulled over and asked again. "You don't want to go?"

She was barely looking at me. Now I was really nervous. I studied the Porsche emblem on my steering wheel, running my thumb up and down the raised edges.

"I'm just not in the mood to go out," she said simply.

"Okay, yeah, I can cancel it," I began. "Do you want me

to leave?" My heart was beating so fast, I was afraid she could hear it from the passenger seat. Was she going to tell me to go? My palms were sweating. I didn't know what to do.

"No, I just don't want to go out. Maybe you can come in? Have a drink?" she suggested.

I suddenly felt a wave of relief. "Yeah, okay. I'll drop you back off then find a spot."

The door to the apartment was open. I walked in, and she was standing in the kitchen, pouring me a scotch. She was still really quiet. "That was fast, you found a spot?" she asked.

"Yes, I pulled into a lot—everything okay?" I asked again, afraid of the answer she was going to give.

She came over and handed me the drink. I took a sip; she was still silent.

"You just want me to taste like scotch," I said, joking around, hoping to lighten the mood.

She finally smiled. "You're right," she said, and then kissed me. That kiss was just as passionate as our first. I melted into her lips. How did I survive without seeing her for so long?

"Where have you been?" she finally asked.

"I've just been busy, end of the year bullshit." For the first time ever, I lied to her.

She pulled away and looked up at me, almost as if she was afraid to ask the next question. "Are you falling out of love with me?" she hesitantly asked.

My heart literally broke right there. I put my drink down and shook my head. "No, no, no," I said, pulling her into me and kissing her. I lifted her chin with my hand. "It's just the opposite, really. I am so in love with you. It gets stronger each day. I want to tell you..."

I stopped myself. I promised her I wouldn't ever bring it up again. I couldn't tell her, not yet. She couldn't have any involvement. I had to end things with Samantha without Sarah knowing, and then I could tell her. Afterward, so she had no guilt.

"Tell me what?" she asked.

I kept my arms wrapped around her waist. "That. Just how much I love you."

"I just thought we could, you know, be together tonight, here. I missed you," she said.

I lifted her up and carried her into the bedroom. I made love to her that night. Slow, sensual, holding her hand the entire time. Brushing her hair out of her face so I could stare at her, telling her profusely how much I loved her. Telling her she was the most important thing in my life. Telling her how beautiful she was.

I fell asleep in her arms and woke up at 3 a.m. in a panic. "What time is it? Shit, I have to go," I said.

She sat up abruptly, watching me frantically get dressed.

"I'm sorry baby, I have to go," I explained. "I'm on vacation next week, so I won't be here Monday, but I'll see you on Christmas Eve. I'll call you tomorrow. I love you." I kissed her and ran out.

I opened the door to my house very quietly, hoping Rocky wouldn't start barking. He was sleeping on a pillow in the corner of the room. He made eye contact with me, but didn't make a sound. Even the dog didn't care that I was sneaking in. I crept up the stairs, trying not to wake anyone. The kids were already back for the holidays, and I wasn't even sure who was home. As I made my way to the guest room, I couldn't help but stop at the master bedroom. I cracked open the door and peeked in. Samantha was sleeping peacefully, holding onto a pillow. I couldn't stop staring at that pillow. It should have been a man she was holding. A man she loved, who loved her back. She looked so tiny in that king-sized bed.

As I watched her sleep, I wondered if she had any idea what was coming. I'd always been a man of my word. I may have lied, but I never went back on a promise. It killed me that I was going to leave her. I'd sworn to her that I would never hurt her, never leave her. I stood there for a long time before I quietly shut the door. When I turned to head back to the guest room, Nick was standing in the hallway behind me. He must have just gotten home.

"Hey, Buddy," I whispered. "Just getting in?"

He looked me up and down. "Yes, you?" he asked, sounding surprised to see me still fully dressed.

"No," I lied. I looked at my watch. "I was actually just leaving. I could use a drink, still have half an hour for last call, right? I was seeing if your Mom was awake, but she's out cold."

He smiled. "I know a club with a great after-hours party, come on, I'll buy you a drink," he said.

"Oh, you'll buy me a drink with my own money? How nice of you." I laughed as we started back down the stairs and headed out.

The club was packed for four in the morning. Everyone was covered in sweat from dancing all night and loud music blared. Half the people drinking probably should have been cut off hours ago; I couldn't believe they were still serving them. Everyone knew Nick, from the bouncer to the abundance of girls who approached him. One girl kissed him on the cheek and touched my arm. She looked like she was probably attractive, had her makeup not been smeared all over her face.

"Who's your sexy friend?" she asked.

"That's my father," Nick answered, and she looked surprised. "Dad, this is Laura."

"Wow, the apple doesn't fall far from the tree, huh? Well, hello Mr. DeLuca." The girl used a very seductive tone and began rubbing my forearm.

"Please don't make me any older than I am. Vince will suffice," I said.

She told Nick she'd catch up to us, winked at me, and then we walked over to the bar.

"Look at that, you can still pick up," Nick said, like he was proud. He made eye contact with the bartender, who also seemed to know him well. "Two glasses of Johnnie Walker Black, neat please," he ordered.

"Eh, if we're using my money, go straight to Blue," I said.

"Well, now we're definitely using your money, if we're getting Blue," he said, laughing.

We took our drinks and toasted. "It certainly goes down smooth. Whether or not it's worth eighty-five dollars a drink, that is debatable," I said.

Nick was twisted in his seat and watching a group of girls, seemingly unamused by my comment.

"Look at them," he began. "One gets better looking than the next."

I turned around and looked at the girls he was referring to. He was right; they were all really hot.

"You know that girl Ashley I'm seeing? She wants to get serious," he said.

"Like marriage?" I asked.

"Eventually. I mean, she knows I'm going to finish getting my master's before actually getting married, but I think she wants a ring."

"Do you love her?" I asked.

"Yeah, I do. But I'm young, so many other girls out there. What if she's not the right one? I don't want to end up twenty years from now sleeping in the guest room, no offense," he said.

That comment went right through me. I felt like I'd just been kicked in the balls.

"What made you marry Mom?"

I guzzled the rest of my drink and ordered another.

"I mean, I know she got pregnant and all, but what actually made you marry her? You didn't have to," he said, once the bartender slid a fresh scotch to me.

I gazed into the glass. No one had ever asked me that question before. I took a deep breath and another sip of my drink. "You know, I've never told anyone this story before," I began. "Your mother doesn't even know."

He looked up at me, listening intensely.

"I found out she was pregnant and sixteen all in the same breath. Naturally, I freaked out, panicked—didn't know what to do. It was statutory rape. All I could think about was that I was going to get arrested. My whole life was about to fall apart. I went to my baseball coach, told him I was in trouble. Asked him for help. All of a sudden, I'm sitting in this fancy attorney's office in Los Angeles. They were walking me through what to say, what to do. Told me to cut off all contact with her. Don't see her, don't pick up her calls, wait until I got arrested." I took another sip of my drink. I could picture being in that conference room, feeling so far from the attorneys across that huge table. My coach sitting next to me, offering me moral support. Nick had a look of horror on his face.

"They told me to start recording everything she said on my answering machine, hoping she'd admit on the machine that she lied about her age," I said. "They wanted to paint the picture that she was a slut, trying to hold on to an aspiring baseball player for the money. Except she wasn't a slut, at all—she was far from it. It took over a month for her to sleep with me. She was just a stupid kid who liked me, so much that she lied about her age. When I tried to argue, they wouldn't hear it, kept asking me if I wanted to spend the next ten years in jail. They went into explicit detail of what they do to 'rapists' in prison."

Nick ordered another drink. "Wow, that's fucked up," he said, sitting very stiff in his chair.

"I ignored her calls for a week," I continued. "Finally, after about the fifteenth call, she started leaving me a message. She was crying, so hysterically, I could barely make out what she was saying. Begging for me to pick up the phone, she had no one to talk to. Then she began saying it. I can still hear her voice in my head. 'Vinny, I'm so sorry I,' she said. I picked up the phone and stopped recording. I just couldn't do it. I went to get her and brought her back to my place. She said a friend of hers knew someone who could fix her problem, but it cost nine hundred dollars that she didn't have. She asked me if I had the money."

"By 'fix' I assume she meant an abortion?" Nick asked.

"That's word for word what I asked, except she couldn't get the word abortion out, just made her cry more. She couldn't even bring herself to say it. I couldn't be responsible for making her do something that she would regret for the rest of her life. I just couldn't do it. Nor could I walk out on the child I had just made. I told her it wasn't her problem, it was *our* problem, and I had another idea of how to 'fix' it. We would pretend like we were in love, and I was going to ask her father for permission to marry her. Well, you know the rest of that story and how it ended; so, here we are. Me and you, at a nightclub, drinking Johnnie Walker Blue—which never would have happened had I not married her."

We both sat there, silent for a few minutes. "If you love this girl Nick, hold on to it," I finally said. "There's always going to be a better-looking girl or a younger girl. Another girl who will do something she won't—don't put yourself in a situation where you're always asking, *what if*?"

"If Mom didn't get pregnant, do you think you'd be married to her now?" he asked.

"I can't answer that question; I have no idea. It's like asking me if I'd be a retired baseball player now if I didn't get into that accident. Everything happens for a reason. We were put together for some reason, what that reason is, I still have no clue."

I couldn't explain why, but it felt good to finally tell someone that story. Like I'd been carrying extra weight around with me for twenty four years. "Nick, I have something else to tell you that I haven't told anybody."

He leaned in closer, as if he were afraid of what might come out of my mouth next. "What is it?"

I studied my scotch. It was hard to formulate the words, but once I did, they came straight out. "I'm going to be asking your mother for a divorce." I was so afraid to look up at him, to see what his reaction would be. When I finally did, though, he didn't seem upset, or even surprised. "Do you think I'm a dick?" I asked.

"Yeah, young aspiring baseball player marries a sixteen-year-old girl he knocks up to save her reputation, gives her and their kids an amazing life—you're definitely a dick," he said. "Do you think I'm a dick for saying that about my mother? I love her, and I love you, I just want both of you to be happy. Do you want to live the rest of your life saying, *what if*?" he threw back at me.

I stared at him, so proud of the man he'd become. Of the way he was able to see past the fact that we were his parents and look at me like no one else seemed to, like I was just a regular guy.

"I still have no idea how you got so smart. You know, if you weren't so damn good looking, I'd question whether or not you're really my son," I said, laughing.

We bonded that night in a way unlike any other night. We stayed at the bar talking for another hour, didn't even get home until six in the morning. For the first time since he'd been born, I felt like I was talking to my friend, not my son.

SARAH

I couldn't get the image of Vincent running out of my apartment out of my head—running back home to her. Even if I told him to leave her and he did, he would eventually cheat on me too, right? I didn't care how rich he was; I couldn't give him a license to cheat. I couldn't be one of those wives who was okay with her husband sleeping around. I loved him too much. I was too jealous. I wasn't okay with any of that. With the situation we were in now, even if he slept with someone else, *I* wouldn't be the one he was cheating on; he'd still be cheating on *her*. But he'd been acting so weird those past few weeks, so distant, that I knew something was wrong. Something was *really* wrong. I had so many questions running through my head. Had he met someone else? Had my show become a reality, with our affair somehow ultimately making his marriage stronger?

I knew there was no future for Vincent and me. So, when Brendon asked me to marry him that Friday night, I had no good reason to say no. Isabel was right. Brendon had everything I wanted. Sex was never on my list of requirements, so why should it be now? I was going to turn thirty. My friends had all started getting married. I was in love with someone who wasn't available. Someone who couldn't give me what Brendon could, no matter how much he wanted to.

We walked up to the rooftop together that Christmas Eve. Our fifth Christmas Eve together. Our three-year anniversary. It was a routine now—also, the warmest Christmas Eve in New York City history, warmer than the year before. Temperatures had reached into the seventies, and it was strange not to be wearing jackets at the end of December.

We drank the first glass of wine, and then he put our song on, and we started dancing. He passed a joke that the song wasn't appropriate this year, and we should be singing "Baby, It's Warm Outside." I half-smiled. I held on to him so tight. I knew it would be the last time we did this.

As I held him, I kept thinking of what to say—how I was going to tell him. I was taking in his whole aura. The smell of him, and the way my fingers felt, running through his hair. The way my hand slid down his neck to his chest, and how I felt so secure and safe in his arms. These were all the things I knew I was never going to experience with him again.

The song stopped, and we just kind of stood there; his arms around my waist, mine around his shoulders. He lifted my chin and kissed me. I didn't want him to stop. I felt the same about that kiss as I had about our first, back when he'd asked me permission. He walked over to the nook to pour us another glass of wine. I didn't move, just stood in the same spot. I was so nervous. My heart was beating so fast.

"Vincent, I need to tell you something," I said.

He brought the wine over, smiling at me—gazing really, how he always did. I could tell he had no idea what was coming. He handed me the wine.

"Tell me," he said.

I couldn't stop looking at his dimple. That perfect smile that I was never going to see again. I opened my mouth, but the words wouldn't come out. I tried again. Still nothing. His face went from awe to concern.

"What's wrong? Is everything okay?" he asked.

"Vincent, I'm... I am..." I couldn't say it. I couldn't get the words out.

Now he looked distraught. He put his wine down on the ground, and came closer to me.

"You're what?" he asked.

I closed my eyes. I couldn't even look at him when I said it.

"I'm getting married," I blurted out. There was silence. I opened my eyes as he stood there for a few seconds, speechless, his mouth dropped open.

Finally, he started shooting out questions, a mile a minute. "You're what? To who? How long have you been dating him for? What does he do? Do you love him?"

I'd never seen him like this. He was upset, mad, nervous. Heartbroken. "A year. I've been seeing him for a year."

"A year? So, when we were in Puerto Rico, you were seeing him?" His voice grew louder as he backed away from me.

"Yes, you told me not to tell you until absolutely

necessary. At this point, it's pretty necessary. He's a gamer," I said, answering his second question.

"A gamer? What the fuck is a gamer?" he asked.

"I don't know, he does something with video games."

He picked the wine up from the floor and downed the whole glass. Then he started laughing. "This is a joke, right? You're fucking with me—you're getting married to a guy who plays video games for a living?"

He had to stop talking because he was laughing so hard that he almost sounded insane. He returned to the bottle to refill his glass again.

"Tell me, Sarah—this is a fucking joke, right?"

I didn't have to answer the question. My expression told him I wasn't kidding. He stood there staring at me, still in shock.

"Do you love him?" he asked again.

"He's a good guy; I'll learn to."

"No...no, no, have you learned anything from my marriage at all? That doesn't work!" he yelled. After finishing the second glass of wine just as quickly as the first, he got this crazy look in his face. "No. Nope. I am not allowing it! You're not marrying him!"

Now I started raising my voice. "You're not *allowing* it?! You're not my father, don't speak to me like I'm your daughter."

"Don't tell me how I speak to my daughter! You have no idea how I am with my daughter!"

Now he was screaming, too. He slammed the glass down on the nook so hard, I was surprised it didn't crack.

I looked at him, lowered my voice and said, "You're absolutely right—I have no idea how you are with your daughter, or with anybody for the matter, because I don't exist in your world!"

"Whose fault is that?" he yelled. "I wanted to leave her—you said no. You said over and over NO. Guess what? I'm leaving her. I wasn't going to tell you because I didn't want you to have any guilt, but we are over, Sarah! Samantha and I do not have a marriage, not a normal one. You know, when Nick was ten years old, we were at an open school night, and the teacher was concerned by a picture he drew. He drew a house that was supposed to be his when he was all grown up. He drew exactly what his bedroom looked like and then what his wife's bedroom looked like. We laughed it off, didn't think anything of it. I'm just a bad sleeper, right? But then you slept with me and apparently, I'm not! Maybe it's more about the woman who's been sleeping next to me all these years."

"Why do you even want to be with me? So, you can cheat on me too? You're forty-six years old. You lived your life; you have your kids. I'm going to be thirty, don't you think I deserve the same?" I demanded.

He went still. "You don't trust me? I have never lied to you, ever. Well, except for the past few Mondays. Look, there was an incident in Aruba, I...." He looked down at the floor and rubbed his forehead. "I slept with her. I slept with Samantha, and I can't get it out of my fucking head, it's driving me fucking crazy!"

He started choking up, and a single tear trailed down his cheek. He quickly wiped it away and tried to compose himself.

"I was afraid I couldn't look at you. I felt like I cheated on you. Think of that statement—I felt like I cheated on you with my *wife!* What about me? I don't deserve to be with a woman who loves me? Or even her, she doesn't deserve the same?"

As he started walking towards me, I turned my back to him. I couldn't look at him.

"Sarah please," he pleaded, clutching my waist from behind. "It's Christmas Eve, tomorrow is Christmas—give me until the 26th. I am leaving her. Yes, you deserve all of that, and I will give it to you. All of it, and more, I promise. Please, you can't marry this guy."

I didn't answer.

"There are so many things I still don't know about you," he started arguing. "Things that are going to drive me crazy. Look at how I went crazy for an entire year, just wondering if you could sing—what if I have another question? What if I need to know something?"

"What could you possibly need to know about me that you don't already? Go ahead, ask me now."

He paced the rooftop as he searched for questions. He was in panic mode. It was really hard to see him like that. Then, he started firing off ridiculous questions.

"What's your middle name?" he asked.

"Danielle."

"How old were you when you lost your virginity?"

"Really? That's what you *need* to know?" I asked. He shot me a look, so I sighed and answered. "Nineteen."

"And your first kiss?"

I rolled my eyes. This was absolutely insane at this point.

"Six," I said, completely unamused.

"I mean your first real kiss," he specified.

I took a deep breath. "That was my first real kiss. He wasn't six; he was much older."

He looked at me, disgusted. "If he was anywhere over

the age of ten, I don't even want to hear this story," he said.

"It's actually a beautiful story," I replied. There was silence.

"Okay, now that's going to drive me crazy. Go ahead, tell me the 'beautiful' story about the older guy who kissed the six-year-old," he said.

I paused for a moment. I'd never told anyone this story. Vincent was now bringing me back to a place that I wasn't sure I wanted to revisit.

"I was six," I began.

"I heard that part," he said.

"I had, have a sister. Much older than me, by ten years. She had a boyfriend who was even older than her. I don't know how old he was, but I know old enough that it was a big problem in the house."

He sat down on the nook, now drinking the rest of the wine directly from the bottle. He was so disinterested in this story.

"I thought he was gorgeous; I was so enamored by him. He drove this little red sports car. I don't know what kind of car it was, but it was small, and it was fast. And loud. I heard him pulling up, and I heard him driving away."

"Yeah, you and your guys with hot cars," he said, taking another slug.

"Anyway..." I continued, "I devised a plan. It was Christmas, and I had just learned what mistletoe was. I made a bouquet of mistletoe with cardboard and hung it in my room. I lured him in by asking him to help me with something, fix a toy—I don't know, I don't remember my exact excuse. I do remember having him under this cardboard mistletoe and looking up and saying in the sexiest six-year-old voice possible, 'Do you know what it means to be standing under mistletoe?'"

I remembered back to that moment.

"He had looked up, realized we were standing under the mistletoe, and then squatted down to get to eye level with me. He explained to me that customarily it meant you kissed the person you were standing under there with. I puckered up, waiting for his kiss. He kissed me right on the cheek. I begged him to run away with me, told him I was in love with him. I told him I wanted to be his wife. He smiled and told me that unfortunately, he was already spoken for, but that one day I was going to have a man fall so madly in love with me that he didn't know what to do with himself."

I was smiling at the reenactment while Vincent now stared at me, the bottle of wine dangling from his hands between his legs.

"Then my sister came in. Asked me if I was trying to steal her man. I didn't know what to say, we both knew I was. She told him they had to go. He winked at me to indicate he wouldn't tell her and get me in trouble. Like it was our secret. As they were walking out, she turned around to me and in this firm voice, said, 'And when I get back, we are going to have a long talk about a sister's bond and their men.' I watched them drive away. I *heard* them drive away. They never came back. I never saw either one of them again."

Vincent jumped unsteadily to his feet. "And that's why you hate Christmas."

I nodded. "They ran away together. My parents never spoke about them again. I think they were hoping I was too young to remember, so I never had any ideas of running away. I'd like to think they're still driving around in that little red car, traveling the world. So madly in love, that they can't take their hands off each other. Stopping at rest stops along the way to make love."

He set the bottle down and slowly approached me.

"That's a nice fairy tale you created for yourself in your head, but this is real life. That is not what they're doing."

I looked at him, angry. He was telling me my story was stupid.

"Oh, no? That's not real life? That's so unrealistic? Tell me, Vincent, you know so much, you're so good at rewriting endings. Tell me, what are they doing?"

He looked up to the sky.

"Oh, I don't know. If I had to guess, I'd say she was at some fancy club right now drinking some two-hundred-dollar bottle of wine and bragging with her bougie friends about their make-believe wonderful lives and him...well, he's..." He paused for a moment. "He's on a rooftop, on top of a strip club—staring at the woman he loves so much, he doesn't know what to do with himself. Realizing that when he'd told her about the man who'd fall in love with her twenty-four years ago, he'd had no idea that it would turn out to be him."

I stood there, stunned. In complete shock. What was he saying? That boy, way back then, was him? No, no, it couldn't be. His name had been Vinny.

"And for future reference when you tell that story, that red car was a Camaro. We didn't run away, Sarah. We told your father that night that she was pregnant. He kicked us out; he kicked her out. Threatened to have me arrested, amongst other things. We struggled for years to make ends meet after moving to New York. He told us we would fail. We spent all this time just trying to prove him wrong," he said.

I stepped back with my hand over my mouth. I had no words. His name was Vinny—who later became Vince, and then Vincent.

Not only had I been sleeping with a married man, but I was in love with a married man. And that married man was my sister's husband. All of a sudden, I remembered everything he'd said in the past three years; things that I'd never put together before. They'd moved here from California. She was naturally blonde with green eyes, Irish. They'd been together since they were kids, and he was always a guy with a hot car. His smile that seemed so familiar. How comfortable I was around him from the very beginning. The fact that he was the first man who I'd ever introduced myself to as Sarah.

He wrapped his arms around me.

"Sarah, come on, you don't think this is a sign? A sign we're meant to be together? You begged me at six to run away with you, and here I am, over two decades later, begging you to be with me." He put his hand over my mouth to prevent me from speaking. "You know what, don't say anything. I am going to take my hand off your mouth, and I am going to kiss you. When I'm done, if you can look me in the eyes and tell me you don't love me then..." He choked up again. "Then, I'll leave you alone. I'll walk away, and I promise I will never bother you again."

He removed his hand and started kissing me. Slow, passionately, like this might be the last time he ever kissed me. His hands cupped my cheeks, pulling my lips to his. All I tasted was the wine on his breath mixed with salty tears now streaming down my face.

He pulled back. "Tell me. Tell me you don't love me."

I looked him in the eyes. "I can't," I admitted.

He took a step back, slowly raising his voice again. "I'm leaving her on the 26th. It's over. And I'm going to tell you two things. One—my marriage is over, whether you're going to be with me or not. It's done. And two—the second I'm through with it, I'm showing up at your door. That guy, that gamer, well, he better not fucking be there."

That said, Vincent stormed off the roof.

When I walked back to my apartment, I was crying so hard, I could barely see. What was I going to do? I loved him so much. Would he eventually get tired of me if we were a couple? Or was he right? Was it a sign, a sign that we were meant to be from the start? How could he have been married to my sister? I'd never even known that they'd moved to New York; I hadn't remembered Vinny even being a baseball player. The image of him squatting down to talk to me all those years ago, was suddenly all I could see. The same position he'd demonstrated for me while explaining the requirements of a being catcher. It made all the sense in the world now.

How had I not put it together?

So many emotions were running through my head. Knowing how my sister had grown up, picturing how my father had treated her. I was so happy that she'd escaped—and now I was going to take her marriage from her? But Vincent was right. She also didn't deserve a man who didn't love her.

I picked up the phone and called Isabel; she would talk some sense into me.

VINCE

"Hey, it's Bianca, leave a message."

I got her voicemail, again. I'd called her at least twenty times over the past two days, but she never picked up. "Hey baby, it's me—again. Please call me back. I know you're mad, or maybe you're with him, I don't know anymore. I just know I need to hear your voice. Please, please call me back."

Christmas came and went. I was in a daze. Practicing over and over in my head what I was going to say to Samantha. If only I could hear Sarah's voice. I was scared she was going to marry that gamer guy. I was still in complete shock that she was Samantha's sister. The parts of that story that she didn't remember, I graphically did.

That night, I had just gotten into a fistfight with their father. Their mother had somehow pulled me off of him, and told me to walk away. I went into the bathroom to cool down. I was washing my face when through the mirror, I noticed this little girl crouching in the corner behind me; the same little girl who used to keep a lookout for us when

Samantha would sneak me into the house.

"You can't hear the yelling in here," she had said. She did ask me to help her fix a toy. I remember walking into that room with her, and her handing me a doll with all of its limbs torn off—no way could that have been accidental. Then, when I looked up at that cardboard mistletoe, I realized she must have been plotting the scheme for a while.

It was now the 26th, though. I needed to have the conversation with Samantha, and this was going to be even more of a blow to her. How was I even going to explain this? She stood in the kitchen by the sink, surrounded by all the plates from Christmas. There were so many plates. They couldn't even all fit in the dishwasher. When she heard me come in, she didn't even look up. She kept washing, scrubbing away with her hair tied up, no make-up on, and still in pajama pants and a tank top. "You know Vince, we spend all this money on catering, next year we need to spring for a cleaning staff."

I looked down at the floor. "Next year? How long are we going to do this for?" I asked.

Her attention remained on the plate she was washing. "You're right; the kids are grown. We don't have to do this anymore. Maybe we'll just go on vacation like we do on Thanksgiving. Italy, maybe?"

"I wasn't talking about hosting Christmas," I said.

She finally put the plate down, shut the water off, and looked at me. "Then what exactly are you talking about?" she asked, but it was obvious she knew exactly where I was going with this.

I put my hand up, pointing at the house. "This—everything. The lies, the façade..."

"No, shut up," she said, pointing her finger at my face. "Stop, no, if you're implying a divorce, we are not getting a divorce! I am not going to give up—"

"Give up what exactly?" I interrupted, yelling now. "The money? Guess what, you're getting half of everything, congratulations you're still rich! The image?"

Her phone started ringing. She ignored the call. "No Vince, no...what, do you think I am stupid? You think I don't know you have a girlfriend? The tattoo, the stupid way you shape your beard! The Wednesday night poker games you haven't shown up to in ages? Yeah, I know all about that!"

Her phone started ringing again. She pressed ignore again. "We're going to keep doing what we've always done. You go do whatever the fuck it is you want to do, and I'll keep closing my eyes to it. But you are absolutely not ending this!"

"Why?" I shouted. "You can't even stand me! How long are we going to keep proving this point? We were never in love—not the way we should have been. We got dealt a hand that we played. And we played it well, we raised two amazing kids. We went into survival mode, and we won. The kids are adults now, though, so why are we still doing this?"

"Yeah, easy for you to say, you look better than ever at forty-six, men always age better. I'm forty. I get worse and worse as the years go on!"

I rolled my eyes and snickered. "Oh please, give me a break—you're hot, and you know it. You will have no problem getting a man. Don't you want a man you love so much you can't wait 'til he gets home at night? Don't you want a man who can't take his hands off of you? Don't you want a man who gives a fuck when you come home at 2 a.m. dressed like a whore?!" I screamed.

She grinded her teeth and clenched her fist, stalking closer to me. Her phone started ringing again.

"Who the fuck keeps calling me?" She picked it up and screamed, "What!"

I had no idea who was on that other line, but I felt bad for them.

"What?" she repeated. "Who? Speaking, who is this? I can barely hear you—*Mom*?"

I hung my head. That would be just my luck, to have my mother call during the middle of this. Of all the people in the world who would disapprove of me leaving my wife, my mother would top the list. She'd compare me to my father and the way he'd left her when I was a kid.

Samantha continued, "What? How? Oh my god...yeah, okay. Thank you for calling."

She hung up. She walked over to the kitchen table and slowly sank into the seat.

"Was that my mother?" I asked, afraid of what she was going to say next.

"No," she said quietly. "It was mine."

"Your mother? The same mother who hasn't spoken to you in twenty-four years? The one who stood by when you got abused. The one who did nothing when you were kicked out of the house, *that* mother??" I asked.

She held up her hand to stop me from coming any closer. "Vince, just shut the fuck up, please. I'm trying to process what even just happened. Just give me a second to breathe!"

I stood there patiently waiting, studying her facial expression. She looked upset. Really upset. She was leaning her elbows on the table now; her head in her hands, rubbing her temples with her thumbs. Like she didn't know what to say.

Finally, she spoke. "Do you remember...?" She paused, and looked up at me, glassy eyed. "Do you remember when I was living at home? I had a sister? A pretty little girl. She had a huge crush on you."

My heart dropped. I stood there paralyzed. Sarah must have told her mother. Was she calling Samantha after all these years just to tell her they were right about me all along? Could she be that malicious and vindictive?

"Yes," I answered simply, not moving.

Samantha looked up at me, tears forming that were about to drop any second. I shifted my gaze toward the dishes. I couldn't even look at her, just braced myself for the words. Anticipating her asking me how I could do this, or telling me how I was an even a bigger asshole than she had originally thought.

"She, um..."

She paused again. I started biting my thumbnail, waiting for her to get the words out, already trying to think of a rebuttal.

"She was murdered on Christmas Eve. The police found her body yesterday. They arrested her fiancé today. Apparently, they think she was trying to leave him, and he strangled her."

At that moment, I felt a knife slice deep into my heart and my soul leave my body.

"No." I shook my head. "No, she's lying!" I was now screaming. "She's a vindictive bitch; she's lying to you! It isn't true...it isn't!"

But suddenly, Sarah not picking up the phone made

sense. I collapsed to the kitchen floor. I was on my knees, balling. The ugliest crying you could ever imagine coming out of a man. I kept repeating the same thing, over and over: it isn't true; she's lying to you.

Through her own tears, Samantha looked down at me on the floor with a sudden revelation.

"It was her? It was my *sister*?"

I couldn't even answer her. I just nodded.

Yes.

I didn't remember much of the next three years. I barely remembered the divorce proceedings, or moving my things into a new apartment. I wasn't sure when I started drinking so much, or when I stopped shaving. Or even when I started smoking again. Casey's graduation, Nick's wedding—all a blur. I was miserable to be around; I was pathetic.

Sarah had died that Christmas Eve, and I'd died two days later.

No one knew what had happened. No one knew she'd even existed. I had no one to grieve with. I couldn't even mourn her death.

The next Christmas Eve, I showed up on that roof, with the same bottle of wine. I had a whole speech prepared in my head that I was going to tell her. It didn't turn out quite that way. I just sat in that nook, by myself, drinking the entire bottle of wine and crying.

The second Christmas Eve was even worse. I couldn't even get through the bottle before I threw it against the wall. The same wall we first had sex against. I had so much hatred in me. I was so angry—I wanted to kill him. If he wasn't in jail, I probably would have. He'd taken her from me but also, I'd failed her. I'd always told her that I'd never let anything happen to her. I didn't know who I hated more: him or myself.

It was almost Thanksgiving when my assistant, Amanda, came into my office. "Vince, there's a very attractive woman waiting for you in the conference room."

"Who?" I asked.

"She wouldn't say, just said a friend. I'm hoping a romantic friend?" she asked with a grin.

Amanda was an attractive girl in her early thirties,

very into the dating scene. She'd been urging me to date for months; constantly trying to persuade me to create a profile on some sort of online dating site.

"I have no idea who is there, but I can assure you it's no one romantic," I replied as I made my way to the conference room.

Amanda was right; the woman who waited for me was very attractive.

"Isabel?" I said, surprised.

"Hi Vincent, it's been a while," she said.

"Yeah, it has been. How are you?" I asked.

"Hanging in there, thanks. Sit down, I need to tell you something."

I sat across from her, staring at her like I was looking at a ghost. I hadn't seen Isabel since before Sarah died.

She got right to the point. "I wrote a book about Bianca."

"Her name is Sarah," I said firmly, looking her straight in the eye.

She paused, her expression sympathetic. "I wrote a book about Sarah. About you and Sarah. The publicist liked it so much it went straight to Hollywood. The movie comes out on Christmas Eve. They're going to start playing previews this week. I didn't want you to be caught off guard."

I stood, walked over to the cabinet, and took out a bottle of Johnnie Walker and a glass. I poured myself a drink.

"Would you like one?" I offered.

"No, I didn't realize you can drink at work," she said.

I walked back over to the table and sat down. "Nice thing about being the boss, you can do whatever the fuck you want."

I couldn't stop my leg from moving. Up and down, up and down, uncontrollably. I took a sip of my drink. I didn't even look at her, just stared at my glass.

"Isabel, three years ago, I lost everything. My wife, my house, half my bank account, and most importantly, the woman I love. My heart, my soul...my dignity. Are you trying to take what little I have left?"

Isabel glanced down at the shoebox in her lap.

"You know," she began. "I was the last person she called that night, right after she got off the roof with you. She was crying. So upset. Hysterical. She asked me what she should do. I think she wanted me to tell her what she assumed would be my answer. Once a cheat, always a cheat. You need to break up with him. You'll never be able to trust him. You need someone your own age. That's not what I said, though. You know what I said?"

I took another sip of my drink. I could see Sarah's face in my head. The last vision I had of her, crying on that roof. Now, I pictured her on the phone with Isabel that night.

"I said, 'Vincent loves you, unlike any man I have ever seen love a woman. They don't make men like him anymore. If what he is saying is true, if he's truly who he says he is—well, everything happens for a reason. There are no mistakes in life. If he is really going to leave his wife, let him. You're the one who's supposed to be with him. You know what you have to do—you have to end it with Brendon.'"

She paused before continuing. "I think even if I hadn't told her all that, she still would have gone running to you. She was so in love with you. You're not the only one who lost something that night, you know. I started the fight that took her life. I even introduced her to him. Sarah deserves for people outside this room to know that someone out there loved her more than life, and that she loved him just as much. She deserves a better ending than 'that Broadway actress who was found dead in her apartment.'"

I looked up at her. I couldn't watch the news about Sarah's murder on TV when they'd aired it. I could never even bring myself to read the articles. But suddenly, there was something I needed to know, even though I was scared to ask.

"Who found her?"

"Her mother," she answered.

I dropped my head. Now I finally understood why, after all that time, she'd felt the need to call Samantha. She'd had no one else. Sarah had been the only other person left. All this time, I'd been grateful that I wasn't the one who'd found Sarah, but after hearing about their mother, I found myself wishing that it had been me.

Amanda poked her head in and noticed the drink in my hand. "Oh, I'm sorry. I came in here to offer you beverages—I didn't realize you already had one."

Isabel smiled up at her. "Thank you, but I'm just leaving."

Amanda walked out while Isabel stood. I looked back down at my drink, silently absorbing everything she had just said. She slid the shoebox to me.

"When we cleaned out her apartment, I found this on the bottom of her closet. I didn't know what to do with it and didn't want to throw it out. I think it belongs to you."

She started walking out and then turned back around.

"Vincent," she said, with so much empathy in her voice

that I finally looked up. "You are still young, super successful, and I'm guessing still extremely attractive under that bush on your face. You have so much going for you. Don't die with her, live for her."

I still had no words. She walked out, and I picked up the shoebox and escaped into my office.

I placed the box on the edge of the desk, sank into my chair, and picked up the phone. I sat there and listened to the dial tone for so long that the sound eventually stopped. I hung up and then picked it up again. I was trying to think of the words to say. Samantha was going to be so upset. She was happy now, even dating someone. She'd moved on. Despite the fact she'd been initially so opposed to the divorce, she had finally come to terms with it. She'd accepted that our marriage was over, knew it wasn't intentional. In fact, she'd assumed that I'd always cheated on her. She was genuinely shocked when she found out that I never had, until Sarah. Finally, she'd admitted to herself that we didn't love each other the way we should have, and that we both knew she could do better.

I was fortunate. For a divorced couple, we had a good relationship. The past coming back up now was going to crush her. I hung up the phone again and rested my face in my hands, desperately trying to think of how to tell her. From the corner of my eye, I saw the shoebox. I pulled it over to me and slowly opened the lid, not quite sure what to expect. There they were. All five corks she'd saved from every Christmas Eve we'd spent on that roof. They still smelled like wine.

I sifted through the contents of the box. Tucked inside was every card from every bouquet of flowers that I'd ever sent her. "Congratulations!" "Happy Valentine's Day!"

"Happy Birthday!" "Happy Thursday!" All signed the same way: "Love you more than life, Vincent."

I picked up a bundle of mesh. At first, I had no idea what I was holding. Then I realized: they were the stockings I'd ripped open that night. She'd saved them. I sat there, holding them for a while. When I finally went to tuck them back into the box, a piece of paper on the bottom caught my attention. I reached for it and saw that it was thicker than paper. Glossier. A photo.

I turned the photo over, and there she was, with her beautiful green eyes staring back at me. It was the picture the photographer had snapped of us in Puerto Rico, when Sarah was wearing that coral dress. She must have bought it when she'd gone back inside to use the bathroom. I was holding the one piece of evidence in the world that proved we'd existed. Maybe Isabel was right. Maybe this movie was going to keep the legacy of her, of us, alive. I just missed her so much.

I went to Samantha's for Christmas Eve. She still hosted, just to a much smaller crowd now: her new boyfriend, Mark, Casey, Nick and his wife, who were expecting their first child. When dinner was over, Nick and his wife left to go home. Casey went upstairs, and I watched awkwardly as Samantha kissed Mark goodbye. I cleared my throat to indicate I was in the room, but neither seemed to care.

Once they'd finished, Mark came over to me and extended his hand. "Good to see you, Vince."

I shook his hand. "You too, Merry Christmas."

Then, he left too, leaving Samantha and I alone in the living room. The entire room was different than when I'd lived there; there wasn't a single piece of evidence remaining to suggest I ever had. We never went into that kitchen together again. Maybe she was on to something with the kitchen demons. All I knew was, I didn't want to find out.

"I spoke to the attorneys today," she began. "Our names aren't mentioned, so there's not much from a legal standpoint we can do."

"Look, the more I think about it—I mean, a stockbroker cheats on his wife who was from an estranged family? Of eight million stories in New York City, that's seven million of them. No one will ever realize it's us," I said.

She shot me a look to stop talking. I turned around, and Casey had just come down the stairs. Wow, she looked beautiful, in a tight, very flattering red dress.

"Where are you going?" Samantha asked her.

"Tyler's taking me to see the movie *The Christmas Fairy*. The one about that Broadway actress," she replied.

I wouldn't even look at Samantha. "You're a little overdressed for the movies, no?" I asked.

"I think...well, I know he's going to propose to me tonight!" she said in an excited voice. "A little birdie told me."

Samantha and I didn't say a word. That was it. Both of our kids were now real adults.

"Wow, congrats! Have a great time," I said, kissing her on the cheek.

Samantha and I stood looking at each other after Casey left. "You know, this time next year there's going to be another one. Except he's going to be calling us Grandma and Grandpa," she said.

I walked up to her. "For what it's worth, you'll be the hottest grandmother I've ever seen," I said.

She smiled at me—a pure, genuine smile. "Vince, I know you have regrets..."

I stopped her. "I do," I said, nodding. "But marrying you, that's not one of them. We made some incredible children, and if I had to do that part all over again, I would."

She hugged me. It was the first time we'd hugged in years. I embraced her for a while before backing away. "I should go."

"Don't go," she said.

I looked at her, confused.

"You've been drinking," she said.

"I'm not driving," I said.

"Yeah, but other people are. Look, Casey is getting engaged tonight! This may be the last Christmas you ever wake up with your daughter in the same house. I'm sure you remember where the guest room is. Consider it my Christmas gift to you."

I couldn't argue. I smiled and agreed. "Hey, what's that movie you used to make me watch every Christmas when we were younger?" I asked.

"*Miracle on 34th Street*," she said, laughing that I couldn't remember the name of such a famous movie.

"Yeah, that one! Let's watch it."

"It's 2018, I'm sure they don't still play that movie on Christmas. It's probably been replaced with *Home Alone*," she said, still laughing.

"I'm sure we can get it On Demand or something," I said, flipping through the channels.

"$4!" I exclaimed dramatically when I found it. "Everyone knows how it ends!"

"Do they?" she asked. "Because if I remember

correctly, I don't think you have ever stayed awake long enough to actually see the end."

She had a point.

"Fuck it." I pulled a five-dollar bill out of my wallet and put it on the coffee table. "I'm spending the $4. We're watching it, and I'll stay up to see the end—consider that my Christmas gift to you." I purchased the movie and sat on the couch, patting the spot next to me.

Reluctant at first, she settled uncomfortably beside me. While watching the movie, though, she gradually loosened up. At one point, I even put my arm around her the way I used to, and she rested her head on my chest. I ran my fingers through her hair like I did when we were in our twenties. It was really nice.

When the movie was over, I said, "So *that's* how it ends! Now I get it!"

She smiled as we sat there, and our eyes locked. "Glad you could finally stay awake to see it."

"I'm making up for lost time," I replied. Still looking at her, with my fingers woven through her hair, I pulled her toward me and kissed her forehead.

"I'm going to sleep," she said, slowly pushing herself off my chest.

"Goodnight."

I poured myself a glass of scotch and walked out on the balcony. It was freezing. I cupped my hand on my mouth and blew into it, trying to warm up. I remembered the night that Sarah was breaking up with me, how I'd been so concerned about having questions that I wouldn't be able to ask. Questions that I'd been afraid would drive me insane, if left unanswered. In that moment, I realized there was nothing I needed to ask her that I didn't already have the answer to. Instead, I wanted to tell her so many things. I wanted to hold her in my arms and smell her hair. I wanted to dance with her.

I sipped my drink and looked up at the sky, focusing on this one star.

"Hey, baby," I began. "I'm late this year. I did go to the roof, but, well, I'm sure you know Isabel made a movie about you, and it's now a tourist trap. $40 to get on! I would have spent the money, but there wasn't enough wine to share with the hundred tourists up there. Look at that—you're still a star! You know, Isabel thinks it's her fault. We know better. It's not her fault that she couldn't prevent what happened. It's my fault. I never should have listened to you. I should have left two years before. You would never have gone out with him to begin with, and you wouldn't be where you are now. God, I miss you. *So* much."

I paused, and then started again. "You once told me your loved ones look over you from heaven. Do you see me? Do you feel me? Do you feel the enormous amount of love I still have for you? If you do, please just feel the love, not the pain. I would never want you to feel pain. Give me a sign, baby, anything. Tell me you feel me, tell me you're with me, tell me you forgive me. A shooting star? A twinkle? A lightning bolt through my chest, take me with you..."

I stood there for a few minutes, waiting for a sign. Any sign. "Nothing, huh? It's okay, you don't need to. When you're ready, you will. Happy Anniversary, Sarah—I love you more than life."

I took another sip of my drink and lit a cigarette. I heard the balcony door open, and I froze. Oh no—had

Samantha misread what had happened on the couch? I mean, cuddling had been nice, but not romantic at all. Why'd I kiss her?

"Please, Samantha, don't make me turn you down, not tonight," I begged silently.

I slowly turned, cigarette still in my mouth. Casey stood at the door.

"Aren't you a little old to start smoking?" she asked, walking toward me, pulling her coat in tighter.

"You were always smarter than me; it's a filthy habit," I said, putting the cigarette out.

"I'm glad you're still here." She shivered.

"Your mom thought I should stay over tonight. How was the movie?"

She smiled with a hopelessly romantic gaze in her eyes. "Beautiful," she answered. "One of those sappy, tragic love stories that makes you leave the theater appreciating life."

I smiled and then snapped myself into father mode. "Speaking of love stories, let's see it. Let's see the ring. Do his diamond picking abilities meet my approval?"

"I didn't give him a chance to propose."

I was taken back. "What? Why? Having second thoughts?" I asked.

"No. If he loves me, that ring will be there tomorrow. I wanted to give you your Christmas present."

I looked at her like that was the most ridiculous thing that I'd ever heard come out of her mouth, well because it was. "My Christmas gift will be there tomorrow," I said.

"I wanted you to have it today," she replied, handing me a Christmas bag.

I took the gift from her and opened it. There in my

hand, I held the bottle of wine. Our bottle of wine. I sighed.

"This was way too expensive for you to get me. It happens to be my favorite wine, though, did you know that?" I asked, looking at her in surprise.

"I figured," she replied.

Then it hit me. She'd just watched the movie. Of all the people in all the world, my daughter—with her psychology degree—was the one person on the face of this earth who could make the connection.

I put the bottle down on the balcony ledge. I turned around and faced her, with my arms folded across my chest in a defensive position. I looked her straight in the eye.

"Say it. I can take it." Honestly, I wasn't sure I could.

She tilted her head and peeked up at me. "Say what?" she asked.

"What you're feeling. I know you too well not to know when wheels are turning in that pretty little head of yours, so say what you're feeling." I was deathly afraid of what was going to come out of her mouth.

"Gratitude," she responded, and my arms dropped. "Thank you," she continued.

"For what?"

"For everything," she said, before throwing her arms around me.

I lost it. I lost control right there in my daughter's arms. I cried like a baby into her shoulder, probably getting snot all in her hair. Nothing a daughter should ever see her father do. I pulled back, wiped my face with my arm, and tried to control myself.

"I'm sorry," I began. "Dads don't do this; Dads don't cry."

She had tears in her eyes. "Humans do," she answered.

Still trying to compose myself, I looked at the bottle of wine on the ledge. "Stay right here."

I hurried into the kitchen. I started to look through the cabinets, searching for the fancy crystal wine glasses we used on special occasions. When I found them, they were covered in dust; I guess it had been a while since there'd been a special occasion. I rinsed them out, grabbed a bottle opener, and went back out to the porch. "You ever have this wine?" I asked her.

She shook her head, so I opened the bottle, "Well, I'm glad I can be the first man you try it with, while I'm still the most important man in your life," I said. I poured two glasses.

She went to take a sip, but I stopped her.

"You're supposed to smell it first," I said. Once she'd sniffed it, I lifted my glass for a toast. "Merry Christmas, sweetheart."

"Merry Christmas." She took a sip. "Wow that *is* good!"

"Right?" I said, smiling.

We stood there and stared at the sky, drinking our glasses of wine. Then out of nowhere, she looked at me and asked me if I wanted to dance. I shook my head. "You know I don't dance," I said.

"That's not true." She started playing a song on her phone. It was "Someday at Christmas," by Stevie Wonder. "You danced with me to this when I was a little girl."

I was in shock. "You were four," I said, "How could you possibly remember that?"

"It's one of my favorite memories of you," she said, taking me by the hand to the middle of the balcony. She

STEVIE D. PARKER

lifted her arm and put her fingers through mine. Her other hand rested lightly on my shoulder. I followed her lead, with my free hand on her waist.

"You brought me out to the middle of the living room," she continued. "You were on your knees so I could reach you to hold onto you. You told me to take a good look at that shitty Christmas tree we had. Said that one day, I was going to have a Christmas tree so big, I didn't know where it began and where it ended. You told me you were going to make sure that I had everything I ever wanted in life, and I would never have to worry about anything, especially a stupid Christmas tree. Halfway through the song, you picked me up, guess you were tired of dancing on your knees."

She smiled at the memory, one that I remembered vividly. Her laying her head on my shoulder as I held her in my arms, her little feet dangling. That was so long ago. She was so tiny then. Samantha had been waitressing, and Nick sleeping. It was just her and me. And now here I was, dancing with that same little girl who had grown up to be such a beautiful young woman.

Suddenly, a memory of Sarah came back. We were lying in bed one Monday afternoon listening to Christmas songs, and this song had come on. I'd told Sarah that it reminded me of my daughter.

"Tell me about your daughter," she'd said.

"Well," I told her, "She's beautiful, takes after my wife. Extremely smart and very strong. But I worry about her. She's one of those hopeless romantics dying to fall in love, ever since she was a little girl. She has so many boys chasing her, I just hope she picks the right one."

"Who's the right one going to be?" Sarah had asked.

260

I remembered staring into her eyes when I answered. "The one who loves her at least *half* as much as I love you."

"You really love me that much?" she'd asked, like she hadn't believed me.

"I love you more than life," I'd responded.

Casey spoke, bringing me back to the present. "You told me that would be the last time we danced until my wedding. See? You were wrong." She'd always loved telling me when I was wrong.

As we swayed to the music, I looked at her and said, "Yeah, it turns out I'm not always right."

We danced for the whole song, neither of us speaking again until near the very end.

"Hey, Dad?" she said.

I didn't even look up. I was caught up in the moment, just dancing with her. "Yeah?"

"I'm so sorry for your loss."

I'm pretty sure I was still moving, but in that moment, the world stopped. I looked straight at her, to see her staring back at me with such empathy in her eyes. So many responses ran through my head. "I'm not sure what you're talking about," "There must be some misunderstanding," "What loss?"

Then it occurred to me. This was it. This was the sign I had just asked for. That bottle of wine she'd handed me—that was from Sarah. A sign telling me that not only was she still with me, but that she forgave me. That love was more than just feelings. Love was sacrifice, and forgiveness.

Still staring into Casey's eyes, I opened my mouth, and the words came out. Uncontrollably and naturally.

"Thank you."

SAMANTHA

I watched them dance from my bedroom window. Vince had always been a great dad—that went without saying. But he was right, we'd raised incredible kids. To watch his daughter dance with him like that was truly a beautiful sight. I'd watched him for twenty minutes before Casey had joined him. Watching him talk to that spot in the sky, looking so lonely and miserable. So broken. I'd contemplated going out and consoling him, but I didn't want him to misread what had just happened on the couch. I mean, the couch thing had been nice, but it wasn't romantic or anything.

Vince and I had shared a lifetime together. We had been through so much. Affair or not, it was hard to see him that way. On so many different occasions, I'd wanted to ask him about her. What she'd grown up to be like? What he'd loved so much about her, and if she'd loved him just as much. I wanted to believe that she did. Before she died, I'd thought about her from time to time, even tried to look

262

her up once. I hadn't known then that she'd changed her name. I couldn't help but wonder: would our fates have ended the same way had I looked up Bianca Evans and not Sarah O'Malley? I never did ask him, though. After seeing him devastated on the kitchen floor that day, watching him sob—I couldn't bear to put him through that again.

I looked up at the sky, toward the same spot he'd been looking earlier.

"Merry Christmas, Sarah. I wish I'd gotten to know you as well as he did."

VINCE

Well, Samantha was right. That next morning would be the last Christmas that I'd wake up with my daughter in the same house. The three of us had breakfast together—I made pancakes. Casey's boyfriend did ask her to marry him that night, and she accepted. Good looking guy, doctor. Provides a good life for her, and you know what? He loves her a little more than half the amount I love you, which is still pretty impressive. I can't complain.

After breakfast, I took an Uber back to my apartment and took a shower. Shaped my beard just like you like it. Picked out the nicest black button-down that I could find, one I knew you would approve of. I even left it out. I walked over to the church and lit a candle for you. I told you I couldn't wait to reunite with you in heaven, but I now knew it wasn't time yet. I walked three blocks to the movie theater and bought two tickets to see *The Christmas Fairy*. I bought two because I knew you were with me. I liked it. It was pretty good. No, it was *really* good. I watch it every Christmas now. And sometimes on Thursdays. The actress doesn't hold a candle to you, but in her defense, no one ever will.

ABOUT ATMOSPHERE PRESS

Atmosphere Press is an independent, full-service publisher for excellent books in all genres and for all audiences. Learn more about what we do at atmospherepress.com.

We encourage you to check out some of Atmosphere's latest releases, which are available at Amazon.com and via order from your local bookstore:

Saints and Martyrs: A Novel, by Aaron Roe

When I am Ashes, a novel by Amber Rose

Melancholy Vision: A Revolution Series Novel, by L.C. Hamilton

The Recoleta Stories, by Bryon Esmond Butler

Voodoo Hideaway, a novel by Vance Cariaga

Hart Street and Main, a novel by Tabitha Sprunger

The Weed Lady, a novel by Shea R. Embry

A Book of Life, a novel by David Ellis

It Was Called a Home, a novel by Brian Nisun

Grace, a novel by Nancy Allen

Shifted, a novel by KristaLyn A. Vetovich

Because the Sky is a Thousand Soft Hurts, stories by Elizabeth Kirschner

ABOUT THE AUTHOR

Born and raised in New York City as a "nineties teenager", Stevie D. Parker grew up studying journalism. When life took her in a different direction, she spent the past two decades as a Public Relations Executive, a position that involved traveling throughout the US and dealing with many different types of people. A self-proclaimed "realist" with an astute sense of people and situations. She is fun-loving, open-minded and spontaneous but believes that everything happens for a reason. Passionate about everything she does, Stevie now spends her time writing fictional stories based on real life experiences.